SOME CHAMPIONS

SOME CHAMPIONS

SKETCHES & FICTION BY

RING LARDNER

EDITED BY
Matthew J. Bruccoli & Richard Layman

WITH A FOREWORD BY
RING LARDNER, JR.

CHARLES SCRIBNER'S SONS · NEW YORK

818

L

Library of Congress Cataloging in Publication Data

Lardner, Ring Wilmer, 1885–1933.
  Some champions.

  1. Lardner, Ring Wilmer, 1885–1933—Biography—Jour-
nalistic career—Addresses, essays, lectures. I. Title.
PS3523.A7Z518 1976   818'.5'209 [B]   75-38544
ISBN 0-684-14582-0

To Lewis L. Layman

July '76   1847.   5.77

Contents

Foreword

The more famous a writer becomes, the less posthumous protection he has against literary archaeologists who want to exhume the very artifacts he chose to have buried with him. In the cause of scholarship every word he ever set down on paper is served up between covers to a long-suffering public, from his first grasp of how to arrange them in sentences to the sometimes slow decline of that facility in his last years. In between, material considered suitable for collection may include contributions to his high school magazine, letters meant only for the eyes of mail-order houses or dunning creditors, and notebooks and rough drafts meant only for himself.

As a result some twentieth-century American writers have, in my opinion, been overcollected, and I would not like to see that happen to my father. To date, however, only a small fraction of his nonfiction has been reprinted in books, and of his short stories there are just about as many uncollected as collected. Even so, when a proposal was made to me some years ago to make a book from a selection of those stories, my decision, after considerable thought, was against it.

Most of them fell into one of two categories. The first consisted of stories he had chosen not to include in his definitive 1929 collection *Round Up*. I believe heirs should respect such judgments but not be absolutely bound by them, for they can be mistaken or the values behind them altered by time. In this case I felt that too many of the stories, especially those written when he was first venturing into fiction, were inferior to those on which his fame largely rests.

The second category was tougher, for it consisted of stories written in the four years remaining after *Round Up*. No new collection was discussed before he died at the age of forty-eight, so he had expressed no preferences among them. Some of them were clearly turned out under the pressures of illness and lack of money, but others indicated he was probing into new areas of style and content. In the end there just weren't enough stories in either category that I would classify

ix

as first-rate Ring Lardner. I concluded that the proposed collection would do more harm than good to his reputation.

There is no such danger with *Some Champions.* By incorporating a cohesive body of his nonfiction, Bruccoli and Layman have not had to strain for enough material to make a book. Three of the nine short stories do not belong in either of the categories I have cited. "Call for Mr. Keefe!" and "Along Came Ruth" are clearly superior to any of the chapters in two of the Jack Keefe books, *Treat 'Em Rough* and *The Real Dope.* "The Battle of the Century" didn't get into a short story collection because my father didn't think of it as a work of fiction.

As for the "dark stories," none of them is flawless in the way that "Haircut" is, or "Some Like Them Cold" or "A Day with Conrad Green." But each of them has the mark of Ring Lardner's superlative talent, and collectively they show how the area of his concern was broadening in what should have been the prime of his life.

RING LARDNER, JR.

Introduction

The last great concentration of American humorists came in the 1920s, when Robert Benchley, Donald Ogden Stewart, James Thurber, S. J. Perelman, Frank Sullivan, Dorothy Parker, George S. Kaufman, and Corey Ford were active. Ring Lardner, the best and most popular of them, enjoyed a vast readership and the respect of the literary community during his own time. In the middle twenties when Lardner's syndicated column was appearing in more than 150 papers with a combined circulation of over eight million, his fiction was acclaimed by sound judges. H. L. Mencken stated that Lardner was writing "some of the most satisfying and searching stories that have been done in this country since the beginning of the century." Lardner was admired by F. Scott Fitzgerald and Virginia Woolf. He was imitated by Ernest Hemingway, Sherwood Anderson, and a throng of others. Hemingway paid him tribute by writing for the Oak Park High School paper as "Ring Lardner Junior," and William Faulkner once remarked that he kept a copy of Lardner's "Sun Cured" until it fell apart.

Since his death in 1933 at the age of forty-eight, Lardner's reputation has diminished. Although a few of his stories—"Champion," "Haircut," "Golden Honeymoon," and "The Love Nest"—have become anthology standards, most of his books are out of print. He is unknown to many younger readers. Yet the scope of Lardner's work entitles him to permanent stature as a humorist, as an artist, and as a social historian. F. Scott Fitzgerald loved Ring Lardner, but he was wrong about one thing: "However deeply Ring might cut into it, his cake had the diameter of Frank Chance's diamond." Other commentators have taken the position that Fitzgerald elucidated in "Ring" —that Lardner's material was incommensurate with his genius. The proper evaluation of Lardner's career has been impeded by the circumstance that he never wrote a novel; all of his twenty volumes are collections of short pieces. His career has been judged in terms of a handful of his best-known stories. Nonetheless, Lardner's total output forms one of the most useful accounts of American life from World War I to the Depression. Happily, there are signs that Lardner's career is now receiving broad attention, that an impending revival will place his work in the mainstream of American literature —where it belongs. At the time of this writing, at least five books about Lardner are in press or in progress.

Ring Lardner was one of the American writers who emerged from the newspaper sports desk. He began his professional career as a sports reporter for the *South Bend Times* in 1905. During the next fourteen years he became known as an expert on baseball as well as one of the most entertaining sports reporters in the country. His column "In the Wake of the News" in the *Chicago Tribune* (1913–19) has been called "one of the municipal glories" of Chicago. In 1919 Lardner became a syndicated columnist with his "Weekly Letter," which was tremendously popular for the nearly seven years of its duration.

Lardner began publishing fiction in 1914 when the first Busher story appeared in *The Saturday Evening Post.* In less than twenty years he published 128 short stories while pursuing his journalistic careers. At the peak of his popularity in the twenties, he was one of the highest-paid fiction writers in the country, receiving $4,500 per story. In 1926 Lardner learned he had tuberculosis, which, compounded with alcoholism, forced him to give up his daily column in March 1927. By this time he had been working under the pressure of newspaper deadlines for twenty-two years. He continued to write regularly for magazines, commencing an association with *The New Yorker,* and pursued his lifelong interests in songwriting and playwriting. Although two of his plays were produced—and *June Moon* (1930) was a success—the collaborative effort necessary to produce them conflicted with Lardner's pride in his work. Lardner continued to write fiction, largely impelled by financial considerations, and in the early thirties his stories became increasingly pessimistic. As *Some Champions* shows, Lardner remained a fiction writer of the first rank.

In 1924 when Fitzgerald persuaded Ring Lardner and Maxwell Perkins of Scribners to publish *How to Write Short Stories,* he was amazed to learn that Lardner had not preserved copies of his stories.

The volume had to be assembled by photographing library copies of magazines. Fifty years later, the editors of *Some Champions* were impressed, while compiling *Ring Lardner: A Descriptive Bibliography* (University of Pittsburgh Press, 1976), to discover how much valuable Lardner work remained buried. Throughout most of his career Lardner had to meet deadlines, and much of his uncollected work shows the pressure under which it was written. Nevertheless, a considerable body of first-rate Lardner is entombed in back-number magazines and disintegrating newspapers. We expressed our sense that the best of this material merited republication to Ring Lardner, Jr., who generously assisted in selecting these seventeen articles and nine stories—none of which had been collected previously.

The plan of *Some Champions* is to represent two aspects of Lardner's work—the humorous articles and the short stories. It is our contention that these twenty-six pieces are of permanent value to the general reader—not just the Lardner specialist—for at least two good reasons: they stand up as examples of Lardner's best work; and the material itself provides useful insights into his career.

The first section of *Some Champions* is organized around autobiographical nonfiction and concentrates on Lardner's journalistic apprenticeship, even though half of these articles were retrospectively written near the end of his life. The two earliest articles, "Oddities of Bleacher 'Bugs' " (1911) and "The Cost of Baseball" (1912—Lardner's first magazine article), though not autobiographical, are included because they show Lardner's awareness of the ignorance of sports fans as well as his expert knowledge of a type of baseball different from today's game. The core of the autobiographical section is the series of eight reminiscences of Lardner's years as a sports reporter, which appeared in *The Saturday Evening Post* between 1931 and 1933. They not only provide the most trustworthy account of Lardner's early newspaper days, but they also contradict the sloppy critical assumption that he hated baseball and baseball people. Some critics have found it impossible to respect Lardner's work unless they convince themselves that he wrote from a sense of despairing misanthropy. It is certainly true that Lardner was a hater. He hated stupidity and cruelty and insensitivity. But he did not generalize his hatred to the human race; nor did he feel degraded by his occupation as a sportswriter. As these articles show, Lardner had an unfeigned appreciation for pre–"rabbit-ball" baseball and a sincere affection for some of the players. Indeed, his friendships with players, reporters, and sports figures became lasting influences on Lardner. Two of his *New Yorker* articles, "Jersey City Gendarmerie, Je T'Aime" (1929) and "X-Ray" (1930), are included as examples of Lardner's experiments with the essay form late in his career. The first section closes with "Insomnia" (1931), a stream-of-consciousness sketch detailing the agony commercial writing became for Lardner during his last years of failing health.

The fiction section consists of three early humorous stories and six dark stories from the thirties—three of which were published after Lardner's death in 1933. The first two stories belong to the enormously popular Busher series about Jack Keefe of the *You Know Me Al* stories. "Call for Mr. Keefe!" (1918) was not included in *Treat 'Em Rough* because Keefe's attempts to evade the draft seemed harmful to wartime morale; and "Along Came Ruth" (1919) was written too late for inclusion in the final Busher collection, *The Real Dope*. "Battle of the Century" (1921) is transparently about the Dempsey-Carpentier fight, which Lardner rightly believed was pure ballyhoo. The six late stories reveal Lardner's search for new material in the thirties. Although he has been typed as a writer of vernacular baseball fiction, most of Lardner's stories after 1920 do not, in fact, deal with sport. In these six late stories the subjects are domestic incompatibility, alcoholism, and the Depression. Only "Bob's Birthday" employs the familiar Lardner technique of the uneducated narrator; the others demonstrate Lardner's ability to write straight fiction without relying on speech or spelling idiosyncrasies. "Mamma" (1930) and "Second-Act Curtain" (1930) are among Lardner's most effective stories. Although the playwright in "Second-Act Curtain" is treated as a fictional character, the story is clearly an account of the frustrations Lardner experienced as a playwright whose work was tampered with by directors, actors, and producers. Together with "Insomnia," it reveals Lardner's anxiety about the diminution of his writing ability. As such, they deserve consideration with Fitzgerald's "Crack-Up" essays as self-studies in the psychology of authorship.

A misleading critical approach to Lardner's career is to depict him as a broken writer in the 1930s—an embittered man no longer able to write funny stories, desperately grinding out potboilers. It is, therefore, worth emphasizing that sixteen of the pieces in this volume were written in the thirties, during the last four years of Lardner's life. These late articles and stories belie that description of the ruined Lardner. Despite his anxieties, he was writing as well as ever. The words came hard, for he was a sick man; but they came. Moreover, his work was evolving, and he was seeking new material and new forms.

Americans don't feel quite comfortable about their humorists. Perhaps we secretly feel that humor isn't an occupation for a serious person. Critics like to regard humorists as spoiled writers who failed to develop. The problem has been handled by canonizing Mark Twain and largely ignoring the rest. Since his death, Ring Lardner has been treated better than his colleagues. He has received a certain amount of critical respect, but with the built-in reservation that he never fulfilled his potential. Although this position is an indirect compliment, it is also a distorted way of regarding literature. A writer deserves to be judged in terms of his achievement, not in terms of what he did not attempt. Lardner was not a Swift, but then Swift was not a Lardner. All genius is unique. There are as many kinds of great writers as there are great writers. Ring Lardner never wrote for critics or even for other writers. He wrote for a wide readership and was unimpressed by his intellectual following. We hope that *Some Champions* will please the audience which always came first for Ring Lardner.

M. J. B.

R. L.

UNIVERSITY OF SOUTH CAROLINA

SOME CHAMPIONS

Who's Who—and Why

RING LARDNER—HIMSELF

REMARKS BY HIMSELF
(The Saturday Evening Post, 28 April 1917)

The Public will doubtless be dumfounded to learn that I recently celebrated my thirty-second birthday anniversary. We had a cake and candles.

CHRONOLOGY

1885
Began to eat at Niles, Mich.

1889
Could tell by the sound of the whistle the number of the engine that was passing on the Cincinnati, Wabash & Michigan's main and only track, which lay across the street and down the hill from our house.

1895
Determined to be a brakeman.

1896
Determined not to be a brakeman. Smoked a cigarette.

1897
Decided not to be a clergyman.

1901
Was graduated from the Niles High School.
"And so young!" said they.
Accepted an office boy's portfolio with the Harvester Company in Chicago. Canned.

1

Served a prominent Chicago real-estate firm in the same capacity. Canned.

Was appointed third assistant freight hustler at the Michigan Central in Niles. Canned for putting a box of cheese in the through Jackson car, when common sense should have told me that it ought to go to Battle Creek.

1902
"Studied" mechanical engineering at Armour Institute, Chicago. Passed in rhetoric. Decided not to become a mechanical engineer.

1903
Rested. Recovered from the strain which had wrought havoc with my nervous system.

1904 and Part of 1905
Became bookkeeper for the Niles Gas Company.

Part of 1905, 1906 and Part of 1907
Society reporter, court-house man, dramatic critic and sporting editor for the South Bend, Indiana, Times.

Part of 1907
Sports reporter for the Chicago Inter Ocean.

1908 to 1912
Baseball writer on the Chicago Examiner, the Chicago Tribune, St. Louis Sporting News, Boston American, and copy reader on the Chicago American.

1913——
Resting on the Chicago Tribune.

1914——
Started writing for THE SATURDAY EVENING POST. Its circulation was then only a little over a million.

19??
Died intestate.

TASTES

Favorite author—Ring W. Lardner.
Favorite actor—Bert A. Williams.
Favorite actress—Ina Claire.
Favorite composer—Jerome Kern.
Favorite flower—Violet.
Favorite bird—Buzzard.
Favorite recreation—Bronco busting.

SUMMARY	Jobs	W.	L.	Pct.
	13	8	5	.616

What I Ought to of Learnt
in High School

(*The American Magazine*, November 1923)

*I won a chanct for a scholarship to college but took a job in a freight
depot instead—Mr. H. G. Wells thinks a feller ought to study
up on a lot of things, but as for me I claim that from
12 to 17 or 18 ain't no time to waste on books*

A little wile ago I read a article by H. G. Wells where he says in
it that when a person has obtained the ripe old age of 16 yrs. old they
should ought to be able to (1) draw a picture of a monkey wrench
so that even a monkey could guess what was it, (2) answer practally
any decent question in regards to geography, and (3) talk and understand 3 live foreign languages so as you could travel through the
different countries where these languages is sprachen without loosing
your temper.

According to Mr. Wells the above items would be duck soup for
all 16 yr. olders if the system of education was perfect.

Well it looks like the system in usages when I was around that age
must of been off color to say the lease, any way I was one of these
smart Alex that graduates from high school at 16, and if I had been
ast the next day to dash off a monkey wrench's portrait, those not
in the secret might of been excused for christening it Long Tailed
Animal Cracker. (2) I was under the impression that Nice was in
Italy and (3) I had mastered just enough of one live foreign language
to tell Razzle, a gullible bartender, that Ich war ein und zwanzig
Jahre alt.

They was one central school bldg. in Niles, Mich., at this era. It
was 3 storeys in hight and the high school was on the top floor. Hence
high school.

But must state in justice to the lower grades that I did not tend same as us 3 youngest members of the family was too fragile to mingle with the tough eggs from the West Side and the Dickereel. We had a private tutor that come to the house every morning at 9 and stayed till noon and on acct. of it taking him 2 and a ½ hrs. to get us to stop giggling, why they was only a ½ hr. left for work and this was genally always spent on penmanship which was his passion.

The rules of penmanship at that time provided that you had to lean your head over to the left, wind up like they was nobody on second base, and when you finely touched pen to paper, your head followed through from left to right so that when you come to the end of the line, your right ear laid flat on the desk.

I was a complete flop under this system and in after yrs. I changed my stance, kept my head still, took a slower back swing and seemed to improve a little, though 2 of my gal friends told me when I was 20 that my mash notes looked like the output of a 3 yr. old child with a satisfied craving for brandy. The ultimate results of my long battle with the wiles of penmanship is that during the last 15 yrs. I ain't used pen and ink, except to sign letters of apology to golf clubs.

Well in order to get into high school a man was supposed to of either passed through the 8th. grade or else they had to take a special examination. They give me the special examination and after reading my answers to same the supt. of schools swooned, but he was good-hearted though German and he says he would leave me start in high school and how long I stuck was up to me.

At this junction they was 2 items that come to my rescue and one of them was that the high school had a football team but no football, whereas I had a $5.00 football which my great-aunt had sent me from Philadelphia on acct. of me being named after her favorite son, thinking it was a punching bag.

Well the high school team could not play football without a football and they could not play football with my football unlest I played with it too, so I didn't have no trouble making the team and it was a high school team which you couldn't be on it unlest you was a high school student, so I was safe till Thanksgiving day at lease. One Saturday we played the Carroll Hall team from Notre Dame and they could not understand English very good and got the idear that I was the football instead of just the proprietor and kicked me from one end of the field to the other, but that is either here or there.

The other item that helped me along was that irregardless of how big a dumbell the undersigned may of been, they was 31 classmates out of 35 who I could regard as fellow morons without giving myself the best of it. If the principal had felt like it was his duty to weed out the feeble-minded, why the recitation rm. where the freshmen was reciting would of looked like the right field bleachers at a inter-urban chess match.

Well I don't know how it is now, but in those times practally all the teachers in high schools was members of the fair sex. Some of them was charter members. They was one that was kind of hard of hearing, and, as people that has enjoyed my public speeches is well aware, the place to set when I am talking is back of the front row where you can't tell one wd. from another. Well when this teacher called on me I would get up and move my shapely lips like I was answering and finely I would stop and she would say very good. They was a rule that if a person stood 95 in a study, they was excused from examinations in that study. This teacher had me in 4 or 5 studies all told and I never took a examination in none of them.

As near as I can remember, our studies in freshman yr. was composition, English literature, beginners Latin, algebra and U. S. history. I may as well admit that I was pretty good in Latin though even now I have trouble getting what I want in a barber shop. In regards to algebra I don't know nothing yet wile what I have gleaned of U. S. history has been picked up since the kiddies come to bless our home. Every so often one of them asks me who was old Hickory nut or Tippecanoe or something and I tell them to wait a minute till I get a handkerchief, and then I snoop off and spend a few moments among my books and when I come back I say who was that you ast me about a little wile ago.

I never had no trouble in composition as when teacher come to look over our papers she genally always picked out ones she could read.

English literature was the baby that called for deep thought. They would make us buy a little booklet with one of the classics in it like say the Ancient Mariner. Then they would tell us to take it home and study the first 10 stanzas and master the meaning of same. Most of we boys done our studying at a 10x5 table with six pockets in it, but when we come yawning to recitation the next day they was no way for the teacher to know whether we had spent the night trying to get Coleridge or the 14 ball.

One of the boys or gals would get up and read the first few stanzas followed by questions in regards to same.

TEACHER: "Mr. Brown, what is an ancient mariner?"

MR. BROWN: "Why, let's see. It's a it's a kind of a old sailor."

TEACHER: "And what is meant when it says he stoppeth one of three?"

MR. BROWN: "Well well it means it means he stopped a man. They was three men and he stopped one of them, one of the three."

TEACHER: "Mr. Starkweather, what is a loon?"

MR. STARKWEATHER: "It means somebody that is kind of crazy." *(Aside.)* "Like a lot of teachers."

(Laughter from admirers of Mr. Starkweather.)

TEACHER: "Let's have quiet. Now, Miss Millard, explain the line eftsoons his hand dropt he."

MISS MILLARD: "It means that pretty soon right away he dropped his hand."

MR. STARKWEATHER *(aside):* "He didn't even have a pair."

TEACHER: "Let's have quiet."

One month to 6 wks. would be spent solving the hidden meanings in the Mariner and then we would delve into the mysteries of the Lady of the Lake, Idylls of the King and etc. All and all we read six or seven of Tennyson's and Milton's and Scott's best sellers and read some of them twice and studied them line by line, but to show how baffling they must of been, why I can't recite a whole verse correct from none of them to-day whereas I can reel off a verse and chorus of Good-by Dolly Gray which come out that same yr. and which I can't remember studying at all.

Speaking about songs we devoted a hr. every Friday to what was jokingly called music. The singing teacher used to get very angry at we boys because we would not sing out. Louder boys louder was her slocum. But we boys would not sing out.

On the other hand they was hardly a evening passed when some gal's father did not feel himself called on to poke his head out his Fourth Street window and tell these same boys to shut up and go home for the sake of a leading character in the bible.

Another weekly incidence was rhetoricals. This consisted of a program of recitations and songs by members of the different classes. Which suffered the most, those on the program or those not on the program, will always remain a misery.

Well I was assigned to my first recitation along in November and I don't recall the title or who wrote it but the first line was Heap high the farmer's wintry hoard.

Well along about this time they was a family moved to town that had a daughter and I was amongst those that swooned at first sight. Now when a person lose their heart in those days you hoped they would put it in the Star, you wanted the whole town to know how you felt even if the girl herself treated you like you was quarantined.

So any way when I mounted the rostrum that A.M. to speak my piece they was no one in the vast assembly rm. but what was in full possession of the statistics.

"Heap," I started, but the rest of it left me. I choked and tried again, but the only wd. that would come this time was the wd. "winter," a fatal wd. as it happened to be the young lady's name. The faculty joined in the rioting that followed and in fact they was only one person in the rm. that didn't seem to be having the time of their life. The last named might of been on the Chautauqua to-day but for the fear of audiences born of that incidence.

In the sophomore yr. they give us Caesar, botany, some more algebra and literature, higher arithmetic and rhetoric. We was taught in rhetoric class that the main thing to remember in writing was to be terse and concise and etc. and not use no wds. that was not nessary. I don't know if this teaching is still in vogue, but if so I advice young men who expects to write for a living to forget it as soon as possible a specially if they aspire to membership in the Baseball Writers Assn. of America.

Caesar would of been kind of tiresome except for the gals. Their system of translating was to first find out the meaning of the wds. and then read from left to right in the order named. Like for inst. "When Caesar in Gaul hither was as before related he that the Helvetians were in phalanges solid marching heard" and etc. This give it the elements of a puzzle which was lacking when we boys was called on. For we boys had boughten from last yr's sophomores a funny little book which only every other line was latin and the rest English that give you a kind of a broad hint as to what was going on.

Nothing has stuck in my mind in regards to botany only that when the spring come we was told to visit the woods and get wild flowers which was to be analyzed and pressed in a book and handed in at the end of the school yr. They would half to be 50 different kinds of wild flowers in the book if you wanted to pass. Well I don't believe to this day that they's 50 different kinds of wild flowers, besides which a couple of gals would genally always insist on tagging along to the woods and they would get mad if you kept talking botany all the time. Any way they was a couple of we boys that was 26 specimens short with 2 days between us and the end of the school yr. and it looked like the best thing to do was get a hold of 8 pansies, 8 violets and 10 daisies and christen them angina pectoris, in loco parentis, spinal meningitis and etc. We got by with it all right maybe because teacher was in a hurry. And maybe because she was going to be the botany teacher again next yr.

Besides the regular weekly rhetoricals they was a couple of evenings per month devoted to debating. I took part in one or two debates, but for some reason or another was not selected to represent Niles in the contests with Decatur and Kalamazoo. As I recall it now the gen. drift of our debates was always the same, namely whether or not the U. S. should ought to keep a hold of the Philippines, and I suppose President McKinley used to set up till all hrs. waiting for news on the results of the debate at Niles, Mich.

In junior yr. we was introduced to Cicero, German, geometry, gen. history and 2 other studies which I forget. Those that took Cicero was excused from chemistry on acct. of the 2 being so near alike. I passed up chemistry as useless. Nobody had heard of Volstead at that time.

Six studies is all I had, but all I learned was that a man is a sucker to play at Notre Dame without a steel head gear. We was playing Carroll Hall again and the ground was covered with wet snow. We had to punt and I started down the field hoping I would not get there first as their punt catcher was a man named Hogan. Well I did not get there first or last neither one as I decided to stop on the way and lay down a wile. This decision was reached immediately after receiving a special message from admirers on the side lines in the form of a stone carefully wrapped up in wet snow. The message was intended for my ear and came to the right address. For the rest of that fall I was what you might term stone deaf on that side and I thought maybe that was the reason I never heard our quarter-back call my signal. But the quarter-back said that was not the reason.

Junior yr. in fact might of been nicknamed the stone age as far as I was concerned. They was a ½ witted boy in town that thought the school yard was his amusement park. For many yrs. he had spent all his days roaming the grounds and picking up stones which he throwed at no special target, but finely one day the janitor told him to get off of the grounds and stay off by orders of the school board. Well my father was on the school board and after that whenever I hove in sight of the boy, who incidently ignored the janitor's advice, he would say to me your father is on the school board and follow up the remark with a shower bouquet of specially selected stones. My sudden death would not of changed the make-up of the school board, but I never had time to stop and tell him that. In fact I ain't never been in such a hurry before or since as when entering or leaving the Niles central school bldg. during junior yr.

Ovid, Vergil, more German, Shakespeare, more history and physics was the program for seniors. Physics was supposed to reveal the secrets of mechanics, motion, electricity, gravity and what not, but at the end of the yr. they was still secrets to me. Yes and I will state further that in our graduating class of 16 boys and gals they wasn't four that could of made a grade of 80 in a final physics examination. The teacher knew this and excused the class from the final examination. He was coming back next yr. too.

In the fall of that final yr. we boys did learn one lesson which was that a misfortune may be a blessing in disguise. By this time we had a pretty fair football team and we was all wondering what rich alumnus would hear about us first and beg us to go through the university at his expense. We slaughtered Benton Harbor, St. Joe and Buchanan and Decatur and Dowagiac. We was assigned to play Albion, and the winner was to meet the winner of the Ann Arbor-Ishpeming game for the high school championship of the state. We trimmed Albion 6 to 0. This game was played in Niles and the town was so wild about us that a crowd of 46 was on hand to cheer. Well they was a rule in the league that you had to pay the visiting team's R. R. fare and expenses, and if you didn't you was barred from further games. And 46 admissions at 25 cts. a piece wouldn't even buy a round of sardines for a bunch of fat boys like they used to grow at Albion.

So we was barred and Albion was declared winner by default and we went around with a long face till the result of the championship game reached our ear. The Ishpeming boys, who worked in lumber camps all summer and used trees for tackling dummies, had win by the narrow margin of 81 to 0, and the Albion football team's parents had leased the university hospital at Ann Arbor for the winter months.

I hope I have give a pretty clear acct. of what I learned in high school and must not allow modesty to keep me from adding that when our diplomas had been passed around, the supt. of schools said I had win first refusal of the scholarship to Olivet. But Olivet was said to be ran by Presbyterians so the next fall found me pursuing the higher education in the Michigan Central freight house, where I learned that they's only one thing worse to unload than a carload of iron pipe and that is a carload of hides.

However, I do think, Mr. Wells, that you expect too much from sweet 16. From my experience I would say that was about the right age to start in kindergarten and then by the time you got to high school you would be old enough to at lease try to learn. From 12 to 17 or 18 ain't no time to waste on books a specially in Niles, Mich. where gals is gals.

What I Don't Know About Horses

(*Trotter and Pacer*, December 1922)

Dolly and Polly's Record to a Platform Wagon
Was 10 and a ı, Which Still Stands

The editor of this magazine has ast me would I write him up a article on the subject "What I don't know about horses," and I suppose when he give me that subject he figured I would fill up the entire issue and he wouldn't half to do no work this month. But as a matter of fact, I was practally raised in a barn you might say as we had 3 horses of our own and father used to make me tend to their hair when we couldn't afford no hired man and I bet they wasn't never 3 horses in the world that had so much dandruff and got so mad at you when you tried to take it off of them.

Two of these members of the feline tribe was whitish gray twin mares aptly named Dolly and Polly, and when you hitched them up either singly or in pairs and started to drive them they looked like the fore runner of the present day slow motion pictures. We lived about a ½ mile from Main St. and their record as a team halling the platform wagon was 10 and ¼ which I believe still stands.

The other horse was what would be called a b. g. and he was a funny party as he had double action, he trotted part of the time and paced part of the time. When he trotted he could go the mile under 3 min. but when he made it up in his mind to pace he went backwards. This bird's name was Fred but that is the last thing I called him when he begun to pace. However he done me a big favor as 1 night they was a show in South Bend 10 miles from my home town and I wanted to take a gal to it who I thought I was stuck on and

I didn't have no $1.50 to hire a livery rig as we use to call it, so I hitched up Fred and took her over in him and he trotted all the way in fine style and we got there in plenty of time for the show, but when we got in the buggy to come home Fred heard the dame make the remark that she had promised her mother to not stay out later than 12:30 so the minute we left the city limits of South Bend Fred begun to pace and it was after 12:30 already when we got as far as Notre Dame still 8 miles from home which I may as well remark at this time was Niles, Mich., also the home of Frank G. Jones and Bascow Parker, both bugs on your kind of horses.

Well anyway we got to the gal's house at ½ past 3 which was at that time the latest which either she or I or Fred had been up, but mother was still setting up and I tried to tell her the old proverb about how you can trot a horse to South Bend but you can't trot him home but she couldn't hear me on acct. of somebody talking all the time. So that is the last I seen of that special gal except as a friend but afterwards she grew married to another man that couldn't afford livery rigs and she left him flat just like I would of been left only for Fred. So I have got a soft spot in my heart for the old b. g. and also a whole lot of hard spots for the critter.

When I finely ripened into manly yrs. and Dolly and Polly and Fred was all gone, our family brought another horse which turned out to be a former broncho and when anybody went near her she would hoot like an owl and go right after you.

Well father said they must be somebody in the family who she wouldn't be mad at and we must all try out and who ever she seemed to like, why he could take care of her. So I tried out 2d, and you can bet I give her dirty look for dirty look and made sure she wouldn't like me and she didn't.

That is about all I don't know about horses, but if the editor had of asked me to write in regards to what I don't know about thoroughbreds in Cuba, I could of wrote a book and still not told nobody nothing.

Meet Mr. Howley

(*The Saturday Evening Post*, 14 November 1931)

In the fall of 1927 or 1928—and I hope you people won't demand accuracy, because I burned my diary when the Starr Faithful story broke—there was a world series between Pittsburgh and some other club, probably a club in the American League. Now, a world series is a big thrill for a young baseball writer and for a baseball fan of any age, but for dotards like me it is just a golden opportunity to sit around and discuss the game as it was before Mr. Volstead substituted the lively ball for Schlitz in brown bottles.

One evening after I had finished my "work," I set out from my suite in the Hotel Schenley with an open mind, which closed halfway to the elevator, in front of a room that unmistakably contained Bill Hinchman. I walked in without knocking, and there they were—Bill himself, Honus Wagner, Jim Sheckard, Fred Clarke, Chick Fraser, and, far from least, my own personal hero of more than twenty years' standing, Mr. Dan Howley.

"We were wondering," explained Bill, "what Honus, here, would have done to that ball they played with today."

"He couldn't have hit it much farther than he hit the old one," I said, waving myself to a seat on the floor.

"You're right, boy," said the big Dutchman approvingly.

"Where do you get that 'boy'?" said Dan. "This guy was in the Central League with me in 1906, scoring an error against the third baseman if I hit the right-field fence on the fly."

"In South Bend?" said Chick. "I pitched an exhibition game there in 1906. They didn't have fences."

"Not after you got through pitching," said Dan.

"At that," put in Hinchman, "this ball wouldn't have made as much difference to Honus or big Larry as it would to the left-handed, fly-ball hitters like Crawford and Schulte and Lumley and Flick."

"How about me?" said Jim Sheckard.

"One ball will go as far as another if you miss it entirely," said Dan.

"I was looking over the final averages yesterday," said Clarke. "I didn't see the names of any of your men among the home-run hitters or the plain hitters, either one." He addressed this remark to Mr. Howley, who had just gone through a season as manager of the St. Louis Browns.

"You must have been looking at the big-league averages," said Dan. "I did have one fella that was way up around .210 the middle of July, but the boss sold him, for fear Boston would get him in the draft."

"Are you going back there again?"

"Not unless the fans demand it," said Dan. "You know those St. Louis fans. You think they're not paying any attention to you, and all of a sudden you find out you're the one big interest in their lives. Why, the last couple of series we played at home, the entire attendance sometimes running into double figures, they used to hang around after the game till I came out, and they'd follow me all the way home to my doorstep. What I really think I'll do is lay off a year, to get even."

"Who with?"

"The fellas I was supposed to manage."

"You won't have no trouble landin' a job," said Honus soothingly.

"Thanks, Honus," said Dan. "And I believe you're right. If I can't teach them baseball I can at least teach them geography. My slogan is Join Grand Rapids and See the World. And speaking of Grand Rapids, I'll bet I could take the club we had there in 1906 and beat either club we saw out there today. This guy will tell you the same thing."

"This guy" meant me, and I lost no time in voicing an agreement.

"What are you—his press agent?" asked Sheckard.

"No, I'm not," I replied. "But I've got a tender spot in my heart for a fella that saved my life."

"That's putting it a little strong," remonstrated Mr. Howley.

"Get it over with," said Fraser. "One of you is going to tell the story, and the sooner it's told, the sooner we can take up the next order of business."

It was agreed that if Dan was the hero I must be the historian, and as this threatened to be my only chance to talk, I snapped it up. Here it is, and you can take it or leave it alone:

During the late autumn of 1905, the Niles, Michigan, Gas Com-

pany was paying me eight dollars a week to read meters, make out
bills, keep books, try to collect bad debts—and I never heard of a
good one—handle all moneys, get new customers and mop the office
floor at least once daily.

The making out of bills and the keeping of books came under the
head of hard labor. The mopping was a kind of game; I used to see
whether I could do it today faster than I had done it yesterday.
Trying to collect bad debts and get new customers was a set-up; I
have always been a person who could take no for an answer. Reading
meters was the rub, because meters are usually in dark cellars, where
my favorite animal, the rat, is wont to dwell. When I entered a cellar
and saw a rat reading the meter ahead of me, I accepted his reading
and went on to the next house.

My brother Rex was reporter for the Niles Daily Sun and Niles
correspondent for the Kalamazoo Gazette and South Bend, Indiana,
Tribune. He wrote so well that the editor of the South Bend Times,
Mr. Edgar Stoll, coveted him. Mr. Stoll came to Niles and discovered
that Rex was on his vacation. His employer did not know where to
reach him—or why Mr. Stoll wanted to reach him—but was sure
Mr. Stoll could get the desired information from me. Mr. Stoll
sought me out and stated his errand, also inquiring whether my
brother was tied up to a contract. I said yes, which was the truth.
I asked how much salary he was willing to offer. He said twelve
dollars a week. Why?

"Oh," I said, "I thought I might tackle the job myself."

"Have you ever done any newspaper work?"

"Yes, indeed," I said. "I often help my brother." This was very
far from the truth, but I was thinking of those rats.

The upshot was that I promised to report for duty in South Bend
the following Monday morning—or was it Tuesday? Other members
of my family pointed out that while twelve dollars was four dollars
more than eight dollars, transportation on the interurban would
amount to $2.40 a week and I would have to pay for bad lunches in
cheap restaurants instead of getting good lunches at home, free. But
I had given my word.

Well, let's skip the winter and open the Central League baseball
season of 1906—the year of the fire in San Francisco. I may as well
state at this point that the Central, a Class B league, was fully as

strong then as are the AA minors of today, and distributed amongst its eight clubs were athletes like Rube Marquard, Donie Bush, Dan Howley, Jack Hendricks, John Ganzel, Goat Anderson and Slow Joe Doyle, to name only a few. And the president of the league appointed me official scorer at one dollar a game, because the new Tribune man was even newer than I.

Stand by for just a moment. Mr. Howley wishes to say a word or two. Mr. Howley: "An umpire in a minor league has a tougher time than an umpire in a big league, but an umpire in any league can wear a mask and protector. The official scorer's desk at the South Bend ball park was right on the field, in front of the stand, twelve feet from the visiting club's bench and with no barbed-wire entanglements to give him a feeling of safety. A major-league ball player loves his base hits, but a minor-league ball player worships them, because minor-league batting averages are eagerly scanned by scouts from higher up. When a minor leaguer hits a fly ball and the fly ball is cleanly muffed, he wants it scored as a base hit and is apt to lose his temper if the official scorer says 'no.' "

The official scorer at South Bend found this out during the first two series, with Terre Haute and Evansville, but the offended athletes did not threaten him with physical violence. And finally along came John Ganzel and Grand Rapids.

Grand Rapids had a player with a sweet disposition whom we will call Frank. He was well known in South Bend, especially to Chief of Police Jim McWeeny, of the famous Chief of Police McWeenys of that name. And in the course of my police reporting during the winter, I also had become well acquainted with the chief, and he liked me because I laughed at every story he told, though it was always the same one.

Well, Frank came to bat in the first inning and hit a ground ball down the first-base line. It was an easy chance, but Buck Conners missed it and it rolled between his limbs into right field. Frank tallied the first run of the game on a couple of real hits and stopped to speak to me on his way to the bench.

"How did you score that, busher?" he said.

"I scored it what it was—a boot."

"If I was you, I'd change my mind," said Frank.

"No," I said, "I find that a scorer's first judgment is his best."

"If I was you, I'd change my mind," Frank repeated, "and if you ain't changed your mind by tomorrow, you won't have no mind left to change."

That evening I repeated the conversation to Chief McWeeny. "Don't weaken, kid," said he. "If he starts anything, I'll finish it."

The next afternoon Frank showed up late, as usual, but not late enough to suit me. The chief was even later. Dan Howley was standing near my desk, warming up his pitcher, Elmer Bliss.

Frank said: "Well, busher, what did you give me on that first blow yesterday?"

"I didn't give you anything. I gave Buck a boot."

Elmer was through warming up, but Frank asked Dan to wait a minute; he wanted to warm up too. He tossed a couple of slow ones to Dan and then cut loose with as fast a ball as he could throw, and he could throw fast. The ball was not aimed at Dan, and I can still hear it whistling past my ear.

"Look out, Frank," said Dan. "You'll hurt somebody."

"My control's rotten, but it'll get better," said Frank.

Dan edged over toward my desk and made a sidewise dive that stopped a shot which would have blown my head clear across the state line. Dan kept the ball and said, "That's enough." Frank pulled another ball out of his pocket and let it go with everything he could put on it. Dan made another beautiful dive and catch, and the official scorer, white as a sheet and suffering from palsy, remained just conscious enough to see five or six Chief McWeenys running toward the scene. Dan stood directly in front of me, and the chief addressed Frank.

"How do you like South Bend?" he said.

"I don't like it," said Frank.

"Well," said the chief, "if you aren't a good little boy from now on, you're liable to spend the whole summer in a town you don't like."

Frank took the hint and I tried to thank Dan, but my voice refused to function. You can readily understand why it has sickened me to note that his two big-league managerial jobs have been with clubs that had nothing to manage. Perhaps you can also understand why I always laugh when a chief of police tells a funny story.

Between then and now, Dan has played with, managed or coached

Indianapolis, Cleveland, Portland, Detroit, St. Louis, Toronto, Montreal—where he won pennants—Philadelphia, Cincinnati and all local stops. Those superhuman diving catches enabled me to continue a journalistic career so lucrative that I can almost support a day nurse and a night nurse in the hospital to which they have been accustomed.

And that reminds me, when the Cincinnati club was in New York last time, the night nurse confessed that this same Cincinnati was her home town and she was still pulling for the Reds—heaven help night nurses—so I gave her a note of introduction to Dan and careful directions on how to reach the visitors' bench at the Polo Grounds.

She met him face to face in the runway and was seized with a sudden attack of vertigo, so that when he asked her whom she wanted to see, she said, "A ball player. I have a letter of introduction to a ball player."

"Try the other bench," said Mr. Howley.

Me, Boy Scout

(*The Saturday Evening Post,* 21 November 1931)

One day not long after the assassination of President Garfield, my brother Rex and I, in our perambulators, were on a sight-seeing tour of Niles, Michigan, when suddenly we came face to face with a billboard on which had been plastered a large lithograph portraying a ball player floating obliquely in mid-air, about to snatch a ball from a low-hanging cloud with one hand, and announcing—the lithograph—that on such and such a date next week there would be an exhibition game at Spring Brook Park, South Bend, Indiana, between the Cleveland Spiders, who had finished second in the National League and had just won—or, maybe, lost—the Temple Cup Series with the champion Baltimore Orioles, and a strong semiprofessional nine hailing from Bryan, Ohio, and barnstorming our part of the country with the Cleveland club. Moreover, that on the day and date mentioned, CY YOUNG would POSITIVELY pitch for Cleveland.

Loud crows of excitement from the occupants of the perambulators, who even then could rattle off the batting order of any of the National League's twelve clubs, were followed by commands to the female chauffeurs to drive home at once—mother must be "fixed" before father arrived for midday dinner. It developed, however, that father did not need coaxing; he had seen Cleveland play in Chicago, but he had never seen Cy Young pitch.

Though the game was scheduled for 2:30, and Fred, then in his prime, could cover the twelve miles, pulling a buggy, in 1.15, we insisted on setting out in the forenoon and reached the park before there was an athlete in sight or the more expensive—thirty-five-cent—ticket window was open. But when Ellen put up lunches, she put up lunches. The wait did not seem long.

I grieve to state that I cannot recall the Bryan club's line-up. Cleveland had O'Connor catching, Pat Tebeau at first base, Cupid Childs at second, Chippy McGarr at third, and Ed McKean at shortstop. Its outfield was composed of Blake, Jim McAleer and

Jesse Burkett. And, of course, its pitcher was POSITIVELY CY YOUNG. My memory tells me that in spite of the fact Bryan was hopelessly outclassed and the game slow and one-sided, Tebeau and his men, excepting their pitcher, carried on a continuous, bitter quarrel with their umpire and their opponents. I say "their umpire" advisedly, for he was a National Leaguer and as much a part of the troupe as the players themselves. We hicks expected the thing to develop at any moment into a free-for-all fight. This particular hick did not learn until much later that the Spiders were extremely jealous of their reputation for badness, and the way to burn them up was to hint that they were not so tough as their rivals in Baltimore.

Everybody was remarking how quiet and gentlemanly the pitcher seemed compared with the rest of the gang. As a matter of fact, Cy Young was a quiet man and seldom engaged in verbal altercation with umpires, opponents or mates. But the next time I saw the "positively Cy Young" who pitched that day in South Bend, he had changed his name to Bobby Wallace, his position to shortstop and his summer home to St. Louis. And the toughness of the two other members of that Cleveland club—Jim McAleer and Ed McKean— with whom I became well acquainted in after years, was something that could be put on or taken off at will, like bridge work.

Well, when I was twenty-one and spending half the spring and summer afternoons at this same Spring Brook Park, not sitting in a buggy but at the official scorer's bench, an employe of the Central League at one dollar a game and of the South Bend Times at twelve dollars a week, along came the Dayton, Ohio, club for its first series, and with it, naturally, its manager, Mr. Ed McKean, star shortstop of those old Cleveland Spiders. It was not the official scorer's duty to ask the visiting manager his age, but it was his privilege to guess, and my guess was three to five years on the sad side of forty. His weight could not have been far below that of a Tammany district leader, and he was now playing, or attempting to play, second base, a shortstop's first and often last stand prior to unconditional surrender.

"I haven't got much of a ball club," said Ed frankly, in our brief interview before he led his men out for fielding practice. "I don't expect to worry Springfield or Grand Rapids. But I've got a kid playing alongside of me that you want to keep your eyes on, if they're quick enough. This year he's going to lead the league in boots, but when he learns not to pick up the ball till he can reach it, and finds out that the first baseman ain't sitting in the stand, we'll sell him for five or six thousand dollars more than he cost us, which was nothing."

The youngster, Ed went on, had been found on the sand lots of Indianapolis. He was twenty—less than half his new manager's age. He weighed an even hundred pounds, as against Ed's two hundred and forty or more. He was a great deal too fast for the game he had chosen as a career. His name was Owen J. Bush.

All Ed had said about him was true. He covered so much ground that he was constantly trying for, and missing, fly balls that belonged to the center or left fielder, who got out of his way and let him run wild. The center fielder was Dode Paskert, for years afterward a big-league star and the owner of one of the most accurate throwing arms the game has seen. But his—Bush's—most disastrous experiences were with balls hit on the ground, about a quarter of which the third baseman or the pitcher, or even old Ed himself, could have handled satisfactorily if the kid had not frightened them off. He usually managed to do one of three things—fumble, miss contact entirely, or, making contact, throw so far over the first baseman's head that the batsman made two or three bases on what should have been an easy out. His throws—mostly underhand—were beautiful things to watch, even when they sailed so far from their target, and in the years following, when he had acquired control of them, became the wonder of the fans and the envy of rival shortstoppers.

In that series his fielding was atrocious and his batting efforts pitiable, nor could one notice improvement, offensively or defensively, in his two subsequent South Bend appearances as a member of the Dayton club. Nevertheless, even to this inexpert eye—and when I use "inexpert" I don't mean a word of it—young Bush was a born ball player and would rise to the heights with experience and proper training.

One of my duties as sporting editor was to read the sport pages of papers printed in other Central League towns. At some time during the winter of 1906–07, a Dayton exchange made the announcement that Owen—or Donie—Bush had been released outright. I hurried with this news to baseball headquarters—a cigar store run by Bert McInerny and Ed Doran, principal owners of the South Bend club. I am a little bit afraid it was not news, that they had already been informed by some friend in Dayton or elsewhere. But they were tactful and pretended I was giving them a surprise. They were more than tactful; they asked my opinion of Bush. I told them he couldn't be a very bad investment in as much as he would cost nothing at all, and with due respect to Ed McKean, he was likely to overcome his faults very quickly under the tutelage of our manager, Aggie Grant, who was as good and smart a second base-man as you ever looked at and whose weakness with the bat was all that had prevented a long and lucrative big-league career.

Well, whether it was on my enthusiastic though immature recom-mendation, or on the advice of Aggie himself—he was spending the winter at his home in Defiance, Ohio—or on their own initiative, Donie Bush was Messrs. McInerny and Doran's shortstop when the next season opened. And before the season was half done, Manager Grant had transformed him into one of the best of minor-league shortstops and, by making him a turnover batsman—left-handed against right-hand pitchers—had increased his average from .016 to .300, which, in those days, was enough in any league.

Holding a pass on the Grand Trunk Railroad, and a baseball pass besides, I had attended the 1906 World Series between White Sox and Cubs. The victory of the White Sox had just about wrecked my life, but I had been introduced to their owner, Charles A. Comiskey, and to Charles W. Murphy, proprietor of the Cubs. Each of these magnates, on learning that I was a baseball reporter in South Bend, had asked me to keep on the lookout for promising young ball players and to report by wire, collect, if I saw one. I would be financially rewarded if the players I recommended were drafted or bought, and made good.

For several years I had been a friend or, at least, an acquaintance of George Huff, director of athletics at the University of Illinois, one of the smartest and most successful of college baseball coaches and, at the time I am writing of, scout for Boston's Red Sox in the American League. He also had requested that I notify him if any-thing good turned up, and said I would get a split if a deal, profitable to him and to Boston, went through.

I was not the type to keep secret my affiliations with baseball's higher-ups, and I had Messrs. McInerny and Doran pretty well convinced that my word bore weight with Red Sox and White Sox and Cubs.

You must know that six out of eight clubs in a Class B league—even a league as fast as the Central—were run at a loss. Their only hope of breaking even or of finishing a season with a small profit lay in their possession of a ball player good enough to bring a decent offer from a major-league club before the first day of September, when Class B players no longer could be bought but were subject to the draft. It was a cinch that South Bend's only prospect, Donie Bush, would go in the draft for $750 unless some club made an offer for him before September first, and so impressed were the South Bend magnates by my boastings, or else so desperate when the twenty-first of August arrived without bringing an offer from anybody for the best minor-league shortstop in the country, that I was called in, told to pull all the wires I could with the two Chicago clubs and with Boston, and promised a cut if I inveigled my big-league pals into a deal. Thus I stood to make money from buyer and seller both if I succeeded in selling Bush. And thus my journalistic work suffered from neglect between the twenty-first of August and the dawn of September first.

Telegrams to Mr. Comiskey, Mr. Murphy and Mr. Huff elicited no replies. On the twenty-fifth I called up Messrs. Murphy and Comiskey at Chicago and Mr. Huff at Urbana, Illinois. Mr. Murphy was in the East; his secretary, Mr. Thomas, thanked me for my interest, but was sure the Cubs were not in the market for a shortstop so long as Tinker and his understudy, Artie Hofman, retained their health. Mr. Comiskey was on a vacation in the Wisconsin woods; his secretary, Mr. Fredericks, said the White Sox employed a corps of scouts; one or more of them had undoubtedly seen Bush and had not been impressed; moreover, "we're pretty well fortified at shortstop." Yes, they did have George Davis, a smart ball player and, in his prime, equal to the best of them, but now so close to Ed McKean's age that he was casting envious glances at the second-base position, where the lack of speed is less noticeable and the throw is short and sweet. Allow me, drafted into the big league myself that fall and a constant companion of the White Sox all through the season of 1908, when they lost the pennant by one game—allow me to venture the

guess that with Donie Bush———— And I who say this liked George
Davis as well as any ball player I ever knew and found him so human
that it was hard to believe he was a ball player at all.

No one in Urbana could tell me where George Huff had gone. But
on the twenty-ninth of August I had an engagement to meet a friend
arriving from Niles on the 1:55 interurban from the north. My friend
was not on the car. George Huff was.

He told me he had been at his farm in Michigan and that in an
hour or two he was going out to Notre Dame to talk track schedules.
I assured him he was going to postpone his trip to Notre Dame and
was coming with me to the ball game, where he would see the
greatest young prospect in the minor leagues. He asked whom I
referred to. I said he would know before the game was over. We
separated at the press gate, George climbing into the grand stand to
hide. But he was a big man and the ball players knew he was there.

The game went twelve innings and was won on a three-base hit by
Bush. He had played a sensational game afield and had made, besides
his three-bagger, a home run, a two-base hit and three singles. He
had socked three of his six hits left-handed and three of them right.
Believe it or not.

Riding back to South Bend, Mr. Huff said:

"I think that was staged. I saw that kid last year and marked him
down as fast, but impossible."

We hurried to the telegraph office in the Oliver Hotel. There
George sent a wire to John I. Taylor, owner of the Boston Red Sox:

> STRONGLY ADVISE PURCHASE OF BUSH SOUTH BEND
> SHORTSTOP STOP MUST BE DONE IMMEDIATELY

After three long hours the answer came: "What would I do with
another shortstop?"

Bush went into the draft and Detroit got him for $750. I went into
McInerny and Doran's, which I had carefully avoided for more than
ten days.

"Well," I said, "I'm sorry I fell down on the job. It cost me $9.30
in telegrams and phone calls."

They were busy with a customer.

Until the close of the 1931 season, Bush was manager of the White
Sox, the club that should have bought him twenty-four years ago.

There is no telling where 1932 will find him. In his big-league managerial experience—with Washington, Pittsburgh and Chicago —he has had a fair share of success, and probably would have had more if his employers had not been omniscient and, therefore, in a position to criticize and second-guess to their hearts' content.

He did get a laugh or two at Pittsburgh, where the boss, Barney Dreyfuss, summoned him to the office after each game and, no matter what had happened, either that day or in the past century, scolded him for it. For example, three or four or five years ago, Paul Waner had a batting average of .500 the last week in May.

"What's the matter with Waner—Paul Waner?" Barney asked Bush. "What have you done to him?"

"Done to him!" said Donie. "Don't you know he's hitting .500?"

"Hitting .500—yes," said Barney. "But no home runs! No home runs!"

Caught in the Draft

(*The Saturday Evening Post*, 9 January 1932)

This is not an obituary, though if the subject's adventures were all printed in ordinary newspaper columns and laid side by side, they would extend from Kenneth L. Roberts' pine-kissed Maine manor to Bill Rogers' storeroom for cosmetics in Beverly Hills; and despite the fact that it takes a heap o' livin' to do what my hero has done and see what he has seen, he is as far from a shave by the Grim Reaper as anyone in Columbus, his present abode.

I must mention Niles, Michigan, again, and I cannot promise that this is the last time. I am not exaggerating when I say that my family was only one of a great many born and raised there. One of the others was named Jacks, and the Jacks boys were virtually inseparable from the younger Lardners, so that when the Jackses moved to Chicago, the Asmuses, Kaisers, Wolfords and Mantkes, who were employed by the Michigan Central, had a good laugh at the sight of men ranging in age from twelve to twenty frankly shedding tears at a mere parting. As matters turned out, the Jackses, and particularly the Jacks parents, ought to have done all the crying, while the Lardners gave their tribal cheer, for on visits to Chicago during the next ten years the Lardners' hotel was the Jacks domicile, and the rates per day or per week, American plan, were nothing.

In the fall of 1907, approximately a decade after the hegira of the Jackses, I found myself in Ruth Etting's usual condition—heartbroken. It was not because of my failure to sell Donie Bush, but because the only girl I could ever care for had announced her engagement to somebody decent. I saw her and we talked it over, and she said that her family held to the conviction that I, like all other newspapermen, was en route to the gutter. I pointed out that some very famous newspapermen had not landed in a gutter until a special one was dug for them in Woodlawn, Mt. Vernon or Silver Brook. Her reply to this was a haymaker—she preferred the other bloke to me. This meant one of two things: An escape from the scenes that were constantly reminding me of her, or suicide.

The World Series that year was between the Cubs and Detroit. My vacation was at hand. I telegraphed a young Jacks, inquiring if I might have the usual accommodations. The reply came: "Sure."

Talking with Art and Phil the night of my arrival, I gave voice to my desire to quit South Bend and get a job on a paper in Chicago or New York; I realized it would be hard to crash the gate in either town without an acquaintance to lend me aid. Whereupon, Phil revealed the surprising news that he was acquainted with Hugh S. Fullerton, baseball writer on the Chicago Examiner—he didn't have to tell me that—and would be glad to introduce us, though he didn't suppose anything could come of it. I made him go to the telephone immediately, call up the Examiner and fix a date with Hugh.

The hour was noon the next day; the place, the Examiner office. Phil took me there, made the introduction and tactfully left us, the great Hugh S. Fullerton and the—well, my name is signed to this memoir.

" 'There was a little chicken lived down on the farm.' " Thus Hughey opened on me.

I gazed at him in bewilderment.

"The next line," he went on, "is 'Do you think another drink would do us any harm?' "

I was going to be careful. "I can't have another, because I haven't had one."

"Don't you ever have one?" asked Hughey.

"No," I said.

"Phil," said Hughey sadly, "gave me to understand on the phone last night that you wanted to get a job in the sporting department of some paper here."

"I do," said I, "but I guess there isn't much chance."

"I'm afraid not," said Hughey. "There's one opening in town that might lead into a baseball job, but 'Do you think another drink would do us any harm?' "

My slow-motion Michigan mind began to function. "Is there any place we could get one—I mean, in this neighborhood?"

"If there weren't, why would we have our office in this neighborhood?"

Though my favorite beverage was and is a bourbon highball, I wanted to show off on this occasion, and I took several big shots in small glasses, straight and neat. I do not recommend this as a regular diet—the intermissions are too brief—but I think it worked to my advantage in this crisis, for it did away with my innate reticence, and on the ride from the Examiner office to the White Sox park I discussed, intelligently and in regular baseball idiom, which is the same in a Class B league as in the majors, the merits and defects of the Central's more promising athletes, such as Bush, Marquard, Jimmy Austin, Dode Paskert, Goat Anderson, Joe Doyle, Ostdiek, Osteen and Sheldon Lejeune. Anyway, Hughey stayed awake, and when we got to the ball park, took me up to the office and introduced me to President Comiskey. I expected the latter to remark that we had met a year ago, but for some reason he didn't.

Hughey said: "I'm going to find a job for this boy in somebody's sporting department. He's been writing baseball on the South Bend Times for two years, but he isn't as sappy as that sounds."

"Did you have any good ball players down there this year?" asked Mr. Comiskey.

"South Bend had a shortstop—Donie Bush—whom you'll wish you'd landed."

"I know. I didn't hear of him till too late."

"I telephoned you and telegraphed you when it wasn't too late, but you were up in Wisconsin. I reached Mr. Fredericks by telephone and he didn't seem interested."

"Charley never mentioned him to me."

"That's perfectly natural," I said. "He had no idea who I was or whether I could judge a ball player."

"Well," said Hughey, "Detroit got him in the draft and I understand Jennings intends to farm him to Indianapolis for a year."

Drinks were ordered without a preliminary question as to what harm they might do us. I got rid of mine in a hurry, because I wanted to be in the stand watching the game, though it was the next to the last of the season, the Browns and Sox were playing, and victory meant nothing to either club.

But, "What do you think of the series?" Commy asked Hugh.

"I don't give Detroit a game," was the reply, and, it might be added, neither did the Cubs.

"You haven't seen much of Cobb," said Commy, who had seen too much of the gentleman in question.

"I have watched him and studied him," said Hughey. "He is a

nervous type who will overtry and do his club more harm than good."

"The way he did our club," said Commy.

This may be the proper time to tell of Hughey's first venture in prophesying, which had occurred in 1906 and was referred to, but not accurately, in a New York paper during the recent clash between Cards and Athletics. The New York writer took his tip from a Jersey correspondent. The story was about an almost infallible Jersey baseball seer who had already called the turn on the first two games and predicted that the fourth or fifth game, in Philadelphia, would go thirteen—or maybe fourteen—innings to a tie. The New York writer said that no prophet had ever before been so positive and bold, not even Hugh Fullerton. You all know by this time that tie games and extra-inning games were missing in the recent classic. But you may not know that Hughey was just as positive and bold, and, moreover, right, in his prophecy of twenty-five years ago. I must see that my sponsor is given justice.

It was the year—I have no reference books—in which the Cubs had piled up 116 victories out of 152 games for the biggest percentage in history. The White Sox, notoriously weak in hitting, had come from behind by holding all opponents just about hitless, from the first of September on, through an exhibition of almost incredible pitching, with Ed Walsh in there every other day and Smith, White, Owen, and Altrock helping him along. Now the World Series is usually won by the club possessing two or three masterful pitchers. In this case, there were masters on both sides and the Cubs, outside of their pitchers, were so classy in every position and so well fortified with substitutes that no one but Hughey and the White Sox thought the National Leaguers could lose.

Hughey was working for the Chicago Tribune. He wrote a story for the Sunday preceding the series opening. The story said the Sox would win by four games to two. They did. It gave the scores of all the games.

As I recall, only one score was exactly right, but most of them were nearly so. Hughey turned the story in. A conference of editors decided not to print it. They didn't want people to think one of their baseball writers crazy and they didn't want their paper ridiculed. Hughey was sore, and for all I know, it may have been this incident that made him jump to the Examiner. You can be assured that the editors who made the decison were sore too. But they had kept Hughey's story, and printed it the day after the series ended, accompanied by an apology to him, and an affidavit to the effect that he had written it and handed it in at least five days before the playing of the first game.

Finally I dragged Hughey away from Commy's hospitality, and we went out to see what was left of the ball game. The Browns were in the field and my eyes immediately lighted on their shortstop. It was the Cy Young I had seen pitch for the Cleveland Spiders in an exhibition contest at South Bend sixteen years before.

"That's Bobby Wallace," explained Hughey, when I told him the story of long ago. "He did start out as a pitcher, but was too good a ball player to continue pitching. And of course that old Cleveland gang, when they went barnstorming, advertised Cy to pitch every game. The old boy was probably never even with them when they made those one-night stands."

The World Series of 1907 opened at the West Side Ball Park and Hughey fixed it so I could sit next to him in the press box. The score of the first game was 3 to 3, and unless I am mistaken, Wild Bill Donovan and Mordecai Brown were the pitchers. I know Bill was one of them, and it will help to make Brownie the other, because on that day, or the following, he pulled a beautiful play which spoiled Detroit's main chance and brought a gasp of astonishment from Hugh Jennings, Cobb, Crawford, Coughlin, O'Leary and Schaefer, none of them a dumbbell, a play I want to describe, and I have neither the space nor the memory to write details of the second game; moreover, it will give you, at once, an idea of Mr. Fullerton's foresight.

It was in one of the early innings—probably the third. Davy Jones, the lead-off man, had been disposed of in the preceding round. Charley O'Leary, who was to be deposed in a year by Bush, but never in danger of lacking a big-league job as manager or coach, owing to his shrewdness and popularity, had reached second base. Crawford was on first—Sam Crawford, who, if he could have remained in the pastime until the introduction of this crazy ball, would have led the Babe in home runs, not because of superior strength but because of his faculty of laying off the bad ones. Sam was at that time hitting third in the order, and as there were men on first and second, none out, Donovan going great and Rossman yet to come, it was pretty safe to predict that Cobb, a swell bunter, would bunt, nominally with sacrificial intent, but with the real purpose of beating it out and filling the bases.

"He's bound to lay it down," I said to Hughey.

"I imagine Brownie knows that," said Hughey. "And I imagine Brownie'll outfox him."

Brownie, whose control was perfect, threw the first one so high that Ty would have been insane to offer at it. I heard a couple of reporters suggest a possible purposeful pass. I knew better than that. A man with Brownie's brains is not deliberately filling the bases with Claude Rossman swinging two bats and the score nothing all, or close to that figure. The purpose of the unbuntable ball was to see what the runners were apt to do, provided it was pitched within Cobb's reach. The runners had both been on the run and had to scramble back to escape death at the hands of John Kling, sharp-shooter. I expressed this theory to Hughey, whose reply thrilled me.

"You're ready for this league," he said. "But also, if they did start running, there was a good chance for Johnnie to nail one of them."

The next delivery was a fast ball on the extreme outside corner of the plate, a ball that could be bunted only toward third base. The runners started with the pitch and so did Brownie—toward the third-base line, in time to field Ty's beautiful bunt and force O'Leary, and almost in time for Steinfeldt's relay to double up Crawford at second. Crawford got to second and Cobb to first, and they were still on those bases when the half inning closed.

Another word about Brownie before we leave him for the nonce. You youngsters may not know that the forefinger on his pitching hand was missing, that one of his nicknames was Three-fingered Brown, and that he had lost the finger in an accident—not just as a childish prank. Once, years later, we—the Cubs—had a pitcher named Harry Higginbotham. He was taller than anybody but Eppa Jeptha Rixey, and that's all I can say for him. It made him kind of mad to spend the season in the bull pen and watch Brown, Overall, Reulbach, Richie and Kroh win ball games. One day Brownie was pitching and he wasn't so good as usual, but he had a three-run lead going into the ninth. Two men got on and the next three went out on hard line drives straight at fielders.

"The lucky stiff!" said Harry to Lou Richie, who was sharing the bull pen with him and Tom Needham.

"Yes, he's shot with luck," said Tom, as they walked toward the club-house.

"If," said Harry, "I had half as much luck as him, I'd win twice as many ball games."

"I've got an idea," said Lou, "that his success can be attributed to his missing finger. He's got the best curve ball in the league, and that must be the reason. If you'd cut off your whole right hand and cultivate a wrist ball, you'd out-Brownie Brownie. As for luck, you're ten times as lucky as him. You've got nothing to lose."

Two more games were played in Chicago, the Cubs winning them both. Then we moved on to Detroit and the Cubs won the series in two days there. It was a whole week since I had met Hughey, and all through that week I must have been pretty much of a pest. Not since our first day together had he mentioned "job," and I was growing nervous. But in the rain-soaked, tremulous press coop at Detroit, I was introduced to Frank B.—alias Duke—Hutchinson in the following speeches:

HUGHEY: Here's your man. I turn him over to you.

DUKE: With reluctance?

HUGHEY: With more baseball sense than you've got.

DUKE: That's damning with faint praise. But it isn't important just now. *(To me):* Do you know any football?

ME: I played it in high school, and I've seen it played often by Michigan———

DUKE *(interrupting):* That's enough. *(To Hughey):* Does he know what paper he's going to work for and what salary he's going to get?

HUGHEY: The paper is The Inter-Ocean and the salary is eighteen-fifty a week.

They watched me anxiously. The Inter-Ocean needed a sporting writer and was not particular.

"I am getting fifteen in South Bend," I said, and I was telling the truth; the Times had raised me, but if the Inter-Ocean had offered me just that, I'd have accepted.

"Have you figured how you're going to live in Chicago on eighteen-fifty?" asked Duke.

"I can get on the wagon."

"You can get on the wagon," said Duke, "but nobody can work for us and stay there. However, kid, there's one advantage in starting on the I.-O. Including you, there'll be four people in the sports department, and every one of the four is bound to have an assignment every afternoon or night."

When the series was over, for no reason excepting an unwillingness to part from Hughey and Duke, I went back to Chicago on their train. The distance between Detroit and our destination, was, and still is, two hundred and seventy-two miles. The train left Detroit at midnight and was due in Chicago at seven A.M. We boarded our car and the first people we saw were the two series umpires, Hank O'Day and an American League official who shall remain anonymous. They were sitting in a section that had not been made up. Hank, seated on the aisle, was bored and sleepy, and anxious to get away.

"Hank's trying to walk out on me, but I must have somebody to talk to," said the American Leaguer.

"You can talk to me," said Hughey.

The anonymous ump paid no attention to this kind offer.

"Furthermore," he said, "he won't be sensible; he won't sit by the window."

"What would be sensible about that?" asked Duke.

"Why, I get off first. I get off at Sixty-third Street."

"Oh, so-and-so!" said Hank, and moved over.

Heap Big Chief

(*The Saturday Evening Post*, 23 January 1932)

When I returned to South Bend from my 1907 vacation and the lopsided World Series of that fall, and announced to Mr. J. B. Stoll and his sons, Ed and Elmer, my immediate bosses, that I had decided to quit and go to the Chicago Inter-Ocean to work, the cheering was as subdued as that of which Yale has recently complained; not, please understand, because I was so hot, but when you own a paper in a town of 50,000—the red he-blooded citizens called it 65,000—population, stray out in the sticks, pick up a green kid and in two years develop him into a fairly competent and literate reporter of court and general and society news, a sporting "expert" and a "dramatic critic," start him out at twelve dollars a week and hold him with one raise to fifteen dollars, it is not a gala occasion when he calmly saunters in and says, "Good-by, boys, I'm through."

However, there would have been less weeping and gnashing of Stolls if the Times had not just hired a young "assistant" to me by the name of J. P. McEvoy, who, by the way, soon followed me to Chicago, afterward followed me to New York and finally passed me by writing a novel that he sold to the movies. I had never been able to sell my literary works to the movies; the prices had always been prohibitive—from my viewpoint. Other South Bend newspaper contemporaries of whom I brag are Eddie Cochrane, president of Kansas City and fight and football official, and Bill Orr, who was secretary to Governor Whitman, of New York, and now owns Metro-Goldwyn-Mayer or at least is chairman of Yuma the lion.

The real requiem was held in the old manse in Niles, Michigan. Twice before, I had gone to Chicago to live. Once was to Armour Institute to study mechanical engineering, which I mastered in one semester and was in accord with the dean when he told me I had progressed as far as I could in the subject. On the second occasion I was engaged as telephone boy for the McCormick Harvesting Machine Company at a salary of four dollars a week, and you can believe me when I say that the more mistakes I made, the more salary I deserved. The head men around the place were too busy to answer the telephone, but they were never too busy to dog-trot the whole length of the corridors in order to get close enough to me to tell me I was a heel. Their idea about telephones was widely at variance with mine. I thought the things were invented so that people might converse without putting on their topcoats and hats, walking four or five miles and meeting in the vestry room of a church. So when someone would ring a buzzer on my switchboard and say he wished to speak with Mr. Cyrus or Mr. Harold, I would immediately connect him with Mr. Cyrus or Mr. Harold and let them go to it. Ordinarily the talk did not last more than an instant, though I am positive I made very few mistakes; in fact, I believe to this day that I am a born switchboard operator. But almost invariably, as soon as Mr. Cyrus or Mr. Harold hung up, he would start a sprint for my sacred cubby-hole and say all the things he had meant to say to the person who had telephoned him. I was fired in two weeks, and returned to Niles, where, it pleases me to state, *ma mère* fully agreed with me that the fault had lain with the McCormicks.

My mother, I think, was the person I was going to speak of before I sliced off on this long dissertation about Armour Institute and the McCormick Harvester Company. For reasons perhaps known to herself, she had not grieved a lot over my first two "permanent" departures from home. But this time she knew I was going for good. Chicago, to her, was a huge collection of Gomorrahs, though in those days it was a cloister compared with its present condition. Anyway, she fixed things as nicely as possible for me. She obtained board and lodging for me, by correspondence, in the home of an eminently respectable Episcopal lady in reduced circumstances, whose other boarders and lodgers were all Episcopalians and members of the Brotherhood of St. Andrew. I was assured of decent, congenial company, a likable roommate, clean linen and three home-cooked, wholesome meals a day. The expenses exceeded the salary I was to be paid; that, however, had also been true in South Bend. My newspaper career was not promising to support me in the style to which I had been accustomed; not nearly the style to which had been accustomed those seven bold muscle men of Bugs Moran's gang, who had been found perforated on St. Valentine's Day, 1929, right around

the corner from the eminently respectable home that had been chosen for me.

I am not alleging that twenty-two years constitute a narrow escape
or that I ever should have had the courage to participate in Moran's
game, but merely asserting that Chicago's decent neighborhoods
cannot be pointed out with the same assurance as in the century's
younger days, and then hastening on to say that my mother had
made a small error in her prognosis.

Excepting established baseball writers and other specialists, a man,
and particularly a beginner, employed in the sporting department of
a morning paper, goes to work at two or three o'clock in the afternoon and stays in the office until two or three o'clock in the morning,
leaving only for a hurried dinner or to cover an assignment or two.
When I explained this to my Episcopal lady friend on the North Side,
she agreed that I must seek other quarters. I got myself a single room
at the corner of North State and Goethe—at least, that's what they
were then—and ate in terrible restaurants. I wrote home about the
necessity for making the change, but wrote convincingly that my
sleeping quarters were grand and I had found a restaurant the very
thought of which made me hungry.

I was kept glued to the desk, writing heads and reading copy, for
two rather dull weeks. The only excitement was an occasional visit
from Packey McFarland, Chicago's prize lightweight pugilist,
lesser pugs and their managers seeking publicity, and once—memo-
rable night—Frank Gotch, champion of all the wrestlers and, I
think, conceded the greatest wrestler that ever tortured a Pole or
Turk. Frank was accompanied by Jack Curley, for no reason save
that Jack couldn't spend an evening without a champion on the
leash.

"When youse fellas gets through work," said Jack, "I and the
champ would like for you to go somewheres with us and put on the
feed bag."

Duke Hutchinson, our sporting editor, asked Gotch how many
meals he had eaten that day.

"The champ don't count nothing but money," said Jack. "But I
can tell you he's eat a lot of meals. They wasn't nothing else to do.
Doc Roller's stole all his gals. The champ, here, thought it was a cute
trick, instead of shaking hands with a gal when he seen her, he'd dive

for her foot and twist it till she scrum, no matter if it was the College Inn or the Morrison."

We finished our work and went to a cheap all-night restaurant. I can remember nothing excepting that I was unable to eat; I was too much fascinated by the champion's order and his rapid consumption of it. The order was corn flakes with cream, two glasses of milk, and three poached eggs on toast, smothered with cream.

My first assignment came on a Saturday. It was a football game between Oak Park High School and another high school too unimportant and helpless to mention. Oak Park won by an unspeakable score, and two or three years later you could see the names in that day's line-up sprinkled through the college line-ups of East and Middle West.

Boy, Chicago had high-school football teams—Hyde Park, Englewood, Oak Park and North Division—and if I were coaching, say, Harvard or Minnesota, I should never have thought of scheduling one of these schools for a set-up.

In the summer of 1906, there graduated from North Division a quarterback by the name of Walter Steffen. He entered the University of Chicago and played through the fall there in the same backfield as Walter Eckersall, who was captain, a fourth-year man and completing a brilliant career. Well, the forward pass was a novelty and nobody knew what to do with it, and Chicago, with the two best kickers and two best quarters ever seen under one canopy, failed to burn up the Middle West.

In the fall of 1907, with Eckie gone, Steffen looked a lot better. He and Pat Page, a witch at snaring passes with one claw, gained a great deal of ground with the new toy. Wallie himself ran kick-offs for touchdowns and back again if you wanted him to, sprinted with punts much farther than the guy had punted them, drop-kicked goals from the drum major's hat and was on the road to tying or beating Willie Heston's record for touchdowns. There was no doubt that Chicago would win the new conference title.

On Chicago's schedule was a team called the Carlisle Indians. So far as getting to places was concerned, the Indians made the recent Notre Dame Ramblers look like a switch engine. The Indians' guide and personal conductor was Pop Warner, now at Stanford, provided he can stay in one place long enough. If, in the days I write of, the Indians had a game scheduled with Alabama the second Saturday in

October, they were apt to start South commencement week, and some of the redskins who were supposed to have commenced would think their diplomas were railroad tickets and go right along with last year's squad. Hazing freshmen was unknown at Carlisle. You couldn't find a freshman.

One day Duke said to me these blessed words: "I'm going to let you do the detail of the Carlisle game, and I want some advance stuff on them too. You might as well chase out to Lake Forest and stay there a couple of days. Get what you can out of Warner and Mount Pleasant and some of the other big guys. And don't overlook your expense account."

Fat chance!

It was only Wednesday, but the Indians were not going to be late. Now I am depending on memory and I cannot tell you whether they were using Lake Forest University or Lake Forest Academy field to practice on. It was the field nearest to Ferry Hall, which is a girls' school, and when I got there no one was in sight but girls. The Indians, someone told me, would be out as soon as they had rested from their lunch. I didn't care whether they ever came or not. I had met Wilma Johnson from Niles and Maud Rogers from Adeline, Kansas, and was satisfied.

The "savages" did show up, though, also Pop, their leisurely leader. He was talking with a young Indian in civvies, with bandages around his arm or leg, I have forgotten which. After they had parted and the players were warming up on the field, I approached Pop and introduced myself. He speaks to me now every time he sees me, but has no idea whether my name is Cassidy or Buncutter.

"That's Mount Pleasant," he said, indicating the boy who was walking away from us. "He's out definitely. It's a fracture."

"You'll miss him, won't you?"

"Oh, yes. Miss him."

"Isn't he about your best man?"

"I'll tell you after the game who's my best man," said Pop. "That's when it shows."

"Yes," I said, "but sometimes you know a man is your best man, but he doesn't show up best in a particular game."

Pop seemed bored, for which I didn't blame him, and summoned another player.

"Island," he said, "this is Mr. Gwagwa." And to me, "We may

give Island a chance in Mount Pleasant's place."

Pop left Island and me together.

"Well," I said, after an embarrassed pause, "are you fellas afraid of Steffen?"

"What can he do that we should be afraid of him?"

"He can run back punts."

"Listen," said Island, "did you ever see a man run back punts with six men sitting on him? Listen," continued Island, "we got a man named Thorpe. When you see Thorpe you forget Stevens."

Well, I saw Thorpe the following Saturday, when the Indians beat Chicago 17 to 0, and made a divan of poor Wallie Steffen. And I saw Thorpe, in 1911, beat Harvard almost single-handed or, rather, single-footed. That second time I saw him he must have been a sophomore, I guess.

A Ferry Hall girl approached me shyly as I was about to leave the practice. "Could you tell me," she inquired, "what is the matter with that poor boy with the bandage?"

"A fracture," I said. "He won't be able to play Saturday."

"And how about yourself?" she asked.

Chicago's Beau Monde

(*The Saturday Evening Post,* 20 February 1932)

When the football and soccer seasons are over, when there is no longer anything to keep a morning-paper sports reporter outdoors in the daytime, his life becomes a little bit unhealthy. It also becomes a little bit dull, even in a town of Chicago's size—that is, after the mere sight of a club owner or ball player fails to make him swoon.

I must say, however, that we had a better break in Chi than they had in the other big-league cities. Though Germany Schaefer and Charley O'Leary earned their money elsewhere, they lived with us, and it was a safe bet that they would be encountered at least twice weekly on the winter baseball beat, usually in a place where it was all right to put on a vaudeville act, and they always had one to put on. Moreover, there was a White Sox fan named Joe Farrell who was more or less ubiquitous and omnipresent, and who was a greater natural comic than I have ever seen on the stage.

My December-January assignment during my term of service on the Inter-Ocean and, later, part of the time I worked for the Examiner and Tribune, was to call, every afternoon, on President Murphy, of the Cubs; President Comiskey, of the White Sox; President Johnson, of the American League; President Hickey—or whoever it happened to be—of the American Association, and visit the haunts of Chicago ball players or ball players from out of town, pick up what news there was, and write something, whether there was news or not.

Almost invariably the stuff written could have been left out of the paper without causing one reader to cancel his subscription.

Joe Tinker Signs for Two Years; Johnson Says Games Must be Speeded Up; Billy Sullivan Buys Apple Orchard in Oregon; Two New Umpires Acquired by American Association. Looking back on it, I am convinced that the American Association must have figured up, each fall, its total attendance for the preceding season and then hired an umpire for every fan.

The daily session with Mr. Murphy ordinarily lasted two or three minutes—long enough for him to offer a cigar and say there was nothing doing. Once in a while, though, he had just been in communication with Manager Chance and half a dozen other magnates, and had consummated a whale of a player deal such as only master baseball minds like Chance's or McGraw's were likely even to consider. For example, the Cubs may have just given two pitchers, two infielders, an outfielder and plenty of cash to get Jimmy Sheckard from Brooklyn. As a matter of fact, Chance did give Brooklyn four players and a piece of money for Sheckard, and thereby he made the Cubs a virtually unbeatable ball club for three years. On account of things like that, it was silly for us to pass up Mr. Murphy's office entirely, though the temptation was to hurry on and join Ban and Commy, who provided less news, but a great deal more refreshment.

However, I promised somebody, perhaps the editor, to lay off baseball for a while and come back to it later on. Well, my winter-evening assignments on the Inter-Ocean were wrestling, indoor track meets, swimming meets and one basket-ball game, with an occasional trip to near-by Wisconsin towns for boxing bouts, that sport being then *verboten* in Chi.

To save my life, I cannot tell you now the intimate details of any track meet I attended. All I can remember concerning them was that Michigan or Chicago or Illinois was invariably tied with the Illinois Athletic Club or the Chicago Athletic Association at 1:45 in the morning; that the outcome depended on the pole vault, and that every time anyone got into the mood to vault, the pole broke, or the crossbar fell off, or the guy changed his mind. Meanwhile, of course, my sporting editor, Duke Hutchinson, or his assistant, Dick Tobin, would be murdering me via the Morse code because the result was still undecided and they were without a lead.

The Illinois Athletic Club had a swimming coach named Frank Sullivan. This meant that the I. A. C. won all the swimming meets until Frank was wheedled away from Chicago by Princeton. You could write your swimming story around noon and then drop in at the I. A. C. about midnight just to be sure that Frank's swimmers had not forgotten to show up.

The only basket-ball match—do they call them matches?—I covered was a ghastly affair between Yale and the Central Y. M. C. A. of Chicago. Yale's five—or is it seven?—was making a holiday trip through the Middle West. I shall never know or care whether its team was good or bad. My ignorance of, and disinterest in, basket ball is something that could not be set down in one volume, and when it was announced before playtime that Yale, which had been using intercollegiate rules, must perform according to A. A. U. rules to please our Y. M. C. A., I was baffled still further.

But if I was baffled, what was Yale? Every time I looked up from my Ovid a foul was being called on the Blue, and the latter was more than thirty points behind before you could mention any of the Robinsons. I am proud to state that never since that evening have I consciously been within a block of an armory or gymnasium where basket ball was scheduled.

Wrestling, I guess, has been the same old bowl of cherries ever since Jack Curley imported it to this country. Save when Frank Gotch was performing—and he was beaten once after a lot of rehearsals—the games generally went by service. I remember covering a match in Chicago one night, and after the first fall, I dropped in next door and had a drink with the referee. He asked me how I was betting, and I told him I had five dollars on the Turk. "Hedge and get on the Pole if you can," he advised. "It's his turn." So I hedged and got on the Pole, and the Pole won, though the Turk was one fall up.

Jack Curley it was who introduced this young man and a few of his pals to Chicago society. The city was, and still is, divided into wards, from each of which two aldermen are elected every two years to the Common Council, and when I say "Common" I am not just groping for words.

The First Ward took in the big department stores, with their free lunch. The perennial aldermen from this ward were Bathhouse John and Hinky Dink.

Bathhouse John built a flop house so that some of his constituents might have a place in which to sleep off the effects of their shopping in his and Hinky Dink's bazaars before the hour for balloting arrived. However, as I say, the inclusion of a bathroom in the hotel was an error. One election morning a guest disrobed by removing two sleeves and a trouser, filled the tub with what looked like gin, climbed into it and lost, by drowning, a newt that had nestled against his bosom ever since he left Pennsylvania. Twelve of his comrades spent the entire day trying vainly to resuscitate the fondling with a stomach pump which somebody had brought along as bagpipes. Thus Bathhouse John lost a dozen votes and had his majority cut to two hundred and fifty thousand.

When Bathhouse John went into politics, Tin Pan Alley lost a second Lew Brown or a third Irving Caesar. As I recall, only one of his songs was published.

Well, in those times you were not crudely asked for a contribution to the campaign fund. You were honored with an invitation to the First Ward Ball. You were invited to bring five guests, for each box held six people. The ball was staged at the Coliseum, and the admission fee was ten dollars a person. In addition, the boxes were sixty dollars apiece. You were requested to dress formally, which meant not to come barefooted.

The beautifully engraved invitations were sent to wrestling promoters, dance-hall proprietors and keepers of gilded saloons and cafés. In the lower left-hand corner they bore the initials R. S. V. P. Very few of the recipients knew what these initials meant. But they did know that if they failed to show up and kick in, they would not run any more wrestling shows, conduct any more dance halls, or stay open more than a week at a stretch.

Jack Curley, looking around for people who had black suits, invited Walter Eckersall and me, two others who do not matter, and a man I shall call Paul Heinz, which is very far from his name. He was one of the best rewrite men ever on a newspaper, and last time I saw him was on Long Island, trying to sell refrigerators. In my pretty good opinion, New York newspapers need real rewrite men more than Long Island needs refrigerators.

The waiters were not paid—at least, not by the gents giving the ball. They themselves paid, a hundred dollars apiece and more, for the privilege of waiting. And despite the fact that one of Mr. Kenna's "places" specialized in goldfish bowls full of beer at five cents a bowl, the only drink procurable at this Coliseum function was champagne at ten dollars a bottle. And so far as I am concerned, I would trade all the champagne ever grown in La Belle France for one authentic mint julep.

Anyway, poor Jack had to keep buying and buying, and we had to keep drinking and drinking, but your watchful young reporter kept his vision clear enough to note that the next two or three boxes were occupied by members of the Follies of 1907, the first of all Flo Ziegfeld's Follies shows. In addition to Flo himself, who must have paid a pretty penny for the evening's entertainment, there were—I am quoting from memory and the producer—Harry B. Smith, the librettist, Bickell and Watson, Dave Lewis, Adele Carson, Emma Carus, Tempest and Sunshine, Charles J. Ross, Julian Mitchell, Mlle. Dazie, Billy Reeves, Grace La Rue and The Original Gibson Girl. Some of us had seen the show during its Chicago run—you could buy a balcony seat then for a dollar or so—and had adjudged it the best all-around entertainment ever given in a theater, which, at that time, it probably was. Flo was just as prodigal with girls, costumes and scenery a quarter of a century ago as he is today, and his comedy was unbelievably better.

The proximity of the stage folk had us in more or less of a fever. Even Eckie, who was ordinarily indifferent to matters theatrical, displayed traces of extraordinary excitement. I had an eye for Miss La Rue, Miss Carus and the other ladies, but my real interest was in Harry Watson—whom I have always considered one of the stage's greatest comics—and the fascinating Billy Reeves, who, as you may be too young to know, played a drunk, something like Leon Errol's drunk, always falling or about to fall. His entrance in the Follies was from a stage box, out of which he fell onto the stage, just missing the foots. He was usually dressed in an ill-fitting full-dress suit and his nose was painted a vivid red. Either to get a laugh or because of his eagerness to be on time for the party, he was still in full make-up at the Coliseum.

But Paul Heinz could not see Reeves or Bickell and Watson; he was also blind to the presence of Miss Carus and Miss La Rue. Every other moment I could hear him muttering, "She belongs to me," and after a very few mutterings I deduced that "She" was none other than The Original Gibson Girl.

The latter's identity is something I would gladly reveal to you if it were possible. But my copy of the old program does not tell, I was not introduced to her myself, Mr. Gibson did not select her for the part, and Mr. Ziegfeld cannot remember her name. All I can say is that she was beautiful and that she belonged to Paul Heinz right up to the instant he started toward her box to claim her.

At that instant there was the unmistakable crack of a revolver, and a bullet, plowing a groove in the floor, just missed one of Paul's unsteady feet. It also drove into the night all the featured members of the Follies of 1907. And it caused Jack Curley, our host, to order Eckie and me to "get that guy out of here"—an order which we gladly and speedily obeyed.

No one seemed to know or care who had done the firing. It was just an incident of the ball, which, now I think of it, was a peculiar ball in that there was no music or dancing. Eckie and I put Paul to bed and left him asleep. Then we dropped in at Sol Bloom's, on Twenty-second Street, knowing the Follies crowd would be there. We found also a crowd of University of Chicago undergraduates, giving their yells and those of other Middle Western colleges. They were interrupted by Billy Reeves, who, though an Englishman, had memorized some Princeton, Yale and Harvard cheers, and, standing on a table, delivered them amid wild applause.

"I am an English citizen," he boasted, "but I know the cheer of every school in the United States."

As he spoke, we saw entering—and nobody could help see entering—a pale-faced young man of twenty-two or twenty-three, whose hair had been carefully combed and brushed by the roof of a taxi, whose ready-made St. Louis dinner clothes had been freshly rehabilitated by a half hour's tussle with a mattress, whose eyes were ablaze with an *idée fixe,* and whose every lunge forward knocked a defensive waiter sprawling to the floor with a trayful of Sol's almost priceless grog.

Straight-arming, hurdling, dodging and spinning, our hero, whom you surely have recognized by this time, reached Billy Reeves' table and lifted the great British comic down onto the floor.

"Now," he commanded, "you give me my girl! She belongs to me! And after that I want to hear the cheer of the Peekskill Military Academy!"

Eckie

(*The Saturday Evening Post,* 20 February 1932)

There was great excitement around the Chicago Inter-Ocean office during the last two or three days of January, 1908. The prophets had declared that if we found the place still open at noon on February second, the paper would exist for six more weeks. Since the beginning of the year it had been common gossip in the town that we were on our last limbs, and the issuance of weekly pay checks was always followed by a foot race downstairs to the bank; the theory being that only the first five or six to reach the paying teller's cage would land in the money.

However, according to the best of my knowledge and belief, all the employes of the I.-O. were paid in full when publication finally ceased. I was not on hand for the funeral, because I received, on February first, an offer from Harry Shroudenbach, sporting editor of the Examiner, to join his staff immediately at the noble salary of twenty-five dollars a week, an increase of $6.50 over what I had been getting. My Inter-Ocean boss, Duke Hutchinson, advised me to grab the offer before it was withdrawn; whether from kindliness or from the fact that he was tired of seeing me around, I shall never know.

With Hugh Fullerton, star baseball writer, hibernating, the Examiner's sporting staff was numerically equal to the Inter-Ocean's. We had Shroudy, the sports editor, Duffy Cornell, his assistant, and Sam Hall and me, domestics. It was important, of course, to get the news into the paper, but more important than that, it seemed, was to write startling, pretty, perfectly fitting headlines of an intricacy which still makes me shiver in retrospect. The sport pages' first and last columns had to be crowned with what were called "Whitney heads," and I don't believe the best copy reader in the world would call them simple. They were triangular in shape, with the base on top and the vertex on the bottom; thus:

GOTCH BREAKS BEALL'S
FOOT WITH TOE HOLD
AS RECORD CROWD
AT COLISEUM
GOES STARK
MAD

Below that was a single cross line, then a double, uneven cross line —both of them common in the heads of today—and finally a symmetrical bank, in small type, that was supposed to tell everything you hadn't told before.

These headlines were undoubtedly a delight to the eye of the reader, but a pain in the neck to the person or persons who wrote them. One in an evening, if you could take your time, was no trouble at all. But when you had to tear off four or six, with a two-minute limit for each, you were ready to spend your off day seeking oblivion.

And that reminds me of three successive off days I took—one of them on the office and the other two on myself—during which so much oblivion was found that it is a wonder the Examiner did not advertise at once for another maid of all work. On Monday, my regular day of recess, I began a preliminary reconnaissance of the South Side. There was so much ground to cover that my explorations were far from complete when someone told me it was Tuesday afternoon and time to report for duty. I reported, and received a note from Shroudy stating that he and Mr. Cornell and Mr. Hall had all left for Milwaukee to handle the big fight. Shroudy was going to write the lead, Mr. Cornell the detail, and Mr. Hall the notes. I can't remember what fight it was, possibly one of the terrific battles between Billy Papke and Stanley Ketchel.

Well, all three of them were good fight writers and any Papke-Ketchel fight was bound to be a good fight; particularly good for a Chicago paper because Papke's home was in Illinois and Ketchel's —whether he ever saw it or not—in Michigan. Just the same, it seemed kind of quaint to leave a hick like me alone in the office to take care of their copy and all the other sport copy that would come in, while the three experienced guys went on a junket to Milwaukee for the simple reason that they were wild-eyed fight fans. Shroudy's instructions said I would have to watch my step, because the stuff would arrive by wire a piece at a time; I would have to figure out whose stuff was whose and keep it all straightened out.

Unseen audience, I wish I had preserved the Examiner's Papke-Ketchel story of that Wednesday morning. Not even a broadcaster could have got things more messed up. Lead, detail and notes were all jumbled together and Round 1 probably read something like this:

> The boys were called to the center of the ring and received instructions from William Hale Thompson, Ernest Byfield, Percy Hammond, Charles Richter, the Spring Valley Thunderbolt tore in as if he had never heard another crowd made the trip as guests of William Lydon on his yacht the Lydonia Steve cut loose with a left uppercut that nearly this makes certain another meeting between the Battling Nelson and Packey McFarland were also introduced. Steve slipped as he was about to. Seven special trains but the majority thought the round was even it was Papke's round.

That and three or four columns more of the same. The stuff had come in just in time to make the first edition; there was no chance for proofreading or rearranging. And when the edition reached the main copy desk it was greeted with such hilarity that even I woke up and took the advice of a reporter friend who told me to get out of the office before the Milwaukee train bearing my boss and his colleagues arrived back in town.

I sought a quiet spot where I knew Walter Eckersall would eventually appear. When a fellow needed a friend, there was none to be found more satisfactory than Eckie. On this occasion he convinced me that it was not my fault and escorted me in a taxi to my lodgings, leaving me, as he thought, to woo forgetfulness in sleep.

But for some reason I was still restless, and ten minutes after he had gone I was in another taxi, on another sight-seeing tour of Chicago. An account of this trip would be extremely dull, even if I were able to recall any of the details. My chauffeur and I probably called on a great many people who have moved since then. Late Wednesday afternoon it occurred to me that the sooner I knew I was fired the sooner I could start looking for a new job. I asked to be taken to the Examiner office. The meter, I was told, read $132 and this was $130.20 more than I had. The chauffeur appeared vexed at my suggestion that we meet later and talk things out, and he was searching his tool box for an instrument with which to express his mortification when who should pour forth from the office door but Shroudy himself!

"What's the matter?" he said, and was soon informed. And within the next ten minutes he saw the cashier, settled with the taxi man, assured me I was still on the staff and that he realized he had overburdened me the night before, and sent me home to sleep till six o'clock Thursday evening, "when," he added, "we'll start all over."

You will realize by this time that my bosses were pretty well supplied with the so-called milk of human kindness. This pleasant surprise, however, was a double play in which Eckie ought to be credited with an assist. I learned long afterward that the latter had pleaded my cause for hours and had even gone to his own boss, Harvey Woodruff, of the Tribune, and persuaded him to make room for me in the event I got the air from the Examiner, though the Trib already employed so many people in the sporting department that half the writers had to buy seats from the agencies or work lying on their stomachs.

Eckie would do almost anything for anybody, but his friendliness toward me was a natural—I was the only person he knew who shared his horror of going to bed. Night after night, until it was almost the next night, we would sit and just talk; nearly always on one subject —football. And I want to testify that never did I hear him brag of his own skill at that sport, skill equaled—in my opinion and that of other experts who have visited or dwelt in the wilderness west of the Hudson River—only by Jim Thorpe, of Carlisle, and George Gipp, of Notre Dame.

Thorpe and Gipp were quadruple-threat men—they could pass, run, point-kick and punt. Eckie was a triple threat; the forward pass was introduced too late for him to work on it. Nevertheless, when you consider his all-around athletic prowess and his ability as a baseball player, you must conclude that he would have been even more valuable in the modern game than in the old.

Study his equipment for a moment. As a track man at Hyde Park High School, he had done the hundred repeatedly in 10 flat. After he entered the University of Chicago, he got down to 09 4/5 in practice a couple of times and continued to do his 10 consistently in competition. Once, as a stunt, he went the route in 10 1/5 dressed in his football costume. As a quarterback he was a cool, smart director of play. Perhaps not so hard to bring down as Heston, Mahan or Grange, he was harder to catch because of his terrific speed; he played back on defense, and when an opposing team punted to him it was not punting out of danger but into it. I firmly believe Eckie was the reason for Fielding Yost's insistence that his punters learn to punt out of bounds; when a punter boots a high spiral straight down the field for fifty yards, it disheartens a coach to see the punt brought back forty of those yards in spite of faultless covering by competent ends and tackles. As safety man, he was eluded, so far as I know, just once, and that was by Willie Heston. And when Willie eluded you, you were not disgraced. You were merely grateful that you had not been killed.

Now for his kicking. In the Middle West only Pat O'Dea, of Wisconsin, not a contemporary of Eckie's, was the latter's master in drop-kicking and punting, just as he—Pat—was everybody else's superior in these two specialties. It is unnecessary to take my word for that last clause; the record books will bear me out. But Eckie's punts, well aimed and high, averaged close to forty yards, and if he failed to score on a drop kick from thirty yards out, it was almost as much of a shock to the community as seeing Jimmy Walker in a Mother Hubbard.

Seven or eight years after the close of Eckie's college career—and by this time I was a Tribune man, too—there came into the office one Saturday night a story from Harvard—or wherever Harvard had played that day—saying that Charles Brickley had kicked five goals from field in the game with Yale, breaking the world's record so far as major university competition was concerned. Well, everybody around the office knew that Eckie had done the same thing in a game against Illinois, but to make sure, Harvey Woodruff, the sporting editor, asked him.

"Why, yes," he replied, "but maybe Chicago and Illinois are just prep schools." Then, after a pause, "Listen, Woody; I didn't break a record that time any more than Brickley did this afternoon. Mr. Stagg looked it up and found that I had only tied an old record made by a fella at Purdue."

Now you mustn't ask me who the Purdue fella was. The only

prominent athletes from that university whose names I can recall are
G. P. Torrence, Elmer Oliphant and George Ade, and I know it was
none of these.

I discovered years ago that the best way to judge an athlete's worth
was by learning what his opponents, past and to come, really thought
of him. It was from the people who had tried to hit, or were about
to try to hit, Walter Johnson in his good years that I gleaned the
knowledge that no other pitcher of our times was in his class. And
the men of Yost's great, but not greatest, Michigan elevens of 1904
and 1905 were unable to hide the fact that the very name of Walter
Eckersall gave them a headache.

Eckie's first start against Michigan, however, was a life-sized flop.
It was on Thanksgiving Day, 1903, when freshmen were still permit-
ted to play on the varsity. Snow had been predicted, and Marshall
Field, in Chicago, was covered with hay until an hour before game
time. As soon as the hay was removed, the snowfall began and in an
incredibly few minutes there were six inches of it on the ground. The
start of the game was delayed until it had ceased falling and the
ground keeper and his crew had succeeded in removing it from the
field and piling it up a yard out of bounds and behind the goal line.

During the game, which Michigan won, 28 to 0, the regular
Chicago quarterback, Lee Maxwell, was hauled from a drift and
taken to the locker room by relays of dog teams, to be scraped off
and thawed out. Eckie replaced him, and I can still remember his
chef d'oeuvre of the day—a pitiable attempt to punt from a pile of
snow in which he was buried a couple of yards behind his own goal.
The ball traveled nearly two yards and a half. It was Michigan's ball
now and Michigan called Heston's signal, either through sheer
venom or because it was the only signal Michigan had. You can guess
what happened with half a yard to go.

In 1904, Heston's last year, the Wolverines maintained their proud
record of victories which had begun with the engagement of Fielding
Yost as coach three seasons before. They beat Chicago 22 to 12, I
think, but Eckie's beautiful open-field running, which was responsible for his team's twelve points, had my old home state frightened
to such an extent that for months afterward, children hid in the cellar
if you said, "Eckersall." In the same year the late Walter Camp
discovered that the United States was not bounded on the West by

Pennsylvania, and honored both Eckie and Heston with positions on his All-America team. Eckie was chosen again the following season, and five years later when Mr. Camp selected his All-America Team for All Time, positions were awarded Eckie and two other Middle-Westerners, Schulz and Heston, of Michigan.

The 145-pound Chicago quarterback really came into his own in 1905. This was the season in which he kicked five goals from field against Illinois, and he added to the latter's embarrassment by running twenty-five yards for a touchdown. The battle with Wisconsin was tough, but Eckie won it with a twenty-five-yard drop kick, after dashes of fifty, forty and thirty yards had failed to subdue the battling Badgers.

But all games in my memory fade into insignificance compared with the Thanksgiving Day struggle at Marshall Field, Chicago, when Michigan, thanks to Eckie, suffered its first defeat in the reign of Yost. This game was so close and so bitterly fought, and the hostility it aroused between two formerly friendly states so marked, that the Chicago ambassador to Ann Arbor asked for his passports, and vice versa, and athletic relations were severed and stayed severed for years and years and years.

In common with everybody else from Michigan, I felt murderously inclined toward Eckie that day, and not until I got to know him would I admit to myself or anyone else that all he had done was play a great and victorious game of football against a school that had held a monopoly on football glory in the hinterlands since 1900. I could write you, from memory, whole books about that game. Instead, I shall let you off with a paragraph or two.

Chicago was badly handicapped because one of its star halfbacks, Leo De Tray, was sitting in the stand with a bandage over one damaged eye. Michigan became equally handicapped when its star tackle, Joe Curtis, was disqualified for alleged roughing of Eckie on a punt. Michigan made two or three of its familiar marches toward touchdowns, but was always stopped just short. The kicking duel between Eckie and Johnny Garrels was nearly an even thing. The Chicago line was playing over its head and Michigan's defense, led by Tom Hammond, was doing well to keep Bezdek's terrific attack from becoming fatal.

Along in the second half, Chicago had possession of the ball right up against its own goal line. Eckie dropped way back of the goal to punt, but he didn't punt. He ran the ball out nearly to midfield. This is the kind of play that is great if it works, and bone-headed if it doesn't. I have seen Thorpe and Gipp get by with similar plays, which would indicate that Lady Luck is with the stars. Chicago, with Bezdek plunging, was stopped again, and this time Eckie did punt. It was a whale of a punt and came down within inches of Michigan's goal line, where Clark, a substitute back, began to toy with it. He could not make up his mind whether to let it go for a touchback or to run it somewhere. He finally decided on the latter alternative, but it was too late. Just as he gathered the ball into his arms, he was hit, and hit hard, by Catlin and Speik, of Chicago. He was knocked, not for a goal but for a safety, and that's how the game ended, 2 to 0. And it was the first time my girl friend had ever seen me cry.

Ten years elapsed and I was doing a sport column on the Chicago Tribune. My readers had never learned to write, so I was entirely without contributions, and therefore hard up for material. On Thanksgiving morning I printed a dream story of a Michigan-Chicago game that was supposed to take place that afternoon. I wrote an introduction and followed it with a probable line-up, naming players who had been stars ten or twenty years in the past.

Now, there had been no hint of a resumption of athletic relations between Chicago and Michigan. Moreover, Thanksgiving games had been ruled out of the Middle West long, long before, because they interfered with church or turkey or something. Nevertheless, believe it or not, a crowd of more than five hundred people—this is Mr. Stagg's estimate—went to the University of Chicago's football field that day and stood around for hours, waiting for the gates or the ticket windows to open. At length they returned home mad, and many of them telephoned indignant messages to my boss.

This just goes to show that I had Chicago pretty well under my thumb when I sold it to the Sicilians. Also that the typewriter is pretty near as mighty as the rod.

Alias James Clarkson

(*The Saturday Evening Post*, 16 April 1932)

Within the space of fourteen hours of a day in March, Lardner Common, a purely speculative stock, reached a new low and a new high for the year 1908. Employes of the Chicago Examiner received their pay on Monday afternoons. At half-past two or three o'clock Tuesday mornings, a septet composed of our sporting department and three men from the main copy desk would go to a room in a Loop hotel and play a game known as poker until five of us were flat and had signed as many I O U's as the winners saw fit to take. The hotel always had a room ready—a table, chairs, a waiter and accessories. We played dollar jackpots, with an occasional hand of stud. It was before the era of deuces and treys wild, the lively ball, and mellow, twenty-hour-old Bourbon, distilled and aged in the Blue Grass of Little Sicily.

The gang was amazed when, on this particular March morning, I bought thirty dollars' worth of checks instead of my usual twenty-five; everybody knew that twenty-five was what the Examiner paid me, and in 1908 a newspaperman got no salary excepting from his newspaper. Like Mr. Seabury's witnesses in New York, I cannot recall the source of my additional wealth, and besides, it has nothing to do with the story. But the gang was still further amazed when I started out as if to make a killing; my luck had been notoriously bad. Now, at the end of an hour and a half, I was more than one hundred and fifty dollars ahead and wishing that someone would suggest an armistice.

A high official of the state of Illinois entered our den of vice and asked to be dealt in. We were all acquainted with him; he had once been a newspaperman himself. He was first told that eight was a crowd, but he promised he would stay only a little while. He wrote a check for fifty dollars and inquired who would cash it. The silence was so embarrassing that I couldn't stand it. I cashed the check. It was the break of the game; in a very few minutes my winnings had

55

been wiped out and I had twenty dollars left of my original stake.

Then occurred something that simply could not happen in eight-handed poker. The pot was passed five times in a row. Bill Hallowell dealt the sixth hand and I was under the gun. I looked and saw four aces. I looked again; the first look had been right. I thought, "Here is where I get it all back and some more." And I passed. So did everybody else.

That afternoon, accompanied by a man who could and would identify me, I visited the bank on which the statesman's check was drawn. The check bounced back and hit me just below the eye, causing an ugly flesh wound and severe internal injuries. Around six in the evening I reported at the office and was called aside by my sporting editor, Harry Shroudenbach.

"Did you cash So-and-So's check?" he inquired.

"It was no good," said I.

"You're the only one who thought it would be. Don't worry about it though. The gang will split it with you. Just the same, it's my duty to get you out of Chicago before you buy Lincoln Park."

He went on to tell me that I was to join the White Sox in the South, travel with them through the rest of their spring tour and, if I made good, Stick With Them All Season! O diary!

Never since that night have I criticized anyone for fickleness! Happy beyond words, I jumped from the National to the American League, and the Cubs, whom I had idolized all my life, became nonexistent so far as I was concerned. Ed Walsh, formerly an object of hatred, was now my hero and soon to be my friend. Mordecai Brown and Ed Reulbach—theretofore objects of my worship—were suddenly as unimportant as going to bed.

As a matter of fact, I was not being highly honored. The Cubs looked like a cinch to repeat. They deserved an experienced and able historian, and Hughey Fullerton was all of that. The Sox were old and faded and out at the heels. If anything happened to Walsh, they would be lucky to finish in organized baseball. In any case, so the Examiner, and most Chicagoans, thought, they had all the earmarks of a Class B outfit, and I was a Class B scribe. But what did I care? At least I was through with trying to write hot heads on West Side Y. M. C. A. basket-ball games.

"Will my stuff be signed?" I asked timidly.

"Sure," said Shroudy. "You are James Clarkson now, and don't disgrace that grand old name."

James Clarkson, if you must know, was the Examiner's perennial expert. Hughey Fullerton and Charley Dryden might come and go, but James stayed on forever. I don't know who originated him; I only know his job was safe and that the fans swore by him. And why not? He had been writing baseball day after day, year after year, and how were the fans to guess that he never was the same person two years in succession?

The Sox were in New Orleans, at the old St. Charles Hotel. It was evening when James Clarkson, vintage of 1908, arrived. Secretary Fredericks was out. Manager Jones was out. I found George Rice, correspondent for the Chicago Daily News. He suggested that I accompany him upstairs and get acquainted with some of the boys.

Three of the boys—Walsh, Doc White and Jiggs Donohue—were sitting on a bed, singing. As is customary in hotels, the bed was in a room, and the room, I learned, was the temporary home of Doc White and Frank Isbell. Five of the boys—Izzy, Billy Sullivan, Pat Dougherty, Nick Altrock and Frank Smith—were playing ten-cent limit. The limit had been ordered by Manager Jones, who judged, and judged rightly, that the loss of large sums of money at cards often made the losers mad, and sometimes they stayed mad for several days and were hit on the head by fly balls which they would have caught if they hadn't been thinking of those large sums of money. Mr. Jones, christened Fielder by prophetic parents, was one of the smartest managers the game—not poker—has seen, but he did err in presuming that you can't lose large sums at a ten-cent limit. I found out different, as Eddie Hahn used to say.

The gamblers looked up and the singers paused while I was being introduced.

"Are you going to travel with us all season?" asked Nick Altrock.

"If I don't get canned," I said.

"Well, don't get canned," said Nick. "Every place we light in, some goofer wants to know 'Who is that homely guy with your club?' and these guys say, 'You must mean Altrock.' After this they won't be so unanimous."

Nick, of course, meant this as a joke. I was twenty-three years old and constantly being mistaken for John Barrymore.

"Looks aren't everything," said Izzy Isbell.

"Which is just as well for this ball club," said Sully.

It was my turn to speak, so I told Jiggs Donohue that I had been graduated from the Central League and knew his brother, Frank; moreover, that Frank was a sweet young infielder.

"How does he hit?" asked Doc White.

"Well———" I said.

"A born Donohue," said Nick.

"Listen," said Jiggs: "I don't even try to hit like I can hit. It's teamwork that wins ball games, and if I was to try and hit like I can hit, you fellas would think I wasn't with you. Just this afternoon Jones called me down for hitting safe. He told me that he didn't want any innovations on this club."

After a while George Rice escorted me back to the lobby, saying that Manager Jones had probably returned.

"He's a swell fella, but a rough kidder," warned George. "Don't be scared of the way he talks. It's the only fun he has except arguing with umpires."

The manager sat staring into space, his usual occupation when not on the ball field. I had seen him at a distance many times, but never until this close-up had I noticed his resemblance to my conception of Sherlock Holmes. And seven months of association with him convinced me that he could outguess and outsmart Conan Doyle's famous needle snatcher. The following repartee, however, is not offered as evidence of this.

George Rice made the presentation speech and withdrew.

"I suppose," Fielder supposed, "you're just another pest. You'll probably ask a lot of childish questions."

"Undoubtedly," I said.

"Well, go ahead and shoot, and let's get it over. But first, where do you come from? I mean where were you born?"

"Niles, Michigan."

"Have you been working in Chicago long?"

"Three months and a half."

"How old are you?"

"Twenty-three. White. Grandparents on both sides lived to be seventy."

"You're fresh, too, aren't you? What I'm trying to get at is, what qualifies you to write about baseball? You couldn't learn it in Niles. I've been through the place. There aren't enough men to make up a ball club."

"We were shy one, so we used a woman in center field."

"Niles wit! But I'm serious. Why do metropolitan newspapers hire inexperienced kids like you to report big-league baseball?"

"I think it's my turn to ask a childish question. Were you a manager the first year you broke into the big league?"

"All right, Niles. We'll get along if you don't pester me too much. The boys that drive me crazy are the ones who want to know who's going to pitch tomorrow. If I can't tell them and they guess wrong, they're sore."

"I promise never to bother you with a question like that. My paper will be satisfied if I guess right three-quarters of the time. So I'll just stick to Walsh."

That is a more or less accurate account of my first interview with Fielder Jones. I know you are dying to read a similar account of the club's record in New Orleans and the towns in which it played on the way north. I am sorry to say that I failed to memorize this record and I must have left my 1908 scorebook in my other pajamas. And so I shall fill in these few minutes by telling you about a spare-time job which I picked up in Nashville, Tennessee, and held, off and on, for two or three years.

The Sox had a regular infielder named Jack Gibbs. His home was in Brooklyn and his wife's name was Myrtle. He had been graduated from college—*cum laude*—at the age of four, and everybody on the club knew that he could neither read nor write.

When I say his name was Gibbs, his home was in Brooklyn, that he was an infielder and his wife's name was Myrtle, I am not telling the truth. But when I say he could neither read nor write, I don't mean maybe. Give him a sheet of paper with "Jack Gibbs" and "George Washington" written or printed thereon, and he could not tell one from the other. When a new contract needed his signature, he was Madame X.

He suspected that the other players and the veteran scribes were aware of his idiosyncrasy; nevertheless, he persisted in trying to convince them that they were wrong. He would buy a paper and go through it column by column, page by page. He would insist on seeing the bill of fare in hotels or diners and, after a long and careful study, order steak and baked potato, or ham and eggs, or both.

Well, I don't claim to have brightened many a corner, but I certainly was a godsend to Jack Gibbs. Being new, I could not, he thought, have learned his secret; therefore, I was the only one in the crowd who could be of real service to him. When we were traveling and he was tired of steak or ham and eggs, he would maneuver to sit with me in the dining car, knowing that I habitually read menus aloud from top to bottom. It was also my custom, he discovered, to turn to the baseball page in a paper and read that aloud just as I did the menus. So he breakfasted with me as often as he could. All this part of our relationship came after Nashville, where, as I have stated, my spare-time job began.

It is necessary at this point to confess my only failing—a horror of writing anything, even my own name, in script. Longhand is and always has been a terrible ordeal to me, and I hope these few lines are being read by the two or three high-school boys, or girls, fourteen years old, who seem to be collecting autographs.

Anyway, my first order of business when I got to a town was to rent a typewriter, for portables had not been invented—had they?— in 1908. And so it happened that Jack Gibbs heard me clicking away in my room at Nashville, and was struck by a great idea.

"Hello, Eva," he said, entering without the formality of a rap at the door. "I was wondering if you would do me a favor. It ain't really a favor. It's a kind of a joke."

To the rest of the ball players I was always Niles or Lard. But Jack Gibbs had christened me Eva, and perhaps that is what made me feel so close to him.

"You see," he went on, "I just got a letter from the old woman, the missis. I thought it would be a kind of a joke if she got the answer back on a typewriter. She would think I wrote it and wouldn't know what the hell. Would you mind writing me an answer on the typewriter, and I'll send it to her just like I wrote it myself."

"Sure, Jack," I agreed. "But you'll have to tell me what to say."

"Well, let's see. Well, I better read her letter over again first. Or suppose you read it, Eva. Then you'll know what she wants. And you may as well read it out loud."

My recollection is that the old woman's letter was short and businesslike. It said, in effect: "How can you expect me to meet you in Chicago unless you send me some money? I don't intend to make the trip out there on a freight, and I don't want to get my feet all blisters walking."

Jack was no good at dictation. Neither am I—a failing I had forgotten about.

"Well, I guess you better tell her where we are first. No. Start out this way: 'Dear Myrt.' And then tell her she knows damn well I don't get no pay till the last of April, and nothing then because I already drawed ahead. Tell her to borrow off Edith von Driska, and she can pay her back the first of May. Tell her I never felt better in my life and looks like I will have a great year, if they's nothing to worry me like worrying about money. Tell her the weather's been great, just like summer, only them two days it rained in Birmingham. It rained a couple days in Montgomery and a week in New Orleans. My old souper feels great. Detroit is the club we got to beat—them and Cleveland and St. Louis, and maybe the New York club. Oh, you know what to tell her. You know what they like to hear."

Perhaps I didn't tell her all that they like to hear; perhaps my newborn loyalty to the South prevented my mentioning the rainy days in Montgomery, Birmingham and New Orleans. But I think I made her understand.

"Now, what's the address?" I inquired.

"Mrs. Jack Gibbs, 1235 Sterling Place, Brooklyn, New York," said my boss.

" 'Sterling' with an *e* or an *i?*"

"Oh, that don't make no difference. But I'm much obliged, Eva. She'll be tickled to death."

I handed him the finished product, ready for stamping and mailing. He looked intently at the front of the envelope.

"Are you sure you put 'Brooklyn'?" he said.

Oddities of Bleacher "Bugs"

(*The Boston American,* 23 July 1911)

Listen to Some of the Funny Mistakes the "Fans" Make

If reporters of baseball didn't have to sit up in the press box they would probably like their jobs better. Not that said box is such a dull place, with all the repartee of the scribes, operators and "critics." But it would be much more fun to listen to, and take part in, the conversations in the bleachers, where the real "bugs" sit.

Time was when we liked nothing better than to pay our two bits, rush for a point of vantage back of first or third base or out in the neighborhood of right of left field, invest a nickel in a sack of peanuts, another nickel in a score card, and then settle down to try to prove, by our comments and shouts, that we knew more about baseball than anyone around us.

That was when we spoke of "inshoots" and "outs" and "drops" and "outdrops"; wondered who that was hitting in place of So-and-So and thought ball players were just a little bit better than other people, because they wouldn't pay any attention to us if we drummed up nerve enough to speak to them outside the park.

It was before we knew that there's no such thing as an inshoot, that "outs," "drops" and "outdrops" are merely "curve balls"; before we could identify a substitute batter or a new pitcher by just glancing for an instant at his left ear, or his walk, or noting the way his hair was brushed in the back; before we were absolutely positive that the players are just common human beings and that some of them are really no better than ourselves.

But it was lots more joy in those days. There may be a certain kind of pleasure in brushing majestically past the pass-gate man, strutting along the rear aisle of the stand in the hope that some one will know you are a baseball writer, speaking to a player or two and getting answered, finding your own particular seat in the press box and proceeding to enlighten the absent public regarding the important events on the field, in your own, bright, breezy style. But what fun is all that compared with scraping up the necessary quarter, or half dollar, and knowing you are going to SEE a game, not report it?

The man who is on intimate terms with the ball players, who calls at their hotel and takes them out in his machine, goes to the station with them to see them off, gets letters from them occasionally, and knows they are just people, isn't the real "fan" or "bug," even if he does have to pay to get into the park.

The real article is the man who knows most of the players by sight, as they appear on the field, but wouldn't know more than one or two of them if he saw them on the street, struggles hard to keep an accurate score and makes a mistake on every other play, or doesn't attempt to score at all, disputes every statement made by his neighbors in the bleachers whether he knows anything about said statement or not, heaps imprecations on the umpire and the manager, thinks something is a bonehead play when it really is good, clever baseball, talks fluently about Mathewson's "inshoot" believes that Hank O'Day has it in for the home team and is purposely making bad decisions, and says, "Bransfield is going to bat for Moore" when Walsh is sent in to hit for Chalmers.

He doesn't know it all, but he's happy. He is perfectly satisfied when the folks around him believe what he says, and sometimes he almost gets to believing it himself. He's having a thoroughly enjoyable afternoon, if his team wins. If it doesn't, he knows just why and can tell his wife, his brother or his pal, that evening, how the tables could have been turned if only Manager Tenney had used a little judgment.

His imagination is a wonderful thing. Without it he would be unable to make any sort of an impression on his fellows. He must talk unhesitantly, as if he had all the facts, and never stammer or back up when his assertions are questioned.

Pat Moran is catching for the Phillies. Everybody knows Pat. He is getting a chance to work because President Lynch has set down Charley Dooin for a "bad ride." A tall foul is hit. Pat gets under it but makes a square muff.

"He's a rotten catcher," says a nearby fan.

"He's a mighty good catcher when he's right," replies our friend.

"Why isn't he right?" queries the nearby one, sarcastically. "He's had time enough to get in shape, hasn't he?"

"No ball player can keep in shape and drink the way Pat does," is the come-back. "I was down town last night and I saw the whole Philadelphia bunch. Pat was certainly pouring in the strong stuff. He's a regular reservoir."

This remark is greeted with silence because no one has nerve enough to come out with a positive denial of the tale. As a matter of fact, Pat never touches the "strong stuff," and if he bunched all his annual drinking into one night, he'd still be thirsty. But that doesn't make any difference with our friend. He has scored a point by seeming to know why Pat dropped the foul ball.

Charley Herzog is on first base. He starts for second with the pitch. Kaiser, at bat, takes a healthy swing and fouls one over the third base seats. Charley crosses second, but is called back.

Our friend is in a rage.

"He had it stole," he roars, "and that bonehead Kaiser went and spoiled it by fouling off that ball. It was a bad ball, too. They must have chloroformed Tenney when they handed him that guy."

If you'd tell the angered one that Kaiser and Herzog were trying to work the hit and run, and that Kaiser would have been "called" if he hadn't swung, you would be laughed at or treated with contemptuous silence. It never happens, on a hit-and-run play, where the pitch is fouled, that some one doesn't say "He had it stole," and storm at the batter.

The Rustlers are at bat in the last half of the ninth. The score is 5 to 3 against them. Jones singles, and Spratt, batting for Mattern, sends a double to right. "Buster" Brown, coaching at third, makes Jones stop there. There is a pretty good chance for him to beat Schulte's throw to the plate. There is also a small chance that Schulte's throw will beat him. Coacher Brown's act raises a storm of protest.

"You BONEHEAD. He could have walked in. Get somebody out there that knows something."

And just because Brown DOES know something, he has held Jones at third. What he knows is that a 5 to 4 defeat is just as bad as a 5 to 3 beating, that Jones's run isn't worth six cents if Spratt doesn't score, too, and that Jones's run is almost sure to be scored if Spratt's, the needed one, is.

Sweney fans, Tenney fouls out and Hoffman takes Herzog's long fly. The fan goes home convinced that "Buster" Brown has an ivory dome. If he stopped to think, he would realize that Jones's record of runs scored was the only thing that possibly could be affected by the act of Mr. Brown, and that there was just a chance that Schulte's throw would have hastened the end.

The argument that Schulte might have thrown wild and thus allowed Spratt also to score doesn't hold water, for good outfielders aren't taking any chances of overthrowing in cases like that. They are just getting the ball back into the diamond, so that some one can prevent liberties on the bases.

Here's one that actually did happen. It was at the Detroit game on the Huntington Avenue grounds on the twelfth day of June. With one out, Nunamaker singled through Bush. Hall sent a grounder to O'Leary, who tried to nail the catcher at second, but was too late. Hooper popped a fly which Bush gathered in.

Gardner hit a slow one over second. O'Leary picked up the ball, but saw that he had no chance to throw out Gardner. He bluffed to peg to Delehanty, who was playing first, and then uncorked a throw to Moriarty. Nunamaker had reached third and wandered a few feet toward home. He tried desperately to get back, but it was too late, and Moriarty tagged him for the third out.

Almost simultaneously the following storms broke from two real fans:

"Well, what do you think of that stone-covered, blankety-blank Irish Donovan letting him get caught like that?"

"Well, that fat-headed bum of a Dutch Engle. Who told him he could coach?"

Bill Carrigan was the coacher, and Bill has no strings attached to Mr. Nunamaker's feet. Nor had he done anything to deserve being called a stone-covered Irsh Donovan or a bum of a Dutch Engle.

However, Bill and "Buster" Brown and Pat Moran and all of them are still alive and happy, and the fans are even happier. They go out there to have a good time and they have it. Things are often done which don't please them at all—things that would be done differently if they were in charge. But, believe us, they wouldn't have half as much fun if they were in charge, or if they got in through the pass gate.

Some Champions

(*The Saturday Evening Post,* 3 June 1933)

If the general staff of the Chicago Examiner had foreseen what the White Sox were going to do in 1908, it never would have intrusted this inexperienced hick with the job of covering them. Potential tail-enders with a team batting average of about .006⅞, they hung around the outskirts of the first division until the middle of August, and then put on a sprint that landed them one game shy of the pennant, which they lost to Detroit on the last day of the season.

Their showing may be attributed partly to great master-minding by Fielder Jones and his first lieutenant, Billy Sullivan; partly to an impregnable inner and outer defense, and chiefly to superhuman pitching by Big Ed Walsh, the most willing, tireless and self-confident hurler that ever struck terror to the hearts of his opponents. If, as seldom happened, Ed was not pitching himself, he was in the bull pen getting ready to pitch, and it was anything but a help to the enemy's morale to know that if they started a rally he would be in there to stop it, sometimes not even waiting for Mr. Jones to beckon him.

In 1909 and 1910 I was with the Chicago Tribune, and it was that paper's policy to shift its baseball writers back and forth between the two Chicago clubs. I would be with the Cubs a while and then jump to the Sox, alternating with Sy Sanborn, a Tribune fixture and one of the few baseball experts who deserved the name. Anyway, it happened that I was with the Cubs when they clinched the pennant at Cincinnati in 1910. Manager Chance told the bunch they could take the evening off and celebrate, a thing which—now it may be told—some of them did nearly every evening, whether it was a special occasion or not.

Most of the gang gathered in a place across the street from the hotel and celebrated on champagne, probably because the place was noted for the excellence of its beer. The majority grew more and more optimistic regarding their chances in the impending world's

series with Philadelphia, but there was a minority composed of
Frank M. Schulte, right fielder. Knowing that I had traveled with
the White Sox part of the summer and therefore could give first-hand
evidence about Connie Mack's club, he asked the others to be quiet
while I expressed an opinion.

"Unless you have all the luck in the world," I said, "they'll lick
you four straight games. They've got three pitchers that nobody can
beat and a gang of hitters that spell murder."

"They won't look so good when they see my spitball," said the
modest Harry McIntire.

"Listen," said Schulte: "Those fellas have seen Walsh's spitball,
and when they get a look at yours they'll think we've hired one of
the Boston Bloomer Girls."

I quote this speech merely to show the respect in which Big Ed
was held by a great hitter who had tried to hit him in one world's
series and a couple of series for the Chicago championship.

My career as a regular baseball correspondent ended in May of
1913, when the Chicago Tribune set me to work writing a daily
column on the sporting page, with occasional assignments on the side
—world's series, championship fights, football games, and so on. My
interest in the national pastime died a sudden death in the fall of
1919, when Kid Gleason saw his power-house White Sox lose a
world's series to a club that was surprised to win even one game.

When it became certain that the Reds were going to grab their first
league pennant since the administration of James Monroe, a large
pottery concern in Cincinnati conceived the idea of honoring the
players in a truly unique way. The concern's scheme was to hire a
hall, have all the athletes appear in person on the stage and, in full
view of as large a crowd of fans as the auditorium would hold, be
presented with individual pieces of expensive pottery. It would be
necessary, of course, to engage a speaker to introduce the players and
make the presentations; and for some reason that is still being kept
a dark secret from me, I was the person selected for this job.

I received a long telegram outlining the plan. Naturally, it struck
me at once as a beautiful idea. My years of association with minor
and major league ball players had taught me that they were all
sticking to the game and its discouragements in the forlorn hope that
eventually someone would present them with individual pieces of

expensive pottery. Nevertheless, I wired back the suggestion that another speech maker be chosen, because public speaking was one of the few things I couldn't do.

The pottery people were persistent. They sent me another long telegram, and in it they mentioned the sum of five hundred dollars, which, as luck would have it, was the amount I had lost on Mr. Willard at Toledo. So I broke down and said yes, and from that day to this, whenever a pottery company wants somebody to make a speech, they send a telegram to Will Rogers or Irvin S. Cobb.

Now, I have never seen Chicago's Soldier Field or Africa's Sahara Desert, but I am prepared to swear that neither of them is half as big as the hall hired by those pottery people in Cincinnati. My speech was not helped any by the constant cries of "Louder! Louder!" issuing from the throats of those who didn't know when they were well off. My voice is like my No. 1 iron shot—it simply will not carry —and I was told afterwards that only those in the first two rows could hear a word I said. I was told this in the presence of Heinie Groh, Cincinnati's third baseman, and his comment was that occupants of the third row and all the rows behind it had the choice seats.

I shall always remember that evening as if it were tonight, chiefly because of the What-the-hell expressions on the faces of Mr. Groh, Mr. Reuther, Mr. Sallee, *et al.,* when I handed them pieces of pottery which they didn't know—any more than I did—whether to use as missiles or laundry tubs.

A couple of paragraphs ago I spoke of Mr. Willard and Toledo. I met Jess for the first time when he stopped off in Chicago on his way from Kansas to the battle ground. He was very cordial and invited me and another newspaper guy to accompany him to Kid Howard's restaurant.

"It's dinnertime and I'm hungry," he said.

Well, he certainly was hungry, and the double sirloin he ate made him absent-minded; for when the meal was over he walked out of our private dining room, forgetful of the fact that *l'addition* had not been attended to. The waiter, who had had eyes only for Jess before and during the repast, now became embarrassingly interested in me. I settled with him—a matter of twenty-six dollars—and found my newspaper friend alone on the walk outside.

On the occasion reported, the gentlemen of the press thought they had been invited to dine. As a general rule, however, newspapermen ought to have a heart in their relations with a champion boxer, or a champion anything else. Rube Goldberg thinks so too. Unfortunately for him, the subject came up for discussion between us while Jack Dempsey was training at Atlantic City for the Carpentier "fight." With Dempsey's manager, Jack Kearns, as pilot, five or six of us were dropping in at what were then known as cabarets. We had a couple of rounds at each place and Mr. Kearns was paying all the checks. Finally Rube and I decided to astound him by paying one ourselves. We also decided to toss a coin for the honor. We had spent about twenty minutes in the particular cabaret where this important decision was reached. Rube won the toss and paid the check. It was $167.

Some of us were having dinner at Dempsey's bungalow one evening and in the group was one of these reporters who speak right out.

"Jack," he asked the champion, "are you going to lick this Frenchman?"

"Why, he's kind of small, isn't he?" said Jack, which was the closest I ever heard him come to predicting a victory for himself.

Carpentier's training camp was near Great Neck, which was my home, and I got pretty well acquainted with him. Only once or twice a week did he perform for the newspapermen and the public. The rest of his work-outs were secret, and I think the secret was this: He realized what a fat chance he had and that it was silly to go through a rigorous grind of preparation for inevitable defeat. Two hundred thousand dollars is pretty good pay for a sock in the jaw, which, I am told, doesn't hurt—much. I imagine he wished afterwards that the sock had come in the first round instead of the fourth; Jack's gentle infighting did something more than just tickle his ribs.

While Dempsey was training for Firpo, at a small lake near Saratoga, Paul Gallico, now sports editor of the New York Daily News, handed himself an assignment that showed plenty of courage and scared Jack more than did the Wild Bull's wild right-hand punch. Paul wanted to write a story on How it Feels to Face a Champion, and insisted on the actual experience in spite of Dempsey's protest.

"Of course I won't hit him," said Jack; "but even if we just clinch, he may get hurt."

Jack Kearns appointed himself referee of the bout, which, he confided to us, would go only one one-minute round, and a short minute at that.

Paul entered the ring wearing beautiful white satin trunks and the goggles that are part of his regular attire. The champion objected strenuously to the goggles.

"But I can't see very well without them," said Paul.

"You won't have to see very well," said Jack.

The gong sounded. Paul didn't wait for Dempsey to come to him, but rushed and landed a couple of terrific haymakers on Jack's bulging biceps. He aimed another at the champion's nose and, in raising his left hand to ward it off, Jack accidentally tapped Paul on the chin. Down he went, with no harm done excepting to his trunks, which were no longer beautiful and no longer white. Jack picked him up and Jack Kearns sounded the gong, signaling the end of the round and the bout. Somebody handed Paul his goggles and he came out of the ring smiling.

"I don't know exactly what happened," he said, "but at least I wasn't off my feet."

Jack trained at the same spot for his first match with Gene Tunney. Grantland Rice and I, accompanied by the female members of our families, called on him and, the next day, drove to Speculator to watch Gene work. It was a rainy day and the training program was canceled, but Gene came to see us in the hotel. Mr. Rice had met him before and introduced the rest of us. Gene drew up a chair and laid a book on the table, face down. I immediately resolved not to ask him what book it was. However, one of the ladies did, and he replied:

"Oh, it's just a copy of The Rubaiyat that I always carry with me."

The Cost of Baseball

(*Collier's*, 2 March 1912)

As a baseball fan you may think that a major league ball club would be a money-maker in the hands of a truck gardener, that a big-league franchise is synonymous with success, and that it's all luck and no business ability.

But baseball is a business, a mighty big one, and it requires sound business sense of a peculiar kind to be successful in it. A business ignoramus will fail just as quickly and as surely in the national pastime as in any other walk of life, and a man without nerve will fail. Perhaps you can't figure how nerve is required to run a "proposition" which, as a rule, nets an annual profit of from $10,000 to $175,000 per magnate. It becomes our duty, then, to do the figuring for you, to show you why a "piker" would stand no chance in the game.

If the sun always shone on holidays, Saturdays, and Sundays; if there were no such thing as a training trip; if Bakers, Benders, Schultes, McGraws, Archers, and Barrys were as thick as chop suey and as cheap as rice; if fans could be convinced that their money entitled them to seats only, and not to a part in the conversation as well—what a joy ride Mr. Magnate's life would be.

Unfortunately, it is not thus. To make a barrel of money he must spend three or four barrels, and the worst of it is that the aforesaid one barrel is anything but guaranteed.

It is not difficult to understand that receipts stop with the end of the playing season. Expenses stop never. In fact, Mr. Owner is so busy digging from the first day of November until the twelfth of April that he almost forgets how to do anything else.

The past season's business is finished, between interruptions, by the middle of November. Then start the preparations for the next campaign, the most important and arduous of which are the spring training plans.

If you have never planned and executed a training trip, you have not tasted of life's bitterness. The only things needed to make this jaunt artistically and financially successful are thirty-five consecutive March and April days without rain, a thermometer always above 60, a complete squad of satisfied ball players, a smooth practice field in some quiet Southern town, and a list of dates in big Southern cities, not more than a hundred miles apart, extending over three weeks, and each successive date bringing you nearer home. If only one club had to make this trip, there would be nothing to the task of schedule-making, but it must be remembered that the owners of sixteen teams are all looking for the best dates for the same three weeks. He is a wise and farsighted magnate who books some of his practice games two or three years in advance.

These dates are for the slow journey homeward. The owner must also select and secure his "permanent" training camp, where the athletes can spend three weeks, right at the start, getting into shape by practicing among themselves.

Well, your owner feels pretty good when he has completed his schedule of spring games and landed a desirable "permanent" camp. He continues to feel good till the weather begins cutting up. Bad weather is the baseball magnate's worst enemy, and it usually beats the stuffing out of him in the spring.

To show what rain and other pests can do to a training schedule, take the testimony of John I. Taylor, who thought a California trip the proper caper for his Boston Red Sox last spring. The team did succeed in getting to the Pacific Coast. When it got there it stayed over three weeks—indoors. Some of the youngsters demonstrated to the entire satisfaction of Manager Donovan that they could deal cards gracefully and shoot Kelly pool. What he learned about their ball playing ability they told him, and their accounts were naturally prejudiced.

There were plenty of good dates on the club's return schedule. About two of them were filled, rain and cold weather being on the daily menu. Mr. Taylor said to himself: "I'm certainly glad we've got those four Cincinnati games on the card. They'll give us good practice and a nice bunch of money." Three of the Cincinnati battles were called off on account of bad weather. The fourth was played in a drizzle, and the receipts for the "series" were $40.

Ball players' salaries are not paid until the beginning of the playing season. But their expenses, those which the owner must pay, start with the training trip. To begin with, there is the transportation from their homes or from the rendezvous to the Southern camp. For the average squad, with thirty-five men on its roster, this amounts to $500 or $600. Then, too, a great many big league teams "pay the freight" for newspaper correspondents. For meals on the train—and this holds good throughout the playing season as well—each athlete is given $3 a day, or $1 per meal. There are athletes who eat that case note three times daily. There are others who need sleep so badly that they don't climb out of their berths in time for breakfast, and who are so busily engaged playing cards that the dining car is taken off at noon and in the evening before they realize it. They have just time to rush into a railway eating house twice a day and grab sandwich, pie, and coffee. But the $2.50 thus saved does not go back into Mr. Magnate's purse.

The training camp reached, the players are taken to their hotel in an omnibus, an expense that is repeated every three or four days during the season while the club is on the road. It would never do for these delicate young men to walk.

The hotel bill for the athletes, from thirty to thirty-five of them, for about three weeks at $3 a day, approximates $2,000. Also to be reckoned are transportation to and from the park where the practicing is done, baths, massage, etc. Remember, gentlemen, it's all going out and nothing coming in at this stage of the game.

Once in a decade the owner gets the proper combination of good dates and good weather. Then he breaks even or makes a small profit on the training trip. As a rule, however, his loss is in the neighborhood of $5,000, and he usually counts himself fortunate if none of his valuable athletes breaks a valuable arm or leg. The trip must be made on the chance that the players will get in condition, and also for the advertising.

While the team is being thoroughly soaked in the South, repairs and changes are being made at the home park, whether it's a new one or not. Repairs and improvements on the average park aggregate between $4,000 and $5,000 a year. Counting the cost of the training trip as $5,000, a really conservative figure, and estimating the repairs at $5,000, other lesser expenditures swell the total outlay, before the season starts, to something like $13,000.

That brings us round to the opening of the playing season. The joy of opening day's receipts would be doubled but for the sickening thought that the real expenses have just begun. Of course, the biggest item is the salary list. This runs from $55,000 to $75,000 a year, depending on the make-up of the club. It is a strange fact that the highest salaried teams sometimes come nearest to setting new records for total defeats. That a club wins a pennant or finishes second is no sign that it is well paid.

The Boston Nationals, whose followers went wild with joy if they had a winning streak lasting two days, pulled down more coin for their rather feeble efforts than many of the clubs that were fattening their victory columns at Mr. Tenney's expense. In fact, two privates in the Boston ranks were getting heavier pay checks than two managers in the same league.

The team composed of two or three veterans and a bunch of kids does not part with nearly as much money on the first and fifteenth of the month as the club which boasts several seasoned performers and a few youngsters. Thus, the Chicago Cubs, as they were made up last year, were the highest paid team in either big league, and Mr. Murphy's salary list totaled just about $75,000.

Most of the major league magnates of the present day own their ball parks. Those who do not, pay from $6,000 to $25,000 annual rental, the amount depending on the size of the city, the location of the plant, etc.

The third largest item in the annual expense bill is transportation. Railroad fare is two cents per mile straight, there being no special rate. It is the aim of the schedule makers to have the annual mileage nearly equal for all clubs. Each owner figures about $12,500 for railroad and Pullman bills each year, and that is also a conservative estimate.

The athletes pay their own living expenses "at home." Their transportation and hotel bills on the road are footed by the club. The hotels alone cost each owner $8,000 annually, aside from the training trip.

Nor must it be thought that expenditures are light when the team is at home. Ticket sellers and ticket takers draw from $1.50 to $2.50 a day, to say nothing of a lot of abuse. Police protection costs $20 to $50 per day, depending on the size of the crowd. The total for the year for this protection is about $1,800 on the average. The aggregate paid out for ticket men, ushers, groundkeepers and their assistants, and "handy men" around a ball park will easily foot up to $6,500 annually.

The purchase and printing of tickets may appear a small item, but it amounts to something in a year. Advertising in the papers totals about $1,200 a month when the club is at home.

The wise magnate has new home and traveling uniforms for his players each year, and this entails an expense of about $500, figuring two uniforms for each of twenty-five men.

Each club has a secretary, a man of all work, who is virtually business manager, and an assistant secretary, the former drawing about $2,500 or $3,000 and the latter $1,800: two or more scouts, the "head" scout getting $2,500 and the others $1,500 apiece, and a trainer, whose salary is $1,000 or $1,200, but who usually is handed a bonus which brings the total stipend to $1,500.

The secretary's job is about as far from a sinecure as one can imagine. A good secretary must be a natural born actor. When he enters a railroad office, he must wear a dark frown and impress the agent as a man to be feared. In the presence of the owner, he must act the role of Shylock, varying it occasionally with a portrayal of Chesterfield. With the ball players he must appear a good fellow without actually being one. He must make them think they are stopping at swell hotels or sleeping in lower berths whether they are or not.

The trainer must be a veritable Battling Nelson or Hugo Kelly, able to stand terrible punishment. He is blamed for the loss of every game that is lost, for he is usually considered a "jinx"; held responsible for Mr. Star Pitcher's sore arm, even when the soreness was acquired by sleeping in a taxicab with the arm suspended out of the window; soundly "called" as being the cause of the short stop's headache, even though said headache is the result of the satisfaction of a pent-up thirst; and otherwise generally maltreated.

Scouts are supposed to visit minor league and college towns, discover young, undeveloped stars and secure recruits capable of making good on a big league club, and also to find glaring faults and incurable weaknesses in youngsters on whom the big leaguers have received "tips," thus saving time and money for their employers. They are supposed to do those things, but they generally do the opposite, heralding as wonders young men who can hit curve balls about as easily as they can paint landscapes, passing up as "lemons" youthful Cobbs and Tinkers, and accomplishing all manner of things designed to drive their bosses crazy.

Thus it happens that, of ten or fifteen men added to each big league roster annually, one or two show class enough to be retained. Of course, the club doesn't always suffer a total loss on the players sent back to the "bushes." Minor league owners must pay for them, but the major league magnate never profits on such a deal.

The expenditure for new material, including players bought from other big league teams, and men purchased or "drafted" from the minor leagues, averages around $20,000. The amount varies with the needs of the club and the policy of the owner. The fact that his team has won the pennant one season does not signify that the magnate can afford to stand pat for the next. The Detroit Club was champion of the American League in 1908 and paid out over $10,000 for fresh material between that season and the following one, nor did it increase its strength to any appreciable extent. The New York Giants, finishing second in the National League race the same year, spent $20,000 for three men that fall, besides paying out a lot of money in "drafts." Frequently some minor leaguer gets such a reputation that five or six big league owners are tempted to bid large sums for his release, and, very frequently also, the owner who finally secures him for $7,000 or $8,000 finds that he would have been just as well off if he had spent the money for walnut shucks.

Then, too, there is the league fund. In the American League every club sends to the president two and a half cents for each paid admission to the home grounds. From the fund thus made up are paid the salaries of the president, secretary, and umpires, rental for the executive offices and all running expenses of the organization.

It is the policy of some clubs to travel in style and of others to "go cheap." For that reason it is impossible to compile figures that fit all the big league clubs alike. The following, however, is a fair estimate of the average annual expenditure of a major league baseball club:

Players' salaries	$65,000
Purchase of players	20,000
Transportation	12,500
Rental of park	15,000
Park salaries	6,500
Hotels	8,000
Office expense (including salaries)	5,500
Repairs	4,500
Spring trip	5,000
Players' supplies (uniforms, balls, etc.)	4,000
Park police	1,800
Insurance	1,500
Taxicabs, carriages, etc	900
League fund	10,000
Trainer	1,500
Scouts	4,000
Sundries (advertising, printing, etc.)	3,300
TOTAL	$169,000

The sixteen major league owners, then, have a total annual expense of $2,704,000, and it costs each of them about $463 a day, all the year round, to run his club; or, counting only the playing days, about $1,000 per day. Barney Dreyfuss of Pittsburgh has stated that his daily outlay, during the playing season, is over $800. It is safe to say that the minimum is in the neighborhood of $750 and the maximum almost $1,200.

Ponder these things, Mr. Fan, and perhaps you will be more content with your own lot, and less envious of the gentleman who gets that dollar or half dollar of yours on a summer afternoon. Perhaps, too, you will feel a touch of sympathy for him when, on a Saturday in July, dark clouds gather above you. He's not going to the poorhouse. No, but the asylum is not so far away.

Br'er Rabbit Ball

(*The New Yorker,* 13 September 1930)

In spite of the fact that some of my friends in the baseball industry are kind enough to send me passes every spring, my average attendance at ball parks for the last three seasons has been two times per season (aside from World's Series) and I probably wouldn't have gone that often but for the alleged necessity of getting my innumerable grandchildren out in the fresh air once in a while. During the games, I answer what questions they ask me to the best of my knowledge and belief, but most of the afternoon I devote to a handy pocket edition of one of Edgar Wallace's sex stories because the events of the field make me yearn for a bottle of Mothersill's Remedy.

Manufacturers of what they are using for a ball, and high officials of the big leagues, claim that the sphere contains the same ingredients, mixed in the same way, as in days of old. Those who believe them should visit their neighborhood psychiatrist at the earliest possible moment.

When I was chasing around the circuit as chronicler of the important deeds of Cubs or White Sox, it was my custom and that of my colleagues to start making up our box scores along about the seventh inning in cases where one club was leading its opponent by ten runs. Nowadays the baseball reporters don't dare try to guess the answer even if there are two out in the last half of the ninth inning and the score is 21 to 14.

I have always been a fellow who liked to see efficiency rewarded. If a pitcher pitched a swell game, I wanted him to win it. So it kind of sickens me to watch a typical pastime of today in which a good pitcher, after an hour and fifty minutes of deserved mastery of his opponents, can suddenly be made to look like a bum by four or five great sluggers who couldn't have held a job as bat boy on the Niles High School scrubs.

Let us say that the Cubs have a series in Brooklyn. They get over there at eleven in the morning so they can find the park by the time

79

the game begins. The game develops into a pitchers' battle between Charlie Root, Bud Teachout, Guy Bush, and Pat Malone for the Cubs and Dazzy Vance, Jim Elliott, and Adolfo Luque for the Robins. The last half of the ninth inning arrives with the score 12 to 8 in Chicago's favor—practically a no-hit game in these days. Somebody tries to strike out, but Malone hits his bat and the ball travels lightly along the ground toward third base. Woody English courageouly gets in front of it and has two fingers broken. This is a superficial injury for an infielder of the present, so Woody stays in the game. The Brooklyn man is safe at first. The next Brooklyn man, left-handed and a born perpendicular swatsman, takes a toehold and crashes a pop fly toward Charlie Grimm. The pellet goes over the right-field fence like a shot and breaks a window in a synagogue four blocks away.

Manager McCarthy removes Malone and substitutes Blake, hoping the latter will give a few bases on balls and slow up the scoring. But Blake gives only two bases on balls and then loses control. He pitches one over the plate and the batsman, another left-hander who, with the old ball, would have been considered too feeble to hit fungoes on one of these here miniature golf courses, pops it over the fence to the beach at Far Rockaway, where it just misses a young married couple called Rosenwald. The victory is Brooklyn's and the official puts the names of a lot of pitchers, including Rucker and Grimes, into a hat and the first name drawn out gets the credit.

I mean it kind of upsets me to see good pitchers shot to pieces by boys who, in my time, would have been ushers. It gnaws at my vitals to see a club with three regular outfielders who are smacked on top of the head by every fly ball that miraculously stays inside the park —who ought to pay their way in, but who draw large salaries and are known as stars because of the lofty heights to which they can hoist a leather-covered sphere stuffed with dynamite.

Those who are cognizant of my great age ask me sometimes what Larry Lajoie would do in this "game." Well, he wouldn't do anything after one day. Larry wasn't a fly-ball hitter. When he got a hold of one, it usually hit the fence on the first bounce, travelling about five feet three inches above the ground most of the way and removing the ears of all infielders who didn't throw themselves flat on their stomachs the instant they saw him swing. They wouldn't have time to duck this ball, and after the battle there would be a meeting of earless infielders, threatening a general walkout if that big French gunman were allowed in the park again, even with a toothpick in his hand.

But without consulting my archives I can recall a dozen left-handed batsmen who hit fly balls or high line drives and who hit them so far that opposing right and centre-fielders moved back and rested their spinal columns against the fence when it was these guys' turn to bat.

I need mention only four of this bunch—two from each league—to give my contemporaries a talking point when their grandchildren boast of the prowess of the O'Douls, Kleins, and Hermans of today. The four I will select offhand are Elmer Flick and Sam Crawford of the American League and Harry Lumley and Frank Schulte of the National.

In the year 1911 (I think it was) Mr. Schulte led the National League in homers with a total of twenty-one. Such a number would be disgraceful in these days, when a pitcher gets almost that many. Just the same, I am willing to make a bet, which never can be decided, that Frank, with the present ball in play, would just about treble that total and finish so close to the Babe himself that it would take until December to count the ballots. I have frequently seen, in the dim, dead past, the figures of Fielder Jones and Eddie Hahn backing up against the hay-wire when Flick or Crawford came to bat, and on one occasion, when we travelled east on the same train as the Detroit club, I overheard a bit of repartee between Jones and Samuel. That afternoon Jones had caught three fly balls off Sam without moving more than a yard out of his position, which was a comfortable one, with the fence for a back rest.

"Why," said Sam grumblingly, "were you playing pretty near out of the park for me?"

"Why," said Jones, "do you always hit to the same place?"

Right-fielders were constantly robbing Lumley and Flick of two-base hits or worse by lolling against the bleacher wall—and it must be remembered that in those ancient times bleachers were far enough from the playing field so that the first and third-base coachers couldn't sit in them.

Speaking of Mr. Lumley (if you've heard this before, don't stop me), we (the Cubs) came east one season and we had a pitcher named Edward Reulbach, who was great when he had control and terrible when he lacked it. On this trip he lacked it to such an extent that Manager Chance ordered him to pay forenoon visits to each hostile battlefield and pitch to the rival batsmen in their practice. The latter had no objection—it just meant somebody to hit against without wearing out one of their own men.

Well, we got to Brooklyn and after a certain game the same idea entered the minds of Mr. Schulte, Mr. Lumley, and your reporter, namely: that we should see the Borough by night. The next morning, Lumley had to report for practice and, so far as he was concerned, the visibility was very bad. Reulbach struck him out three times on low curve balls inside.

"I have got Lumley's weakness!" said Ed to Chance that afternoon.

"All right," said the manager. "When they come to Chicago, you can try it against him."

Brooklyn eventually came to Chicago and Reulbach pitched Lumley a low curve ball on the inside. Lumley had enjoyed a good night's sleep, and if it had been a 1930 vintage ball, it would have landed in Des Moines, Iowa. As it was, it cleared the fence by ten feet and Schulte, playing right field and watching its flight, shouted: "There goes Lumley's weakness!"

Well, the other day a great ballplayer whom I won't name (he holds the home-run record and gets eighty thousand dollars a year) told a friend of mine in confidence (so you must keep this under your hat) that there are at least fifteen outfielders now playing regular positions in his own league who would not have been allowed bench-room the year he broke in. Myself, I just can't stomach it, but Brooklyn recently played to one hundred and ten thousand people in four games at Chicago, so I don't believe we'll ever get even light wines and beer.

Jersey City Gendarmerie, Je T'Aime

(*The New Yorker*, 2 November 1929)

Over the river from Christopher Street, that's where the West begins, but if Mr. Greeley ever advises me to go in that direction again, I will detour by way of Miami or Montreal. Jersey City doesn't want me. I had a faint suspicion on the occasion of my first visit; the suspicion was strengthened the second time, and became a certainty when I made a third trip there the other week. The old saying has it: "Three times and out." I am not quite out, but Jersey City is, so far as I'm concerned. I have no desire for another perusal of the handwriting on the wall. Anyway, the letters have grown so much bigger with the years that now I could read them, if necessary, from the Hudson's safe side.

As soon as I had got back to Manhattan and quit trembling after the most recent indiscretion, I looked up the place in the encyclopedia to see whether any of my ancestors had played it a dirty trick which cried for vengeance on their progeny. I learned only that it is the second largest city in its state and the county seat of Hudson County; that the hill section back of the main portion is noteworthy for beautiful residences, and that it has a full equipment of hospitals and asylums, probably for visitors who go there a fourth or fifth time. In 1779, "Light Horse Harry" Lee, with two hundred men, overwhelmed a sizable British garrison and took the town with only five casualties. This was considered quite a stunt, but I have an idea that the English force didn't object much to being chased out, and it is not surprising that Mr. Lee withdrew his gallants the minute he learned where he was at.

Present-day defenders of the dorp point with pride to the fact that though the state of New Jersey is famous for murders, hardly any occur in Jersey City itself. My theory is that the returns are incomplete because the police don't consider such pranks worth reporting,

83

and that a thorough investigation of the slayings which take place elsewhere would reveal that nearly all the assassins had just been in Jersey City and talked with a cop.

In 1921, or maybe 1922, Dempsey and Carpentier "fought" at Boyle's Thirty Acres. Dempsey and I had both trained in Atlantic City, also in Jersey and my favorite town next to San Francisco (who asked you what was your favorite town next to San Francisco?). The police of America's Playground had been so sweet and sympathetic that I thought maybe they were that way all over the state. So my reception in Hudson's county seat was the more mortifying.

I couldn't find my entrance at first, and asked a policeman where it was.

"Who wants to know?" he said belligerently.

"I do."

"What for?"

"It's the place I'm supposed to go in."

"Well, go in there, then!"

"Where is it?"

"If you're so smart you can find it yourself, but you can't stand here!"

"That's the last thing in the world I want to do."

"Then beat it!"

The smartness which he had divined led me to walk around to the opposite side of the enclosure and there, sure enough, was my entrance. With no assistance from ushers, I made my way to the seat my ticket called for. It was a hard seat, and when I happened to catch sight of a girl by the name of McMein a few rows away, I thought I would rest myself and do her a favor by warning her that her hero and Bernard Shaw's was about to get his block knocked off. An overstuffed policeman stopped me in the aisle.

"Where are you going?"

"Just on a visit."

"You can't do no visiting here! Where is your ticket?"

I showed him the stub.

"Well, you get back there and stay there!" he ordered, and poor Miss McMein remained unprepared for the massacre.

My next appearance in the town was, I think, two years later, on the evening of the "battle" between Willard and Firpo. Once more

I found my seat in spite of the feverish apathy of ushers. But the seat was occupied, and by two people. They had a keen sense of humor and my request that they show me their stubs got a bigger laugh than the fight itself. I summoned a uniformed gent who seemed to be in charge of that part of the house and explained the situation in the native dialect.

"Those fellas have got my seat."

"What of it?"

"Nothing, except that no other seats are vacant and I'm tired."

"Go outside and rest."

"But why can't I have the seat my ticket calls for?"

"Because two other fellas is in it. And my best advice is to get the hell out of here before they carry you out on a stretcher!"

"You can't put me out when I've got a ticket."

"Can't I?"

Halfway up the aisle toward an exit, with policemen on both sides of me, squeezing my arms in their boyish rapture, my mercurial flight was suddenly stopped by a terrifying yell from the mouth of a customer, none other than Mr. William A. Brady, who had recognized my forehead and who, whether it be to his credit or not, appeared to have my escort thoroughly cowed. In a short and very abusive speech, he persuaded them to leave go of my arms and conduct me respectfully back in the direction of the ringside. The cops whispered a few words to the gent who had sponsored my tour and he found me a place on the floor not far from my own seat.

Well, it seems there were two Southerners whom we will call Mr. and Mrs. Wild and one night in 1929 they invited me to accompany them to Hoboken to see a show.

It was raining when we came out of the theatre. We asked a taxi-driver to take us to the nearest Tube.

"You've just missed a train," said the driver, who looked disarmingly like the gentle athlete, Eddie Collins. "They won't be no more leaving from here for twenty-five minutes, but I'll drive you eighteen blocks, to Journal Square, and you can catch one right away."

In our innocence we believed him, and we didn't know that Journal Square meant Jersey City. He was a terrible driver with a passion for wet street-car tracks and profanity. When he had skidded and jolted many more than eighteen blocks and we were tired of him and of the ride, which apparently had no destination, we asked him to stop and let us out. He did so with comment that made my friend, Mr. Brady, seem inarticulate. While Mr. Wild was paying, I walked in front of the car and impishly wrote down the license number. In the nick of time I observed that "Eddie" was resenting this bit of byplay by trying to run over me. I jumped out of the way and we went to the nearest corner, where stood a policeman.

"Can you tell me," said Mr. Wild, "how to get to the Tube?"

No answer; not even a look. The question was repeated, and still no answer.

"A Silent Policeman," said Mrs. Wild. "Dere's anudder one across de street. Ah'll done ask him."

"No, you won't! You stay right where you are!" Thus Eddie, who had left his cab and joined us. "Listen," he said to the cop, "I want these mugs arrested. They're mugs!"

Mrs. Wild, heedless of Eddie's shouts of "Come back here!" boldly crossed to the other policeman. Mr. Wild, the first policeman, Eddie, and I followed. The second policeman was as reticent as the first. Both were quite evidently in mortal fear of Eddie and their jobs. A car stopped beside us and one of its two murderous-looking occupants cordially asked Mrs. Wild to jump in. The officers appeared to consider this a natural, innocent piece of gallantry and were a little surprised at her refusal of the invitation.

Questions as to the location of the Tube failed to elicit any reply whatever, and all the time Eddie was urging our arrest, and particularly mine. Curiosity impelled me to ask, "On what charge?"

"You took my number," said Eddie.

"Is that a crime here?"

"You're a mug!" he replied, as the Law gazed into the distance. "You look like a mug to me! I think you're a mug!"

"Can I be arrested for looking like a mug?"

"I think you're a gunman!"

"Maybe these policemen had better frisk me."

It was unpleasant standing in the rain and we started away.

"Come back here!" yelled Eddie, and Mrs. Wild was the only one brave enough to disobey. She ventured down the forbidding street in search of a vocal policeman or another cab.

"All I want of youse," said Eddie to the cops, "is to take these mugs in. I want it to cost them some time. They're a couple of mugs, 'specially that one mug.''

Now I make no claim to physical courage, but Eddie was not much bigger than Miller Huggins and it wasn't fear of being socked by him that restrained me from taking offense at the charge of mugginess. Something told me that it would be a major mistake to hit a Jersey City taxi-driver whose presence struck the police dumb.

Mr. Wild and I went in pursuit of Mrs. Wild, expecting to be followed again, by Eddie or a bullet. But he preferred intimidating the Law to annoying us further, and we saw him still standing there, gesticulating and probably protesting the escape of visiting mugs, when we joyously climbed into a Holland Tunnel bus that said it was Broadway bound.

I will take the encyclopedia's word for the beautiful residences back of the main portion. I am not going to see for myself. There may be coppers in them hills.

X-Ray

(*The New Yorker,* 5 July 1930)

On this occasion I was taking one of my sitting-up exercises which hardly ever last less than forty-eight hours and in fact I hold an unofficial record of sixty hours at the Friars Club, but it has never been allowed by the A.A.U. because it was done in dinner clothes and the only people that get up in such costumes are those who are called on for speeches. I might state four uninteresting facts in connection with this Friars Club sitting: One was that five of the best music-writers in New York played their latest stuff and it all sounded good (at the time); another was that I and whoever happened to be with me at the moment ordered five meals and rejected them as fast as they were brought in; the third was that in this era they had kind of silly traffic laws in New York (not that that differentiates the era from any other era)—the code being that your car could face east for twelve hours and then must face west for twelve hours—and it was necessary to find a couple of bellmen capable of making the desired alterations at six A.M. and six P.M.; and the fourth was that though I was not even a neophyte when I entered the monastery, my long sojourn made me a regular member and I have been a Friar from those days and nights to this, probably because of some obscure squatters' law. Will say in conclusion of this interminable paragraph that the function occurred in June and I had no topcoat and the urge to get home and weed the bathtub came at high noon, and it was kind of embarrassing passing all those policemen in dinner clothes instead of the conventional pajamas.

Now then, we come to the occasion I started out to tell about and I began by visiting the home of George S. Kaufman. I arrived at nine o'clock on the theory that neither George nor Peaches would be up yet and I would have a chance to romp a while with their daughter, Margaret. George was aroused about half-past ten by his pompadour tickling his latissimus dorsi. This was quite a relief, as either Margaret or I—I can't remember which—was by this time tired of romping. George got up and changed his underwear and we sat down to talk about a play that will win the Pulitzer Prize as soon as they get some brains on the committee.

As usual George walked back and forth picking fauna off the rug and now and then giving voice to an idea or line that would have done credit to the master of ceremonies at a night club. There was a slight interruption of three hours while Peaches invited the Manhattan Telephone Directory to dinner. At length she asked me:

"What are you going to do tonight?"

"Nothing," I said.

"Golly Moses!" she exclaimed. "I wish I were in your place."

Along about five o'clock, George said, "Who can you see as the male lead?"

"Well," I replied, "before answering that question, I should like to know what the play is about and whether the male lead is going to be a track-walker or a priest."

"One of us," said George, "ought to spend the evening at the Lambs Club and look over the different fellows between twenty-one and a hundred and twenty-one. And the queer part is that I am not a Lamb and Peaches always likes to have me here at a dinner party to carve the bird."

So the next night at eight I ran into Dorothy ("Spark Plug") Parker and we went places until I got tired of her and I landed at the stagedoor of the Broadhurst hoping I could pick up somebody and it was Harry Rosenthal who his press agent said his left foot had just been insured for sixty-two cents so there would be no temptation for him to fool with the soft pedal. Harry left me with two girls on my hands and I took them to Reuben's hoping the last-named would at least have the grace to christen one layer of a sandwich in my honor, but all the waiters acted as if I were still living in Niles, Michigan, and the girls soon joined another party and the only person in the joint that seemed to recognize me was Rosie Dolly who hadn't seen me for nine years, but she got up and shook hands and said, "I am Rosie Dolly," and I said, "You don't have to tell me that because I can always tell you girls apart the instant you say you are Rosie Dolly." This went over with a bang and I was quickly out in the street with nobody to talk to but a taxi-man and I gave him my home address though I wasn't at all sleepy and when I got home I took some paraldehyde and plunged into the vacant bathtub thinking it was breakfast and along about noon my patella began to hurt and we had to call Dr. Tyson and after five days he persuaded me to go down to St. Vincent's where they could take an X-ray, but I didn't give in until he promised to have me sent there in an ambulance.

It was a private ambulance from Brooklyn and the minute I saw the driver and his assistant I knew who had killed Rothstein.

In an ambulance they make you ride lying down, whereas you can take your choice in a taxi. My nurse was Miss Adelaide O'Donnell, a French-Canadian who can't speak either language, but she made me understand that they would like to know which side I would prefer to ride on. A problem. If I rode on my right side I couldn't see Bergdorf-Goodman's and if I laid on my left I couldn't see Thomas Cook & Son. So I compromised by lolling on my back and couldn't see anything but the roof of the car.

Boy, if you have got expensive tastes, don't ever get the ambulance habit. It didn't make any difference whether the X-ray was taken now or next Advent, but everybody got out of our way and we didn't pay any attention to traffic signals. It cost eighteen dollars, but it was with real regret that I said goodbye to the gangsters when they dropped me four feet from their stretcher to the X-ray man's toboggan. From now on I will walk rather than ride in the taxi.

The X-ray man took some very good likenesses of my leg in different poses and I intend to autograph them and sell them to my fans—ten cents for the calf and a quarter for the entire limb. He made many a wisecrack during the photography, but I am saving them all for the Erie company of "June Moon."

Insomnia

(*Cosmopolitan,* May 1931)

It's only ten o'clock, but I hardly slept at all last night and I ought to make up for it. I won't read. I'll turn off the light and not think about anything. Just go to sleep and stay asleep till breakfast-time.

Then maybe I'll feel like working.

I've got to get some work done pretty soon.

It's all going out and nothing coming in.

That was a song of Bert Williams'. Let's see; it started:

Money is de root of evil, no matter where you happen to go,
But nobody's got any objection to de root, now ain't dat so?
You know how it is with money, how it makes you feel at ease;
De world puts on a big broad smile, and your friends is as thick
    as bees.

Bert sang a song of mine once and I had it published; it was put on phonograph records, too, and I think the total royalties from sheet music and records amounted to $47.50. It's fun writing songs, but I never could make money out of things that were fun, like playing poker or bridge or writing songs or betting on horses.

The only way I can earn money is by writing short stories. Short! By the time I'm half through with one, it's a serial to me.

I wish I were as good as O. Henry and could get by with a thousand or twelve hundred words. I could write a thousand-word short story every day; that is, I could if my head were as full of plots as his must have been. I think of about one plot a year, and then, when I start writing it, I recall that it's somebody else's, maybe two or three other people's.

Just the same, plot or no plot, I'll have to work tomorrow. There's the insurance and notes and interest on mortgages———— But I won't get to sleep that way. I mustn't think about anything at all, or at least, I must think about something that doesn't make any difference.

Sheckard, Evers, Schulte, Chance, Steinfeldt, Hofman, Tinker, Kling, Brown.

91

Twenty years or so ago I was a baseball nut and could recite any club's batting order. Nowadays I hardly know which Waner bats second and which third.

When I was sixteen, I lived in Clayton, Michigan, and sang in the choir. One Christmas day there was a new face in the congregation, a girl's face, the most attractive face I had ever seen. The owner of the face was sitting with a schoolmate of mine, in the fifth or sixth pew from the front.

I saw her at the start of the service and I'm afraid I wasn't of much use to the choir that morning. When the recessional was over, I got out of my cotta and cassock in nothing flat and ran around to the front of the church. My schoolmate generously introduced us. I guess it wasn't generously at that; he didn't lack self-confidence to the extent of considering me a rival.

Her name was Lucy Faulkner. I had always hated the name Lucy, but from then on it was music. We met at several parties and she seemed to like me, in spite of terrific competition. I could say some awfully funny things in those days. I wish I could remember them.

If I had gone to dances, we might have got better acquainted, which probably would have hastened the ruination of my chances, if I had any. You can't be funny all the while, even at sixteen.

Her family, new in town, didn't have much of an opinion of our educational system. They sent her to a boarding school, far away. We started a lopsided correspondence. I wrote her two letters and she didn't answer either of them. But when she came home for spring vacation, she was still quite friendly. As for me, crazy is not the word.

One day our cow got loose and I received the assignment to chase her and bring her home. My pursuit of Cora through the main street of the town afforded the merchants and shoppers a great deal of amusement and me considerable anguish, which developed into suicidal mania when the cow suddenly turned a couple of corners and dashed right into the Faulkners' yard. I realized what a blight to romance would be the spectacle of the perspiring, bedraggled hero chasing a wild, demoniacal cow and losing a length in every two.

My mind was quicker than my feet. I conceded the race, hid behind a tree and prayed that Lucy was not at home, or that if she was, she hadn't seen me and would not recognize Cora.

Luck was with me. The Faulkners were all absent, Cora and I were not observed and Cora, stopping for refreshments on a near-by unmowed lawn, was caught and returned to the owner by a friendly hired man.

It was only a postponement of the bitter ending. One night in July, four of us young men about town drank a great many steins of Meusel's singing beer and, at half past two in the morning, decided to go serenading. Our first stop was in front of the Faulkners'. The night was hot and all the windows were open.

Lucy, blessed with youth, slept through the horrible din. Not so her parents. From one of the windows came the sound of a voice that could talk even louder than we could sing and we decided to go somewhere else while a cloud still obscured the moon and kept our features secret.

Well, they never knew who three of us were. But they knew who one of us was. And yet there is said to be a tendency on the part of medium-sized men to envy tall men their height.

Lucy was given some orders at breakfast and obeyed them until she was safely engaged to a decent fella. There was no ban put on the other members of the quartet, though I swear my bass had been barely audible against their deafening whoops.

It must be after midnight. I'll just turn the light on and look at my watch. Eight minutes after ten. Good Lord! Maybe if I read just a little while——— No; that will only make me more wakeful than ever. And if I have to work tomorrow, I must get some sleep.

Ten or eleven high balls or a shot in the arm would be an effective lullaby. The trouble is, the more habits you have, the more you have to snap out of. At that, I guess too much coffee is as bad as too much Scotch. Too much of anything is bad, even too much sleep.

If I had an idea for a story and kind of laid it out in my mind, it would be a lot easier than facing that typewriter tomorrow with no idea at all. I'll try to think of one. No, I mustn't think. You can't go to sleep thinking up an idea for a story.

It is essential, I'm told, that your mind be a perfect blank. Some might say that in my case it wouldn't take much erasing. It would, though. Perhaps I don't think importantly, but I think just the same.

I wonder if I could make a story out of what Doc Early was telling me the other night. It was about Allan Spears and his wife and his kids. I would have to disguise their names and where they were from or Doc would kill me. I could call the man Leslie Arnold and his wife Amy, and have them live in Janesville, Wisconsin, instead of Rockford, Illinois. I'd have to fake and pad a little, but that's no novelty.

I had heard of Spears, and Mrs. Spears was pointed out to me at the theater, last time I was in Chicago. She is one of the prettiest women I ever saw. A blonde, slight, and with a wonderful complexion. In the story I will make her a brunette and statuesque.

Well, let's see: Spears went to the University of Illinois and won his letter in baseball, football and track three years running. His athletic activities kept him in pretty strict training, but when he got through college, he more than made up for it. He was Rockford's whoopee kid as long as his money held out. It was money (about $6,000) left him by an aunt or something. The money lasted him seven months, and then he had to sober up awhile because everybody knew he was flat and he couldn't even get rat poison on credit.

It was during his involuntary water-wagon ride that Edith Holden fell in love with him. He fell in love with her, too, and I don't suppose he fought very hard against it inasmuch as she was said to have a private fortune of one million dollars. The fortune really amounted to one-fifth of that, but even so———

When Edith broke the news to her parents, their cries could be heard throughout the Middle West. Here was their only child, a young woman so beautiful that when she walked down the street, or up the street for that matter, all of Rockford's male citizens swooned, throwing herself away on a youth who held the world's record for personal consumption of terrible hooch, six thousand dollars' worth in seven months, and who would doubtless try to tie or beat that record as soon as he had the means.

It wouldn't have been so bad if Allan had ever shown an inclination to work. He hadn't.

Mr. Holden made all sorts of threats. He would lock Edith up, he would never speak to her again, he would publicly denounce her, he would shoot young Spears, he would cut her out of his will. (This last item meant something, too, for he was actually a millionaire.) She didn't laugh at him. She cried, and went ahead with plans for an elopement. They ran away to Chicago and were married, and decided to live there. Half of her two hundred thousand dollars was in good bonds, which she put in a safety-deposit box accessible to both her husband and herself. The other hundred thousand in cash was divided evenly and deposited for checking accounts, one his, one her own.

Now you might guess that he was overdrawn within the year, but your guess would be wrong. To his own surprise as well as everybody else's, he stayed on the wagon, went to work for an insurance company, and for the first four years of his married life, earned an average annual income of fifteen thousand.

He and Edith managed to live on this and their coupons without much economizing. And I mustn't forget to mention that he had his own life insured for seventy thousand, with Edith and their twin children, a boy and a girl, named as beneficiaries.

Young Mrs. Spears hoped and prayed that Allan's good behavior and the existence of the twins would soften the hearts of her parents, but not until the beginning of her fifth year away from home did she see an encouraging sign. It came in the form of a letter from her mother, a brief letter to be sure, but still a letter, beginning "Dear Daughter." And Allan chose that otherwise cheering day to fall with a thud.

In two months he had lost his job and thirty thousand dollars, the latter at the race tracks, and had spent five thousand for parties. On the occasions when he came home, unkempt and crazy-looking, the twins ran from him in terror and Edith grew hysterical.

She had no one to call on for help and, besides, she doubted that there was any help for a thing like this. She thought of taking her children to Rockford, but she was not of a temperament that could endure calmly what her mother and father were sure to say.

On the sixty-second day of his bender, Allan was brought to his house in a taxi and carried from the taxi to his bed by the driver and a man Edith had never seen before. Allan was sick, very sick, and she was glad of it. For the moment she didn't care whether he got well or died. However, she did call a doctor.

The doctor said it was a pretty close thing, but that Allan's remarkable constitution would pull him through. That is, it would pull him through this siege. He'd have to stay on the wagon, though, from now on. Another bat would finish him.

When Allan could be talked to, Edith talked to him.

"The doctor says if you ever drink again you'll die. I say if you ever drink again, don't come home. If you do drink again and come home, I'll take the children and go away and never, never come back. I mean it."

Allan was in bed two weeks, up and around the house a week, and then went downtown seeking a job. He was turned down a dozen times a day for a good many days. He was discouraged, blue, despondent.

And then one day he met two alumni of his university, Gilbert White, a classmate, and Harry Myers, an older man credited with having cleaned up in the market and being on the inside of everything that has an inside.

They invited him to luncheon and he accepted. They asked him to have a drink and he declined.

"I'm looking for a job," he said.

"Well," said White, "if you take a drink, Harry will give you something better than a job. He'll give you the tip he's given me and if you play it for all it's worth, you won't need a job."

Allan woke up next morning in a Loop hotel. His head was splitting. He found his coat, which wasn't much trouble since he had not taken it off. He put his hand in a pocket where cigarets might lurk, but the pocket was empty, save for a slip of paper on which Harry Myers' tip was inscribed in his own handwriting.

Allan read the slip with some difficulty and stumbled to the telephone. He called up the brokerage firm of Rogers and King. Sam King, the junior partner, was another alumnus of Illinois.

"What do you think of So-and-so?" asked Allan.

"I think it's the greatest buy there is," said Sam.

"How much margin would I have to put up?"

"Why don't you buy it outright?" said Sam, who had heard, and still thought, that Mrs. Spears had a million in her own name.

"Oh, no," said Allan. "If I did that I'd have to tell my wife and I want to surprise her."

"Well," said Sam, "the amount of margin would depend on the number of shares."

"Make it seven thousand shares," said Allan.

"You're certainly talking big numbers," said Sam, "and your wife *will* be surprised, especially if something happens and the market takes a nose dive."

"What is it selling at this morning?"

"Forty-nine," said Sam.

"Well," said Allan, "you buy me seven thousand shares and I'll be over there inside of an hour with collateral for seventy thousand bucks. And to play it safe, you can sell at forty-four."

Allan hung up the receiver, took it down again and called his home.

"Edith," he said, "I had some drinks last night, as you probably guessed. I'm likely to have some more today. I'm going to stay away from home till I'm all through forever. I may see you a month from now, or it may be a year. Yes, I know what the doctor told you, but doctors are always guessing. You won't hear from me again till it's good news. I send the kids a good-by kiss through you. I'm sure that's the way they'd rather have it. And I hope you'll think of me as I am sometimes and not as I am other times."

Allan went to the safety-deposit box, took out seventy thousand dollars' worth of bonds and delivered them to Rogers and King. He returned to the box and deposited the memorandum and receipt.

"It isn't stealing," he told himself. "If the doctor is wrong and Myers is wrong and I lose thirty-five thousand, I'll work till I can pay it back. And no matter whether Myers is wrong, if the doctor is right, the insurance company will pay Edith seventy thousand."

He exchanged what was in his checking account for travelers' checks. Then he got on a train for New York, an Eastern seaport at which you can usually find a ship that will ride you as far as you want to go.

The story I expect to make out of this would be immoral if I allowed Allan himself to profit by what he had done. But the doctor wasn't wrong. And when news of her husband's death, in some remote corner of the earth, reached Edith several months later, she was able to sell Allan's stock at a hundred and fifty-three dollars a share, a profit of $728,000 minus commissions. This chicken feed together with Allan's seventy thousand dollars' worth of life insurance, her hundred thousand in bonds and her fifty thousand dollar bank balance, almost intact, enabled Edith to prove to her parents that she had loved wisely and just about well enough.

Now that's off my mind and I ought to be able to go to sleep. Maybe if I'd exercise every day———But golf is the only exercise I like and I can't make any money at it. I can't beat anybody. I might if I played three or four times a week.

I'll turn on the light now and see what time it is. Eleven-eighteen. Well, at least it's after eleven. What I should do is get up and make a few notes for my story. And smoke one cigaret, just one. After that, I'll come right back to bed and turn off the light and not think of anything. That's the only way to go to sleep. Not thinking about anything at all.

Call for Mr. Keefe!

(*The Saturday Evening Post,* 9 March 1918)

ST. LOUIS, April 10.

FRIEND AL: Well Al the training trips over and we open up the season here tomorrow and I suppose the boys back home is all anxious to know about our chances and what shape the boys is in. Well old pal you can tell them we are out after that old flag this year and the club that beats us will know they have been in a battle. I'll say they will.

Speaking for myself personly I never felt better in my life and you know what that means Al. It means I will make a monkey out of this league and not only that but the boys will all have more confidence in themself and play better baseball when they know my arms right and that I can give them the best I got and if Rowland handles the club right and don't play no favorites like last season we will be so far out in front by the middle of July that Boston and the rest of them will think we have jumped to some other league.

Well I suppose the old towns all excited about Uncle Sam declairing war on Germany. Personly I am glad we are in it but between you and I Al I figure we ought to of been in it a long time ago right after the Louisiana was sank. I often say alls fair in love and war but that don't mean the Germans or no one else has got a right to murder American citizens but thats about all you can expect from a German and anybody that expects a square deal from them is a sucker. You don't see none of them umpireing in our league but at that they couldn't be no worse than the ones we got. Some of ours is so crooked they can't lay in a birth only when the trains making a curve.

But speaking about the war Al you couldn't keep me out of it only for Florrie and little Al depending on me for sport and of course theys the ball club to and I would feel like a trader if I quit them now when it looks like this is our year. So I might just as well make up

99

my mind to whats got to be and not mop over it but I like to kid the rest of the boys and make them think I'm going to enlist to see their face fall and tonight at supper I told Gleason I thought I would quit the club and join the army. He tried to laugh it off with some of his funny stuff. He says "They wouldn't take you." "No," I said. "I suppose Uncle Sam is turning down men with a perfect physic." So he says "They don't want a man that if a shell would hit him in the head it would explode all over the trench and raise havioc." I forget what I said back to him.

Well Al I don't know if I will pitch in this serious or not but if I do I will give them a touch of high life but maybe Rowland will save me to open up at Detroit where a mans got to have something besides their glove. It takes more than camel flags to beat that bunch. I'll say it does.

Your pal, Jack.

CHICAGO, April 15.

FRIEND AL: Well Al here I am home again and Rowland sent some of us home from St. Louis instead of takeing us along to Detroit and I suppose he is figureing on saveing me to open up the home season next Thursday against St. Louis because they always want a big crowd on opening day and St. Louis don't draw very good unless theys some extra attraction to bring the crowd out. But anyway I was glad to get home and see Florrie and little Al and honest Al he is cuter than ever and when he seen me he says "Who are you?" Hows that for a 3 year old?

Well things has been going along pretty good at home while I was away only it will take me all summer to pay the bills Florrie has ran up on me and you ought to be thankfull that Bertha aint 1 of these Apollos thats got to keep everybody looking at them or they can't eat. Honest Al to look at the clothes Florrie has boughten you would think we was planning to spend the summer at Newport News or somewhere. And she went and got herself a hired girl that sticks us for $8.00 per week and all as she does is cook up the meals and take care of little Al and run wild with a carpet sweeper and dust rag every time you set down to read the paper. I says to Florrie "What is the idea? The 3 of us use to get along O. K. without no help from Norway." So she says "I got sick in tired of staying home all the time or dragging the baby along with me when I went out." So I said I remembered when she wouldn't leave no one else take care of the kid only herself and she says "Yes but that was when I didn't know nothing about babys and every time he cried I thought he had lumbago or something but now I know he has got no intentions of dying so I quit worring about him."

So I said "Yes but I can't afford no high price servants to say nothing about dressing you like an actor and if you think I am going to spend all my salary on silks and satans and etc. you will get a big surprise." So she says "You might as well spend your money on me as leave the ball players take it away from you in the poker game and show their own wives a good time with it. But if you don't want me to spend your money I will go out and get some of my own to spend." Then I said "What will you do teach school?" And she says "No and I won't teach school either." So I said "No I guess you won't. But if you think you want to try standing up behind a cigar counter or something all day why go ahead and try it and we'll see how long you will last." So she says "I don't have to stand behind no counter but I can go in business for myself and make more then you do." So I said "Yes you can" and she didn't have no come back.

Imagine Al a girl saying she could make more money then a big league pitcher. Probably theys a few of them that does but they are movie actors or something and I would like to see Florrie try to be a movie actor because they got to look pleasant all the time and Florrie would strain herself.

Well Al the ski jumper has got dinner pretty near ready and after dinner I am going over North and see what the Cubs look like and I wish I pitched in that league Al and the only trouble is that I would feel ashamed when I went after my pay check.

                                           Your old pal, *Jack.*

CHICAGO, May 19.
DEAR FRIEND AL: Well old pal if we wasn't married we would all have to go to war now and I mean all of us thats between 21 and 30. I suppose you seen about the Govt. passing the draft law and a whole lot of the baseball players will have to go but our club won't loose nobody except 1 or 2 bushers that don't count because all as they do any way is take up room on the bench and laugh when Rowland springs a joke.

When I first seen it in the paper this morning I thought it meant everybody that wasn't crippled up or something but Gleason explained it to me that if you got somebody to sport they leave you home and thats fair enough but he also says they won't take no left handers on acct. of the guns all being made for right handed men and thats just like the lucky stiffs to set in a rocking chair and take it easy while the regular fellows has got to go over there and get shot up but anyway the yellow stiffs would make a fine lot of soldiers because the first time a German looked X eyed at them they would wave a flag of truants.

But I can't help from wishing this thing had of come off before I seen Florrie or little Al and if I had money enough saved up so as they wouldn't have to worry I would go any way but I wouldn't wait for no draft. Gleason says I will have to register family or no family when the time comes but as soon as I tell them about Florrie they will give me an excuse. I asked him what they would do with the boys that wasn't excused and if they would send them right over to France and he says No they would keep them here till they learned to talk German. He says "You can't fight nobody without a quarrel and you can't quarrel with a man unless they can understand what you are calling them." So I asked him how about the aviators because their machines would be makeing so much noise that they couldn't tell if the other one was talking German or rag time and he said "Well if you are in an areoplane and you see a German areoplane coming tords you you can pretty near guess that he don't want to spoon with you."

Thats what I would like to be Al is an aviator and I think Gleasons afraid I'm going to bust into that end of the game though he pretends like he don't take me in ernest. "Why don't you?" he said "You could make good there all right because the less sense they got the better. But I wish you would quit practiceing till you get away from here." I asked him what he meant quit practiceing. "Well" he said "you was up in the air all last Tuesday afternoon."

He was refering to that game I worked against the Phila. club but honest Al my old souper was so sore I couldn't cut loose. Well Al a mans got a fine chance to save money when they are married to a girl like Florrie. When I got paid Tuesday the first thing when I come home she wanted to borrow $200.00 and that was all I had comeing so I said "What am I going to do the next 2 weeks walk back and forth to the ball park and back?" I said "What and the hell do you want with $200.00?" So then she begin to cry so I split it with her and give her a $100.00 and she wouldn't tell me what she wanted it for but she says she was going to supprise me. Well Al I will be supprised if she don't land us all out to the county farm but you can't do nothing with them when they cry.

Your pal, Jack.

CHICAGO, May 24.

FRIEND AL: What do you think Florrie has pulled off now? I told you she was fixing to land us in the poor house and I had the right dope. With the money I give her and some she got somewheres else she has opened up a beauty parlor on 43th St. right off of Michigan. Her and a girl that worked in a place like it down town.

Well Al when she sprung it on me you couldn't of knocked me down with a feather. I always figured girls was kind of crazy but I never seen one loose her mind as quick as that and I don't know if I ought to have them take her to some home or leave her learn her lesson and get over it.

I know you ain't got no beauty parlor in Bedford so I might as well tell you what they are. They are for women only and the women goes to them when they need something done to their hair or their face or their nails before a wedding or a eucher party or something. For inst. you and Bertha was up here and you wanted to take her to a show and she would have to get fixed up so she would go to this place and tell them to give her the whole treatment and first they would wash the grime out of her hair and then comb it up fluffy and then they would clean up her complexion with buttermilk and either get rid of the moles or else paint them white and then they would put some eyebrows on her with a pencil and red up her lips and polish her teeth and pair her finger nails and etc. till she looked as good as she could and it would cost her $5.00 or $10.00 according to what they do to her and if they would give her a bath and a massage I suppose its extra.

Well theys plenty of high class beauty parlors down town where women can go and know they will get good service but Florrie thinks she can make it pay out here with women that maybe haven't time to go clear down town because their husband or their friend might loose his mind in the middle of the afternoon and phone home that he had tickets for the Majestic or something and then of course they would have to rush over to some place in the neighborhood for repairs.

I didn't know Florrie was wise to the game but it seems she has been takeing some lessons down town without telling me nothing about it and this Miss Nevins thats in partners with her says Florrie is a darb. Well I wouldn't have no objections if I thought they was a chance for them to make good because she acts like she liked the work and its right close to where we live but it looks to me like their expenses would eat them up. I was in the joint this morning and the different smells alone must of cost them $100.00 to say nothing about all the bottles and cans and tools and brushs and the rent and furniture besides. I told Florrie I said "You got everything here but patients." She says "Don't worry about them. They will come when they find out about us." She says they have sent their cards to all the South Side 400.

"Well" I said "if they don't none of them show up in a couple of months I suppose you will call on the old meal ticket." So she says "You should worry." So I come away and went over to the ball park.

When I seen Kid Gleason I told him about it and he asked me where Florrie got the money to start up so I told him I give it to her. "You" he says "Where did you it?" So just jokeing I said "Where do you suppose I got it? I stole it." So he says "You did if you got it from this ball club." But he was kidding Al because of course he knows I'm no thief. But I got the laugh on him this afternoon when Silk O'Loughlin chased him out of the ball park. Johnson was working against us and they was two out and Collins on second base and Silk called a third strike on Gandil that was down by his corns. So Gleason hollered "All right Silk you won't have to go to war. You couldn't pass the eye test." So Silk told him to get off the field. So then I hollered something at Silk and he hollered back at me "That will be all from you you big busher." So I said "You are a busher yourself you busher." So he said:

"Get off the bench and let one of the ball players set down."

So I and Gleason stalled a while and finely come into the club house and I said "Well Kid I guess we told him something that time." "Yes" says Gleason "you certainly burned him up but the trouble with me is I can't never think of nothing to say till it's too late." So I said "When a man gets past sixty you can't expect their brain to act quick." And he didn't say nothing back.

Well we win the ball game any way because Cicotte shut them out. The way some of the ball players was patting him on the back afterwards you would have thought it was the 1st. time anybody had ever pitched a shut out against the Washington club but I don't see no reason to swell a man up over it. If you shut out Detroit or Cleveland you are doing something but this here Washington club gets a bonus every time they score a run.

But it does look like we was going to cop that old flag and play the Giants for the big dough and it will sure be the Giants we will have to play against though some of the boys seem to think the Cubs have got a chance on acct. of them just winning 10 straight on their eastren trip but as Gleason says how can a club help from winning 10 straight in that league?

Your pal, *Jack.*

CHICAGO, June 6.

FRIEND AL: Well Al the clubs east and Rowland left me home because my old souper is sore again and besides I had to register yesterday for the draft. They was a big crowd down to the place we registered and you ought to seen them when I come in. They was all trying to get up close to me and I was afraid some of them would get hurt in the jam. All of them says "Hello Jack" and I give them a smile and shook hands with about a dozen of them. A man hates to have everybody stareing at you but you got to be pleasant or they will think you are swelled up and besides a man can afford to put themself out a little if its going to give the boys any pleasure.

I don't know how they done with you Al but up here they give us a card to fill out and then they give us another one to carry around with us to show that we been registered and what our number is. I had to put down my name on the first card and my age and where I live and the day I was born and what month and etc. Some of the questions was crazy like "Was I a natural born citizen?" I wonder what they think I am. Maybe they think I fell out of a tree or something. Then I had to tell them I was born in Bedford, Ind. and it asked what I done for a liveing and I put down that I was a pitcher but the man made me change it to ball player and then I had to give Comiskey's name and address and then name the people that was dependent on me so I put down a wife and one child.

And the next question was if I was married or single. I supposed they would know enough to know that a man with a wife dependent on him was probably married. Then it says what race and I had a notion to put down "pennant" for a joke but the man says to put down white. Then it asked what military service had I had and of course I says none and then come the last question Did I claim exemption and what grounds so the man told me to write down married with dependents.

Then the man turned over to the back of the card and wrote down about my looks. Just that I was tall and medium build and brown eyes and brown hair. And the last question was if I had lost an arm or leg or hand or foot or both eyes or was I other wise disabled so I told him about my arm being sore and thats why I wasn't east with the club but he didn't put it down. So thats all they was to it except the card he give me with my number which is 3403.

It looks to me like it was waisting a mans time to make you go down there and wait for your turn when they know you are married and got a kid or if they don't know it they could call up your home or the ball park and find it out but of course if they called up my flat when I or Florrie wasn't there they wouldn't get nothing but a bunch of Swede talk that they couldn't nobody understand and I don't believe the girl knows herself what she is talking about over the phone. She can talk english pretty good when shes just talking to you but she must think all the phone calls is long distance from Norway because the minute she gets that receiver up to her ear you can't hardly tell the difference between she and Hughey Jennings on the coaching line.

I told Florrie I said "This girl could make more then $8.00 per week if she would get a job out to some ball park as announcer and announce the batterys and etc. She has got the voice for it and she would be right in a class with the rest of them because nobody could make heads or tales out of what she was trying to get at."

Speaking about Florrie what do you think Al? They have had enough suckers to pay expenses and also pay up some of the money they borrowed and Florrie says if their business gets much bigger they will have to hire more help. How would you like a job Al white washing some dames nose or levelling off their face with a steam roller? Of course I am just jokeing Al because they won't allow no men around the joint but wouldn't it be some job Al? I'll say so.

Your old pal, *Jack.*

CHICAGO, June 21.

DEAR AL: Well Al I suppose you read in the paper the kind of luck I had yesterday but of course you can't tell nothing from what them dam reporters write and if they know how to play ball why aint they playing it instead of trying to write funny stuff about the ball game but at that some of it is funny Al because its so rotten its good. For inst. one of them had it in the paper this morning that I flied out to Speaker in that seventh inning. Well listen Al I hit that ball right on the pick and it went past that shortstop so fast that he didn't even have time to wave at it and if Speaker had of been playing where he belongs that ball would of went between he and Graney and bumped against the wall. But no. Speakers laying about ten feet back of second base and over to the left and of course the ball rides right to him and there was the whole ball game because that would of drove in 2 runs and made them play different then they did in the eigth. If a man is supposed to be playing center field why don't he play center field and of course I thought he was where he ought to been or I would of swung different.

Well the eigth opened up with the score 1 and 1 and I get 2 of them out but I got so much stuff I can't stick it just where I want to and I give Chapman a base on balls. At that the last one cut the heart of the plate but Evans called it a ball. Evans lives in Cleveland. Well I said "All right Bill you won't have to go to war. You couldn't pass the eye test." So he says "You must of read that one in a book." "No" I said "I didn't read it in no book either."

So up comes this Speaker and I says "What do you think you are going to do you lucky stiff?" So he says "I'm going to hit one where theys nobody standing in the way of it." I said "Yes you are." But I had to hold Chapman up at first base and Schalk made me waist 2 thinking Chapman was going and then of course I had to ease up and Speaker cracked one down the first base line but Gandil got his glove on it and if he hadn't of messed it all up he could of beat

Speaker to the bag himself but instead of that they all started to ball me out for not covering. I told them to shut their mouth. Then Roth come up and I took a half wind up because of course I didn't think Chapman would be enough of a bone head to steal third with 2 out but him and Speaker pulled a double steal and then Rowland and all of them begin to yell at me and they got my mind off of what I was doing and then Schalk asked for a fast one though he said afterwards he didn't but I would of made him let me curve the ball if they hadn't got me all nervous yelling at me. So Roth hit one to left field that Jackson could of caught in his hip pocket if he had been playing right. So 2 runs come in and then Rowland takes me out and I would of busted him only for makeing a seen on the field.

I said to him "How can you expect a man to be at his best when I have not worked for a month?" So he said "Well it will be more than a month before you will work for me again." "Yes" I said "because I am going to work for Uncle Sam and join the army." "Well," he says "you won't need no steel helmet." "No" I said "and you wouldn't either." Then he says "I'm afraid you won't last long over there because the first time they give you a hand grenade to throw you will take your wind up and loose a hand." So I said "If Chapman is a smart ball player why and the hell did he steal third base with 2 out?" He couldn't answer that but he says "What was you doing all alone out in No Mans Land on that ball of Speakers to Gandil?" So I told him to shut up and I went in the club house and when he come in I didn't speak to him or to none of the rest of them either.

Well Al I would quit right now and go up to Fort Sheridan and try for a captain only for Florrie and little Al and of course if it come to a show down Comiskey would ask me to stick on acct. of the club being in the race and it wouldn't be the square thing for me to walk out on him when he has got his heart set on the pennant.

Your pal, *Jack.*

Chicago, July 5.

FRIEND AL: Just a few lines Al to tell you how Florrie is getting along and I bet you will be surprised to hear about it. Well Al she paid me back my $100.00 day before yesterday and she showed me their figures for the month of June and I don't know if you will beleive it or not but she and Miss Nevins cleared $400.00 for the month or $200.00 a peace over and above all expenses and she says the business will be even better in the fall and winter time on acct. of more people going to partys and theaters then. How is that for the kind of a wife to have Al and the best part of it is that she is stuck on the work and a whole lot happier then when she wasn't doing nothing. They got 2 girls working besides themself and they are talking about moveing into a bigger store somewheres and she says we will have to find a bigger flat so as we can have a nurse and a hired girl instead of just the one.

Tell Bertha about it Al and tell her that when she comes up to Chi she can get all prettied up and I will see they don't charge her nothing for it.

The clubs over in Detroit but it was only a 5 day trip so Rowland left me home to rest up my arm for the eastren clubs and Phila. is due here the day after tomorrow and all as I ask is a chance at them. My arm don't feel just exactly right but I could roll the ball up to the plate and beat that club.

Its a cinch now that the Giants is comeing through in the other league and if we can keep going it will be some worlds serious between the 2 biggest towns in the country and the club that wins ought to grab off about $4500.00 a peace per man. Is that worth going after Al? I'll say so.

Your old pal, *Jack.*

CHICAGO, July 20.

FRIEND AL: Well Al I don't suppose you remember my draft number and I don't remember if I told it to you or not. It was 3403 Al. And it was the 5th number drawed at Washington.

Well old pal they can wipe the town of Washington off of the map and you won't hear no holler from me. The day before yesterday Rowland sends me in against the Washington club and of course it had to be Johnson for them. And I get beat 3 and 2 and I guess its the only time this season that Washington scored 3 runs in 1 day. And the next thing they announce the way the draft come out and I'm No. 5 and its a misery to me why my number wasn't the 1st. they drawed out instead of the 5th.

Well Al of course it don't mean I got to go if I don't want to. I

can get out of it easy enough by telling them about Florrie and little
Al and besides Gleason says they have promised Ban Johnson that
they won't take no baseball stars till the seasons over and maybe not
then and besides theys probably some White Sox fans that will go to
the front for me and get me off on acct. of the club being in the fight
for the pennant and they can't nobody say I'm trying to get excused
because I said all season that I would go in a minute if it wasn't for
my family and the club being in the race and I give $50.00 last week
for a liberty bond that will only bring me in $1.75 per annum which
is nothing you might say. You couldn't sport a flee on $1.75 per
annum.

Florrie wanted I should go right down to the City Hall or where
ever it is you go and get myself excused but Gleason says the only
thing to do is just wait till they call me and then claim exemptions.
I read somewheres a while ago that President Wilson wanted baseball kept up because the people would need amusement and I asked
Gleason if he had read about that and he says "Yes but that won't
get you nothing because the rest of the soldiers will need amusement
even more than the people."

Well Al I don't know what your number was or how you come
out but I hope you had better luck but if you did get drawed you will
probably have a hard time getting out of it because you don't make
no big salary and you got no children and Bertha could live with your
mother and pick up a few dollars sowing. Enough to pay for her
board and clothes. Of course they might excuse you for flat feet
which they say you can't get in if you have them. But if I was you
Al I would be tickled to death to get in because it would give you
a chance to see something outside of Bedford and if your feet gets
by you ought to be O. K.

I guess they won't find fault with my feet or anything about me
as far physical goes. Hey Al?

I will write as soon as I learn anything.

Your pal, *Jack.*

CHICAGO, Aug. 6.
FRIEND AL: Well Al I got notice last Friday that I was to show
up right away over to Wendell Phillips high school where No. 5
board of exemptions was setting but when I got over there it was

jamed so I went back there today and I have just come home from there now.

The 1st. man I seen was the doctor and he took my name and number and then he asked me if my health was O. K. and I told him it was only I don't feel good after meals. Then he asked me if I was all sound and well right now so I told him my pitching arm was awful lame and that was the reason I hadn't went east with the club. Then he says "Do you understand that if a man don't tell the truth about themself here they are libel to prison?" So I said he didn't have to worry about that.

So then he made me strip bear and I wish you had seen his eyes pop out when he got a look at my shoulders and chest. I stepped on the scales and tipped the bean at 194 and he measured me at 6 ft. 1 and a half. Then he went all over me and poked me with his finger and counted my teeth and finely he made me tell him what different letters was that he held up like I didn't know the alphabet or something. So when he was through he says "Well I guess you ain't going to die right away." He signed the paper and sent me to the room where the rest of the board was setting.

Well 1 of them looked up my number and then asked me did I claim exemptions. I told him yes and he asked me what grounds so I said "I sport a wife and baby and besides I don't feel like it would be a square deal to Comiskey for me to walk out on him now." So he says "Have you got an affidavit from your wife that you sport her?" So I told him no and he says "Go and get one and bring it back here tomorrow but you don't need to bring none from Comiskey." So you see Comiskey must stand pretty good with them.

So he give me a blank for Florrie to fill out and when she gets home we will go to a notary and tend to it and tomorrow they will fix up my excuse and then I won't have nothing to think about only to get the old souper in shape for the big finish.

Your pal, *Jack.*

CHICAGO, Aug. 8.

DEAR OLD PAL: Well old pal it would seem like the best way to get along in this world is to not try and get nowheres because the minute a man gets somewheres they's people that can't hardly wait to bite your back.

The 1st. thing yesterday I went over to No. 5 board and was going to show them Florrie's affidavit but while I was pulling it out of my pocket the man I seen the day before called me over to 1 side and says "Listen Keefe I am a White Sox fan and don't want to see you get none the worst of it and if I was you I would keep a hold of that paper." So I asked him what for and he says "Do you know what the law is about telling the truth and not telling the truth and if you turn in an affidavit thats false and we find it out you and who ever made the affidavit is both libel to prison?" So I said what was he trying to get at and he says "We got informations that your wife is in business for herself and makeing as high as $250.00 per month which is plenty for she and your boy to get along on." "Yes" I said "but who pays for the rent of our flat and the hired girl and what we eat?" So he says "That don't make no difference. Your wife could pay for them and that settles it."

Well Al I didn't know what to say for a minute but finely I asked him where the informations come from and he says he was tipped off in a letter that who ever wrote it didn't sign their name the sneaks and I asked him how he knowed that they was telling the truth. So he says "Its our business to look them things up. If I was you I wouldn't make no claim for exemptions but just lay quiet and take a chance."

Then all of a sudden I had an idea Al and I will tell you about it but 1st. as soon as it come to me I asked the man if this here board was all the board they was and he says no that if they would not excuse me I could appeal to the Dist. board but if he was me he wouldn't do it because it wouldn't do no good and might get me in trouble. So I said "I won't get in no trouble" and he says "All right suit yourself." So I said I would take the affadavit and go to the Dist. board but he says no that I would have to get passed on 1st. by his board and then I could appeal if I wanted to.

So I left the affadavit and he says they would notify me how I come out so then I beat it home and called up Florrie and told her they was something important and for her to come up to the flat.

Well Al here was the idea. I had been thinking for a long time that while it was all O. K. for Florrie to earn a little money in the summer when I was tied up with the club it would be a whole lot better if we was both free after the season so as we could take little Al and go on a trip somewheres or maybe spend the winter in the south but of course if she kept a hold of her share in the business she couldn't get away so the best thing would be to sell out to Miss Nevins for a good peace of money and we could maybe buy us a winter home somewheres with what she got and whats comeing to me in the worlds serious.

So when Florrie got home I put it up to her. I said "Florrie I'm sick in tired of haveing you tied up in business because it don't seem right for a married woman to be in business when their husbands in the big league and besides a womans place is home especially when they got a baby so I want you to sell out and when I get my split of the worlds serious we will go south somewheres and buy a home."

Well she asked me how did I come out with the affadavit. So I said "The affadavit is either here nor there. I am talking about something else" and she says "Yes you are." And she says "I been worring all day about that affadavit because if they find out about it what will they do to us." So I said "You should worry because if this board won't excuse me I will go to the Dist. board and mean while you won't be earning nothing because you will be out of business." Well Al she had a better idea then that. She says "No I will hold on to the business till you go to the Dist. board and then if they act like they wouldn't excuse you you can tell them I am going to sell out. And if they say all right I will sell out. But if they say its to late why then I will still have something to live on if you have to go."

So when she said that about me haveing to go we both choked up a little but pretty soon I was O. K. and now Al it looks like a cinch I would get my exemptions from the Dist. board because if Florrie says she wants to sell out they can't stop her.

Your pal, *Jack.*

CHICAGO, Aug. 22.

FRIEND AL: Well Al its all over. The Dist. board won't let me off and between you and I Al I am glad of it and I only hope I won't have to go before I have had a chance at the worlds serious.

My case come up about noon. One of the men asked me my name and then looked over what they had wrote down about me. Then he says "Theys an affadavit here that says your wife and child depends on you. Is that true?" So I said yes it was and he asked me if my wife was in business and I said yes but she was thinking about selling out. So he asked me how much money she made in her business. I said "You can't never tell. Some times its so much and other times different." So he asked me what the average was and I said it was about $250.00 per month. Then he says "Why is she going to sell out?" I said "Because we don't want to live in Chi all winter" and he said "You needn't to worry." Then he said "If she makes $250.00 per month how do you figure she is dependent on you?" So I said "Because she is because I pay for the rent and everything." And he asked me what she done with the $250.00 and I told him she spent it on clothes.

So he says "$250.00 per month on clothes. How does she keep warm this weather?" I said "I guess they don't nobody have no trouble keeping warm in August. Then he says "Look here Keefe this affadavit mitigates against you. We will have to turn down your appeal and I guess your wife can take care of herself and the boy." I said "She can't when she sells out." "Well" he said "you tell her not to sell out. It may be hard for her at first to sport herself and the boy on $250.00 but if the worst comes to the worst she can wear the same shoes twice and she will find them a whole lot more comfortable the second time." So I said "She don't never have no trouble with her feet and if she did I guess she knows how to fix them."

Florrie was waiting for me when I got home. "Well" I said "now you see what your dam beauty parlor has done for us." And then she seen what had happened and begin to cry and of course I couldn't find no more fault with her and I called up the ball park and told them I was sick and wouldn't show up this P. M. and I and Florrie and little Al stayed home together and talked. That is little Al done all the talking. I and Florrie didn't seem to have nothing to say.

Tomorrow I am going to tell them about it over to the ball park. If they can get me off till after the worlds serious all right. And if they can't all right to.

Your old pal, Jack.

P. S. Washington comes tomorrow and I am going to ask Rowland to leave me pitch. The worst I can get is a tie. They scored a run in St. Louis yesterday and that means they are through for the week.

DEAR AL: Well Al the one that laughs last gets all the best of it. Wait till you hear what come off today.

When I come in the club house Rowland and Gleason was there all alone. I told them hello and was going to spring the news on them but when Rowland seen me he says "Jack I got some bad news for you." So I said what was it. So he says "The boss sold you to Washington this morning."

Well Al at first I couldn't say nothing and I forgot all about that I wanted to tell them. But then I remembered it again and here is what I pulled. I said "Listen Manager I beat the boss to it." "What do you mean?" he said so I said "I'm signed up with Washington all ready only I ain't signed with Griffith but with Uncle Sam." Thats what I pulled on them Al and they both got it right away. Gleason jumped up and shook hands with me and so did Rowland and then Rowland said he would have to hurry up in the office and tell the Old Man. "But wait a minute" I said. "I am going to quit you after this game because I don't know when I will be called and theys lots of things I got to fix up." So I stopped and Rowland asked me what I wanted and I said "Let me pitch this game and I will give them the beating of their life."

So him and Gleason looked at each other and then Rowland says "You know we can't afford to loose no ball games now. But if you think you can beat them I will start you."

So then he blowed and I and Gleason was alone.

"Well kid" he says "you make the rest of us look like a monkey. This game ain't nothing compared to what you are going to do. And when you come back they won't be nothing to good for you and your kid will be proud of you because you went while a whole lot of other kids dads stayed home."

So he patted me on the back and I kind of choked up and then the trainer come in and I had him do a little work on my arm.

Well Al you will see in the paper what I done to them. Before the game the boss had told Griffith about me and called the deal off. So while I was warming up Griffith come over and shook hands. He says "I would of like to had you but I am a good looser." So I says "You ought to be." So he couldn't help from laughing but he says "When you come back I will go after you again." I said "Well if you don't get somebody on the club between now and then that can hit something besides fouls I won't come back." So he kind of laughed again and walked away and then it was time for the game.

Well Al the official scorer give them 3 hits but he must be McMullins brother in law or something because McMullin ought to of throwed Milan out from here to Berlin on that bunt. But any way 3 hits and no runs is pretty good for a finish and between you and I Al I feel like I got the last laugh on Washington and Rowland to.

Your pal, Jack.

CHICAGO, Sept. 18.

FRIEND AL: Just time for a few lines while Florrie finishs packing up my stuff. I leave with the bunch tomorrow A.M. for Camp Grant at Rockford. I don't know how long we will stay there but I suppose long enough to learn to talk German and shoot and etc.

We just put little Al to bed and tonight was the first time we told him I was going to war. He says "Can I go to daddy?" Hows that for a 3 year old Al?

Well he will be proud of me when I come back and he will be proud of me if I don't come back and when he gets older he can go up to the kids that belong to some of these left handers and say "Where and the hell was your father when the war come off?"

Good by Al and say good by to Bertha for me.

Your Pal, Jack.

P. S. I won't be in the serious against New York but how about the real worlds serious Al? Won't I be in that? I'll say so.

Along Came Ruth

(The Saturday Evening Post, 26 July 1919)

ST. LOUIS, April 26.

FRIEND AL: Well Al this is our last day here and we win the 1st.
2 games and lose yesterday and have got one more game to play and
tonight we leave for Detroit. Well if we lose today we will have a even
break on the serious and a club that can't do no better then break
even with this St. Louis club better take up some other line of
business but Gleason instead of useing a little judgement sent a left
hander in against them yesterday and they certainly give him a
welcome and the more I see of left handers I am certainly glad I pitch
with my right arm the way God intended for a man.

Well the boys on our club was feeling pretty cocky the 1st. 2 days
about how they could hit but yesterday they could of played in a 16
ft. ring without no ground rules as the most of the time they was
missing the ball all together and when they did hit it it acted like a
geyser and it was Bert Gallia pitching against us and they all kept
saying he didn't have nothing but when he got through with us we
didn't have nothing either and that's the way it always goes when a
pitcher makes a sucker out of a club he didn't have nothing but when
they knock him out of the park he's pretty good.

Well any way I told Gleason last night that it looked like we
wouldn't get no better then a even break here unless he stuck me in
there to pitch the last game today. So he says "No I was figureing
on you to open up in Detroit Sunday but of course if you are afraid
of Detroit I can make different plans." So I said "I am not afraid of
Detroit or nobody else and you know yourself that they can't no club
beat me the way I am going whether its Detroit or no matter who
it is." So he said "All right then keep your mouth shut about who
is going to pitch because if you are going to manage the club I won't
have no job left." Well let him try and run the ball club the way he

wants to but if I was running the ball club and had a pitcher that is going the way I am going I would work him every other day and get a start on the other clubs as the games we win now counts just as much as the games we win in Sept.

Well Al Florrie went back to Chi last night though I wanted her to stick with the club and go on to Detroit with us but she said she had to get back, and tend to business at the beauty parlor so I told Gleason that and he said he was sorry she was going to leave us as it was a releif for him to look at something pretty once in a wile when most of the time he had to watch ball players but he admired her for tending to business and he wished it run in the family. He says "You should ought to be thankfull that your Mrs. is what she is as most wifes is a drug on their husband but your Mrs. makes more jack then you and if she give up her business it would keep you hustleing to make both ends meet the other, where if you missed a meal some time and died from it your family would be that much ahead." So I said "Yes and that is because your cheapskate ball club is only paying me a salary of $2400.00 per annum instead of somewheres near what I am worth." So he said "I have all ready told you that if you keep working hard and show me something I will tear up your contract and give you a good one but before I do it I will half to find out if you are going to win ball games for me or just use up 1 lower birth like in old times." So I told him to shut his mouth.

Well Al I thought the war with Germany was all over but Joe Jenkins joined the club here and now the whole war is being played over again. He is 1 of the catchers on the club and he was in France and if they was any battles he wasn't in its because he can't pronounce them but anybody that thinks the U. S. troop movements was slow over there ought to listen to some of these birds that's came back and some of them was at Verdun 1 evening and Flanders the next A. M. then down to Nice the next day for a couple hours rest and up in the Oregon forest the folling afternoon and etc. till its no wonder the Germans was dazzled. If some of these birds that was in the war could get around the bases like they did around the western front all as the catchers would dast do when they started to steal second base would be walk up the base line towards third with the ball in their hand and try to scare them from comeing all the way home.

Well its Detroit tomorrow and 3 more days after that and then home and I haven't been there since the middle of March and I guess they's 2 kids that won't be tickled to death to see somebody eh Al?

Your pal, *Jack.*

DETROIT, April 28.

FRIEND AL: Well old pal I suppose you read in the papers what come off here yesterday and I guess Gleason won't have no more to say after this about me being afraid of Detroit. The shoe points the other way now and Detroit is the one that's afraid of me and no wonder.

I didn't have the stuff that I had down to St. Louis for the opening but I had enough to make a monkey out of Cobb and Veach and I couldn't help from feeling sorry for this new outfielder they have got name Flagstaff or something and I guess he was about half mast before I got through with him.

Well its a cinch now that I will open in Chi Thursday and I will give St. Louis another spanking and then I will make Gleason come acrost with that contract he has been promiseing me and if he trys to stall I will tell him he must either give me the jack or trade me to some other club and he has got good sence even if he don't act like it sometimes and they's a fine chance of him tradeing me though they's 7 other clubs in this league that would jump at it and Detroit is 1 of them though the Detroit club would be takeing a big chance if they got a hold of somebody that could realy pitch as the fans up here would die from surprise.

Well I had a letter from Florrie today and it was just like the most of her letters when you got through reading it you wondered what she had in mind and about all as she said was that she had a surprise to tell me when I got home and I use to get all excited when she wrote about them surprises but now I can guess what it is. She probably seen a roach in the apartment or something and any way I guess I can wait till I get home and not burn up the wires trying to find out before hand.

Your pal, *Jack.*

DETROIT, April 30.

FRIEND AL: Well Al we leave for home tonight and open up the season in Chi tomorrow but I won't be out there pitching unless Gleason apologizes for what he pulled on me last night. It was more rotten weather yesterday just like we been haveing ever since the 1st. day in St. Louis and I near froze to death setting out there on the bench so when we come back to the hotel they was a friend of mine here in Detroit waiting for me here in the lobby and he come up in the room with me and I was still shivering yet with the cold and he said how would I like something to warm me up. So I said "That's a fine line of talk to hand out in a dry town." So he said I could easy get a hold of some refreshments if I realy wanted some and all as I would half to do would be call a bell hop and tell him what I wanted.

Well I felt like a good shot would just about save my life so I called a boy and told him to go fetch me some bourbon and he said O. K. and he went out and come back in about a half hr. and he had a qt. with him and I asked him how much did we owe him and he said $15.00. How is that for reasonable Al and I guess it was the liquor men themselfs that voted Michigan dry and you can't blame them. Well my friend seemed to of had a stroke in his arm so as he couldn't even begin to reach in his pocket so I dug down and got 15 berrys and handed it to the kid and he still stood there yet like he expected a tip so I told him to beat it or I would tip him 1 in the jaw.

Well I asked my friend would he have a shot and his arm was O. K. again and he took the bottle and went to it without waiting for no glass or nothing but he got the neck of the bottle caught in his teeth and before he could pry it loose they was about a quarter of the bourbon gone.

Well I was just going to pore some of it out for myself and all of a sudden they come a rap at the door and I said come in and who walked in but Gleason. So I asked him what did he want.

So he said "Well you wasn't the 1st. one in the dinning rm. so I thought you must be pretty sick so I come up to see what was the matter." Well it was to late to hide the bottle and he come over to the table where I was setting and picked it up and looked at it and then he pored out a couple drops in the glass and tasted it and said it tastes like pretty good stuff. So I said it ought to be pretty good stuff as it cost enough jack so he asked me how much and I told him $15.00.

So he said "Well they's some of the newspaper boys has been

asking me to try and get a hold of some stuff for them so I will just take this along."

So I said I guest the newspaper boys could write crazy enough without no help from the Michigan boot legs and besides the bottle belongs to me as I payed good money for it. So Gleason said "Oh I wouldn't think of stealing it off of you but I will take it and pay you for it. You say it cost $15.00 but they's only about $11.00 and a half worth of it left so I will settle with you for $11.00 and a half." Well I didn't want to quarrel with him in the front of a outsider so I didn't say nothing and he took the bottle and started out of the rm. and I said hold on a minute where is my $11.00 and a half? So he said "Oh I am going to fine you $11.00 and a half for haveing liquor in your rm. but instead of takeing the fine out of your check I will take what's left in the bottle and that makes us even." So he walked out.

Well Al only for my friend being here in the rm. I would of took the bottle away from Gleason and cracked his head open with it but I didn't want to make no seen before a outsider as he might tell it around and people would say the White Sox players was fighting with their mgr. So I left Gleason get away with $11.00 and a half worth of bourbon that I payed $15.00 for it and never tasted it and don't know now if it was bourbon or cat nip.

Well my friend said "What kind of a bird are you to let a little scrimp like that make a monkey out of you?" So I said I didn't want to make no seen in the hotel. So he said "Well if it had of been me I would of made a seen even if it was in church." So I says "Well they's no danger of you ever haveing a chance to make a seen in church and a specialy with Gleason but if you did make a seen with Gleason you would be in church 3 days later and have a box right up close to the front."

Well Al I have told Gleason before this all ready that I would stand for him manageing me out on the old ball field but I wouldn't stand for him trying to run my private affairs and this time I mean it and if he don't apologize this P. M or tonight on the train he will be shy of a pitcher tomorrow and will half to open up the home season with 1 of them other 4 flushers that claims they are pitchers but if Jackson and Collins didn't hit in 7 or 8 runs every day they would be beating rugs in the stead of ball clubs.

Well any way we go home tonight and tomorrow I will be where it don't cost no $15.00 per qt. and if Gleason walks in on me he can't only rob me of $.20 worth at a time unless he operates.

Your pal, *Jack.*

Chi., May 3.

FRIEND AL: Well Al I have just now came back from the ball pk. and will set down and write you a few lines before supper. I give the St. Louis club another good trimming today Al and that is 3 games I have pitched and win them all and only 1 run scored off of me in all 3 games together and that was the 1 the St. Louis club got today and they wouldn't of never had that if Felsch had of been playing right for Tobin. But 1 run off of me in 3 games is going some and I should worry how many runs they scratch in as long as I win the ball game.

Well you know we was to open up here Thursday and it rained and we opened yesterday and I was waiting for Gleason to tell me I was going to pitch and then I was going to tell him I would pitch if he would apologize to me for what he done in Detroit but instead of picking me to pitch he picked Lefty Williams and the crowd was sore at him for not picking me and before the 1st inning was over he was sore at himself and Lefty was enjoying the shower bath. Gallia give us another beating and after it was over Gleason come up to me in the club house and said he was going to start me today. So I said "How about what you pulled on me in Detroit?" So he says "Do you mean about grabbing that bottle off of you?" So I said yes and he says "Look at here Jack you have got a great chance to get somewheres this yr. and if you keep on pitching like the way you started you will make a name for yourself and I will see that you get the jack. But you can't do it and be stewed all the wile so that is the reason I took that bottle off of you." So I said "They's no danger of me being stewed all the wile or any part of the wile when bourbon is $15.00 per qt. and me getting a bat boy's salery." So he said "Well you lay off the old burb and pitch baseball and you won't be getting no bat boy's salery. And besides I have told the newspaper boys that you are going to pitch and it will be in the morning papers and if you don't pitch the bugs will jump out of the stand and knock me for a gool." So as long as he put it up to me that way I couldn't do nothing only say all right.

So sure enough it come out in the papers this A. M. that I was going to pitch and you ought to seen the crowd out there today Al and you ought to heard them when my name was gave out to pitch and when I walked out there on the field. Well I got away to a bad start you might say as Felsch wasn't laying right for Tobin and he got a two base hit on a ball that Felsch ought to of caught in his eye and then after I got rid of Gedeon this Sisler hit at a ball he couldn't hardly reach and it dropped over third base and Tobin scored and after that I made a monkey out of them and the 1st. time I come up to bat the fans give me a traveling bag and I suppose they think I have been running around the country all these yrs. with my night gown in a peach basket but I suppose we can give it to 1 of Florrie's friends next xmas and besides it shows the fans of old Chi have got a warm spot for old Jack.

Speaking about Florrie Al when we was in Detroit she wrote and said she had a surprise for me and I thought little Al had picked up a couple hives or something but no it seems like wile I was on the road she met some partys that runs a beauty parlor down town and they wanted she should sell her interest in the one out south and go in pardners with them and they would give her a third interest for $3000.00 and pay her a salery of $300.00 per mo. and a share of the receits and she could pay for her interest on payments. So she asked me what I thought about it and I said if I was her I would stick to what she had where she was makeing so good but no matter what I thought she would do like she felt like so what was the use of asking me so she said she didn't like to make a move without consulting me. That's a good one Al as the only move she ever made and did consult me about it was when we got married and then it wouldn't of made no differents to her what I said.

Well she will do as she pleases and if she goes into this here down town parlor and gets stung we should worry as I will soon be getting real jack and it looks like a cinch we would be in the world serious besides, and besides that the kids would be better off if she was out of business and could be home with them more as the way it is now they don't hardly ever see anybody only the Swede nurse and 1st. thing as we know they will be saying I ban this and I ban that and staying away from the bldg. all the wile like the janitor.

Your pal, *Jack*.

CHI, May 6.

FRIEND AL: 4 straight now Al. How is that for a way to start out the season? It was Detroit again today and that is twice I have beat them and twice I have beat St. Louis and it don't look like I was never going to stop. They got 2 runs off of me today but it was after we had 7 and had them licked and I kind of eased up to save the old souper for the Cleveland serious. But I wished you could of heard the 1 I pulled on Cobb. You know I have always kind of had him on the run ever since I come in the league and he would as leaf have falling archs as see me walk out there to pitch.

Well the 1st. time he come up they was 2 out and no one on and I had him 2 strikes and nothing and in place of monking with him I stuck a fast one right through the groove and he took it for a third strike. Well he come up again in the 4th. inning and little Bush was on third base and 1 out and Cobb hit the 1st. ball and hit it pretty good towards left field but Weaver jumped up and stabbed it with his glove hand and then stepped on third base and the side was out. Well Cobb hollered at me and said "You didn't put that strike acrost on me." So I said "No why should I put strikes acrost on you when I can hit your bat and get 2 out at a time?" You ought to of heard the boys give him the laugh.

Well he hit one for 3 bases in the 7th. inning with Bush and Ellison both on and that's how they got their 2 runs but he wouldn't of never hit the ball only I eased up on acct. of the lead we had and besides I felt sorry for him on acct. of the way the crowd was rideing him. So wile he was standing over there on third base I said "You wouldn't of hit that one Ty only I eased up." So he said "Yes I knew you was easeing up and I wouldn't take advantage of you so that's why I bunted."

Well 1 more game with Detroit and then we go down to Cleveland and visit Mr. Speaker and the rest of the boys and Speaker hasn't been going any to good against them barbers that's supposed to pitch for Detroit and St. Louis so God help him when he runs up against Williams and Cicotte and I.

Your pal, *Jack.*

CLEVELAND, May 9.

FRIEND AL: Well Gleason told me today he wasn't going to pitch me here till the Sunday game to get the crowd. We have broke even on the 2 games so far and ought to of win them both only for bad pitching but we can't expect to win them all and you really can't blame the boys for not pitching baseball when we run into weather like we have got down here and it seems like every place we go its colder then where we just come from and I have heard about people going crazy with the heat but we will all be crazy with the cold if it keeps up like this way and Speaker was down to our hotel last night and said the Cleveland club had a couple of bushers from the Southren league that's all ready lost their mind and he told us what they pulled off wile the St. Louis club was here.

Well it seems like Cleveland was beat to death 1 day and they thought they would give some of the regulars a rest and they put in a young catcher name Drew and the 1st. time he come up to bat they was men on first and second and 1 out and Sothoron was pitching for St. Louis and 1 of the St. Louis infielders yelled at him "Don't worry about this bird as he will hit into a double play." Well Drew stood up there and took 3 strikes without never takeing the bat off his shoulder so then he come back to the bench and said "Well I crossed them on their double play."

Well in another game Bagby was pitching and he had them licked 8 to 1 in the 7th inning and he had a bad finger so they took him out and sent in a busher name Francis to finish the game. Well he got through 1 inning and when he come up to hit they was a man on 3d. base and 2 out and Davenport was pitching for St. Louis and he was kind of wild and he throwed 3 balls to Francis. So then he throwed a strike and Francis took it and then he throwed one that was over the kid's head but he took a cut at it and hit it over Tobin's head and made 3 bases on it. So when the inning was over Larry Gardner heard him calling himself names and balling himself out and Larry asked him what was the matter and he said he was just thinking that if he had of left that ball go by he would of had a base on balls.

Well I had a letter from Florrie today and she has closed up that deal and sold out her interest in the place out near home and went in pardners in that place down town and she said she thought it was a wise move and she would clean up a big bunch of jack and it won't only take her a little wile to pay for her interest in the new parlor as with what she had saved up and what she got out of the other joint she had over $2000.00 cash to start in with.

Well I don't know who her new pardners is but between you and I it looks to me like she was pulling a boner to leave a place where she knew her pardners was friends and go into pardners with a couple women that's probably old hands at the game and maybe wanted some new capital or something and are libel to get her role and then can her out of the firm but as I say they's no use me trying to tell her what to do and I might just is well tell Gleason to take Collins off of second base and send for Jakey Atz.

Well Al nothing to do till Sunday and if I beat them it will make me 5 straight and you can bet I will beat them Al as I am going like a crazy man and they can't no club stop me.

Your pal, *Jack.*

CHI, May 12.

FRIEND AL: Well old pal its kind of late to be setting up writeing a letter but I had a little run in with Florrie tonight and I don't feel like I could go to sleep and besides I don't half to work tomorrow as I win yesterday's game in Cleveland and Gleason is saveing me for the Boston serious.

Well we got in from Cleveland early this A. M. and of course I hurried right home and I was here before 8 o'clock but the Swede said Florrie had left home before 7 as she didn't want to be late on the new job and she would call me up dureing the forenoon. Well it got pretty near time to start over to the ball pk. before the phone rung and it was Florrie and I asked her if she wasn't going to congratulate me and she says what for and I said for what I done in Cleveland yesterday and she said she hadn't had time to look at the paper. So I told her I had win my 5th straight game and she acted about as interested as if I said we had a new mail man so I got kind of sore and told her I would half to hang up and go over to the ball pk. She said she would see me at supper and we hung up.

Well we had a long game this P. M. and it seemed longer on acct. of how anxious I was to get back home and when I finely got here it was half past 6 and no Florrie. Well the Swede said she had called up and said she had to stay down town and have supper with some business friends and she would try and be home early this evening.

Well the kids was put in bed and I tried to set down and eat supper alone and they didn't nothing taste right and finaly I give it up and put on my hat and went out and went in a picture show but it was as old as Pat and Mike so I blew it and went in Kramer's to get a couple drinks but I had kind of promised Gleason to lay off of the hard stuff and you take the beer you get now days and its cheaper to stay home and draw it out of the sink so I come back here and it was 8 bells and still no Florrie.

Well I set down and picked up the evening paper and all of a sudden the phone rung and it was a man's voice and he wanted to know if Mrs. Keefe had got home. So I done some quick thinking and I said "Yes she is here who wants her?" So he said "That's all right. I just wanted to know if she got home O. K." So I said who is it but he had hung up. Well I rung central right back and asked her where that party had called from and she said she didn't know and I asked her what and the he—ll she did know and she begun to play some jazz on my ear drum so I hung up.

Well in about 10 minutes more Florrie come in and come running over to give me a smack like usual when I get back off a trip. But she didn't get by with it. So she asked what was the matter. So I said "They's nothing the matter only they was a bird called up here a wile ago and wanted to know if you was home." So she says "Well what of it?" So I said "I suppose he was 1 of them business friends that you had to stay down town to supper with them." So she said "Maybe he was." So I said "Well you ought to know if he was or not." So she says "Do you think I can tell you who all the people are that calls me up when I haven't even heard their voice? I don't even know a one of the girls that keeps calling up and asking for you." So I said "They don't no gals call up here and ask for me because they have got better sence but even if they did I couldn't help it as they see me out there on the ball field and want to get aquainted."

Then she swelled up and says "It may be hard for you to believe but there is actually men that want to get aquainted with me even if they never did see me out there on the ball field." So I said "You tell me who this bird is that called up on the phone." So she said "I thought they was only the 2 babys in this apartment but it seems like there is 3." So then she went in her rm. and shut the door.

Well Al that's the way it stands and if it wasn't for the kiddies I would pack up and move somewheres else but kiddies or no kiddies she has got to explain herself tomorrow morning and meanwile Al you should ought to thank God that you married a woman that isn't flighty and what if a wife ain't the best looker in the world if she has got something under her hat besides marcel wavers?

Your pal, *Jack.*

CHI, May 14.

FRIEND AL: Well old pal it looks like your old pal was through working for nothing you might say and by tomorrow night I will be signed up to a new contract calling for a $600.00 raise or $3000.00 per annum. I guess I have all ready told you that Gleason promised to see that I got real jack provide it I showed I wasn't no flash out of the pan and this noon we come to a definite understanding.

We was to open against the Boston club and I called him to 1 side in the club house and asked him if I was to pitch the game. So he says you can suit yourself. So I asked him what he meant and he said "I am going to give you a chance to get real money. If you win your game against the Boston club I will tear up your old contract and give you a contract for $3000.00. And you can pick your own spot. You can work against them today or you can work against them tomorrow just as you feel like. They will probably pitch Mays against us today and Ruth tomorrow and you can take your choice." Well Al Mays has always been good against our club and besides my old souper is better this kind of weather the longer I give it a rest so after I though it over I said I would wait and pitch against Ruth tomorrow. So tomorrow is my big day and you know what I will do to them old pal and if the boys only gets 1 run behind me that is all as I ask.

That's all we got today Al was 1 run but Eddie Cicotte was in there with everything and the 1 run was a plenty. They was only 1 time when they had a chance and it looked that time like they couldn't hardly help from scoreing but Eddie hates to beat this Boston club on acct. they canned him once and he certainly give a exhibition in there that I would of been proud of myself. This inning I am speaking of Scott got on and Schang layed down a bunt and Eddie tried to force Scott at second base but he throwed bad and the ball went to center field and Scott got around to third and Schang to second and they wasn't nobody out. Well Mays hit a fly ball to Jackson but it was so short that Scott didn't dast go in. Then Hooper popped up to Collins and Barry hit the 1st. ball and fouled out to Schalkie. Some pitching eh Al and that is the kind I will show them tomorrow. And another thing Eddie done was make a monkey out of Ruth and struck him out twice and they claim he is a great hitter Al but all you half to do is pitch right to him and pitch the ball anywheres but where he can get a good cut at it.

Well they never had another look in against Eddie and we got a run when Barry booted one on Collins and Jackson plastered one out between Ruth and Strunk for 2 bases.

Well Al I am feeling pretty good again as I and Florrie kind of made up our quarrel last night. She come home to supper and I was still acting kind of cross and she asked me if I was still mopping over that bird that called her up and I didn't say nothing so she said "Well that was a man that was the husband of 1 of the girls I had supper with and he was there to and him and his wife wanted to bring me home but I told them I didn't want nobody to bring me home so his wife probably told him to call up and see if I got home all right as they was worried." So she asked me if I was satisfied and I said I guessed I was but why couldn't she of told me that in the 1st. place and she said because she liked to see me jealous. Well I left her think I was jealous but between you and I it was just a kind of a kid on my part as of course I knew all the wile that she was O. K. only I wanted to make her give in and I knew she would if I just held out and pretended like I was sore. Make them come to you Al is the way to get along with them.

I haven't told Florrie what this game tomorrow means to us as I want to surprise her and if I win I will take her out somewheres on a party tomorrow night. And now old pal I must get to bed as I want to get a good rest before I tackle those birds. Oh you $600.00 baseball game.

Your pal, Jack.

CHI, May 16.

FRIEND AL: Well Al I don't care if school keeps or not and all as I wish is that I could get the flu or something and make a end out of it. I have quit the ball club Al and I have quit home and if I ever go back again to baseball it depends on whether I will have my kiddies to work for or whether they will be warded to her.

It all happened yesterday Al and I better start at the start and tell you what come off. Florrie had eat her breakfast and went down town before I got up but she left word with the ski jumper that she was going to try and get out to the ball game and maybe bring the rest of her pardners with her and show me off to them.

Well to make it a short story I was out to the pk. early and Gleason asked me how I felt and I told him fine and I certainly did Al and Danforth was working against us in batting practice to get us use to a left hander and I was certainly slapping the ball on the pick and Gleason said it looked like I was figureing on winning my own game. Well we got through our batting practice and I looked up to where Florrie usualy sets right in back of our bench but she wasn't there but after a wile it come time for me to warm up and I looked over and Ruth was warming up for them so then I looked up in the stand again and there was Florrie. She was just setting down Al and she wasn't alone.

Well Al I had to look up there twice to make sure I wasn't looking cock eyed. But no I was seeing just what was there and what I seen was she and a man with her if that's what you want to call him.

Well I guess I couldn't of throwed more than 4 or 5 balls when I couldn't stand it no more so I told Lynn to wait a minute and Gleason was busy hitting to the infield so I snuck out under the bench and under the stand and I seen 1 of the ushers and sent word up to Florrie to come down a minute as I wanted to see her. Well I waited and finely she come down and we come to the pt. without waisting no time. I asked her to explain herself and do it quick. So she said "You needn't act so crazy as they's nothing to explain. I said I was going to bring my pardner out here and the gentleman with me is him." "Your pardner" I said "What does a man do in a beauty parlor?" "Well" she said "This man happens to do a whole lot.

"Besides owning two thirds of the business he is 1 of the best artists in the world on quaffs." Well I asked her what and the he—ll was quaffs and she said it meant fixing lady's hair.

Well by this time Gleason had found out I wasn't warming up and sent out to find me. So all as I had time to say was to tell her she better get that bird out of the stand before I come up there and quaffed him in the jaw. Then I had to leave her and go back on the field.

Well I throwed about a dozen more balls to Lynn and then I couldn't throw no more and Gleason come over and asked me what was the matter and I told him nothing so he said "Are you warmed up enough?" and I said "I should say I am."

Well Al to make it a short story pretty soon our names was announced to pitch and I walked out there on the field.

Well when I was throwing them practice balls to Schalk I didn't know if he was behind the plate or up in Comiskey's office and when Hooper stepped in the batters box I seen a dozen of him. Well I don't know what was signed for but I throwed something up there and Hooper hit it to right field for 2 bases. Then I throwed something else to Barry and he cracked it out to Jackson on the 1st. hop so fast that Hooper couldn't only get to third base. Well wile Strunk was up there I guess I must of looked up in the stand again and any way the ball I pitched come closer to the barber then it did to Strunk and before they got it back in the game Hooper had scored and Barry was on third base.

Then Schalkie come running out and asked me what was the matter so I said I didn't know but I thought they was getting our signs. "Well" he said "you certainly crossed them on that one as I didn't sign you for no bench ball." Then he looked over at Gleason to have me took out but Gleason hollered "Let him stay in there and see what kind of a money pitcher he is."

Well Al I didn't get one anywheres near close for Strunk and walked him and it was Ruth's turn. The next thing I seen of the ball it was sailing into the right field bleachers where the black birds sets. And that's all I seen of the ball game.

Well old pal I didn't stop to look up in the stand on the way out and I don't remember changing clothes or nothing but I know I must of rode straight down town and when I woke up this A. M. I was still down town and I haven't called up home or the ball pk. or nowheres else and as far is I am concerned I am through with the both of them as a man can't pitch baseball and have any home life and a man can't have the kind of home life I have got and pitch baseball.

All that worrys me is the kiddies and what will become of them if they don't ward them to me. And another thing I would like to know is who put me to bed in this hotel last night as who ever undressed me forgot to take off my clothes.

Your pal, *Jack.*

CHI, May 20.

FRIEND AL: Well Al I am writeing this from home and that means that everything is O. K. again as I decided to give in and let bygones be bygones for the kiddies sake and besides I found out that this bird that Florrie is pardners with him is O. K. and got a Mrs. of his own and she works down there with him and Florrie is cleaning up more jack then she could of ever made in the old parlor out south so as long as she is makeing good and everything is O. K. why they would be no sence in me makeing things unpleasant.

Well I told you about me staying down town 1 night and I stayed down till late the next P. M and finely I called up the Swede and told her to pack up my things as I was comeing out there the next day and get them. Well the Swede said that Gleason had been there the night before looking for me and he left word that I was to call him up at the ball pk. So I thought maybe he might have a letter out there for me or something or maybe I could persuade him to trade me to some other club so I called him up and just got him before he left the pk. and he asked me where I was at and said he wanted to see me so I give him the name of the hotel where I was stopping and he come down and met me there at 6 o'clock that night.

"Well" he says "I was over to see your little wife last night and I have got a notion to bust you in the jaw." So I asked him what he meant and he said "She sported your kids wile you was in the war and she is doing more than you to sport them now and she goes in pardners with a man that's O. K. and has got a wife of his own that works with him and you act like a big sap and make her cry and pretty near force her out of a good business and all for nothing except that you was born a busher and can't get over it."

So I said to him "You mind your own business and keep out of my business and trade me to some ball club where I can get a square deal and we will all get along a hole lot better." So he said where did I want to be traded and I said Boston. "Oh no" he said. "I would trade you to Boston in a minute only Babe Ruth wouldn't stand for it as he likes to have you on our club." But he said "The 1st. thing

is what are you going to do about your family?" So I said I would
go back to my family if Florrie would get out of that down town
barber shop. So Gleason said "Now listen you are going back home
right now tonight and your Mrs. isn't going to sacrifice her business
neither." So I said "You can't make me do nothing I don't want to
do." So he says "No I can't make you but I can tell your Mrs. about
that St. Louis janitor's daughter that was down in Texas and then
if she wants to get rid of you she can do it and be better off."

Well Al I thought as long as Florrie was all rapped up in this new
business it wasn't right to make her drop it and pull out and besides
there was the kiddies to be considered so I decided to not make no
trouble. So I promised Gleason to go home that night.

So then I asked him about the ball club. "Well," he said "you still
belong to us." "Yes" I said "but I can't work for no $2400.00"

"Well" he said "we are scheduled against a club now that hasn't
no Ruths on it and its a club that even you should ought to beat and
if you want to try it again why I will leave you pick your day to work
against the Philadelphia club and the same bet goes."

So yesterday was the day I picked Al and Roth got a base hit and
Burns got a base hit and that's all the base hits they got and the only
2 runs we got I drove in myself. But they was worth $600.00 to me
Al and I guess Gleason knows now what kind of a money pitcher
I am.

Your pal, *Jack*.

The Battle of the Century

(*The Saturday Evening Post,* 29 October 1921)

I don't know nothing that you don't know, but if you want to hear it again, all right. I'll have to start back pretty near two years ago, the first time I seen Jim after he stopped Big Wheeler and win the title. He'd signed up with a circus and I happened to be in Omaha when it hit there. I run into them on the street, Jim and his manager, Larry Moon. I had them come to my hotel where we could talk things over.

"Well, Jim," I said, "how does it feel to be champ?"

"Not so good," he says.

"Well," I said, "you never did care much for the glory. But still and all it's pretty sweet to have all that dough."

"All what dough?" says Jim.

"Why," I said, "what you got out of the Wheeler fight, and what you're getting with this troupe, and what you've got a chance to get."

Jim laughed and so did Moon.

"Listen, Pinkie," says Moon. "You're an old pal, so I don't mind telling you a couple of facts. Our net profits out of the Wheeler fight wouldn't pay for a Chinaman's personal laundry. We're making a little money with this show, but we've got to spend it because we're champion. We've got an offer to make a picture, but it ain't so much and we'll have to blow the most of it to show we're a good fella. Further and more, Jim hates that kind of work. They's one thing he can do better than anybody else, and that's fight. And that's all he wants to do, just fight."

"Well," I said, "let him fight! He don't have to fight for nothing."

"Let him fight who?" says Larry.

"Why, anybody that'll take him on," I said. "Let him be a champ like some of the old boys and battle everybody that wants his game."

"That's a grand idear!" said Larry. "Now maybe you'll go ahead and name four or five guys that wants his game; that is, guys that's got enough chance with him so as they'd draw two hundred people at the gate."

134

"Well," I said, "how about——" I had to stop and think.

"Sure!" said Larry. "There you are! Now you'll get some idear of what we're up against. You say, 'Let him be a champ like some of the old boys and fight everybody.' That'd be O.K. if we was living twenty or thirty years ago when they was a bunch round like Fitz, Corbett and McCoy, and Choynski, Sharkey, Ruhlin, big Jeff, and all that gang; any one of them liable to knock each other's block off. But who have we got to pick from? They ain't a man living or dead that's got a chance in God's world to even make this baby prespire, and the worst of it is that everybody knows it. Here I got a champion at a time when everything's big money and he should ought to be worth a million fish to me and himself, and he ain't worth a dime. And he won't be worth a dime, neither, unless I can build something up.

"They's just one chance for us," says Larry, "and that's to have some young fella spring up from nowheres and knock five or six of these 'contenders' for a gool; then we'll have to stall a w'ile and pretend like we're scared of him till we've got the bugs thinking that maybe he has a look-in. The one thing in our favor is that people loves to see a champion get socked, especially my champion, who ain't no matinée idol. So if they think they's a man capable of socking him, they'll pay to see it come off. Believe me, if we do get a break like that, I'll demand a purse that'll knock their eye out. Because fights is going to be few and far between for my little ward. His trouble is that he's too good. He'd be better if he was worse. Right now they's no man in sight that it wouldn't be a joke to match him with. So, as I say, all we can do is watch and pray and hope that some hero pops up before the heavyweight champion of the world dies of starvation. Him and his manager both."

II

It was quite a w'ile after this when I was in New York and dropped in at the apartment where Jim and Larry was living.

"Set down," said Moon. "Jim's out buying new records, but I expect him right back."

So we sat and chinned till the champ showed up. He'd boughten the afternoon papers and he showed us the big headlines about the scrap in London—"Goulet Stops Bradford in First Round."

"That Englishman must be a fine heel!" said Jim. "This little

French boy popped him on the chin and he laid down and rolled over like a circus dog."

Larry grabbed the papers and read the story. "Boys," he says, "this may be it!"

"May be what?" says Jim.

"Our chance!" said Moon. "This thing might be built up till it meant something!"

"Say, listen," says the champ; "I and you have been together long enough so as we ought to be able to speak the same language. But when you say 'This thing might be built up,' I swear I don't know what you're talking about."

"I'm talking about this thing that came off in London," said Larry. "Here's the champion of England and the champion of France, the only two countries over there that has boxing. Well, the champion of France stops this Englishman with a punch and that makes him the champion of Europe. And it makes him look pretty good to the English because they was all stuck on this Bradford. And what looks good to the English looks good to a lot of people here. The way the papers plays it up, you can see they figure they's a good deal of interest in it. Further and more, this guy Goulet is a war hero. He's the idol of Europe and the champion of Europe, and if he was built up right he'd be a great card over here. That's what I'm talking about, a match between their champ and our champ for the championship of the world."

"You don't mean match me with this Goulet?" said Jim.

"That's exactly what I mean," says Moon.

"All right," says Jim. "You're my matchmaker and I fight who you pick out. But I don't see how you come to overlook Benny Leonard."

III

I staid round town and seen Larry two or three times.

"It's going to be softer than I figured," he told me. "Those writers over in England has went cuckoo over the Frenchman. They was so nuts about Bradford that they think the guy that stopped him must be a cave man. And our papers is printing all the junk and their readers falls for it. As a matter of fact, I suppose Johnny Coulon could knock Bradford acrost the channel, but don't tell nobody I said that. Though I guess they wouldn't believe it anyway. The combination of what them big English reporters say, along with Goulet being a war hero and handsome—well, it's making him a popular idol in America.

"But the thing's got to be nursed along and worked up, and that's my job. It'll take time, but it'll be worth it. The tough problem ain't getting the fans steamed up. They'll take care of themselves. What I've to do is convince some guy with money and a lot of nerve that it would be a fight, not a murder. I've already stuck one line in the papers that I'm proud of. Maybe you seen it. I said that while Jim Dugan wasn't scared of nobody in the world, still he felt like he ought to give the American contenders first shot. Because this Goulet has showed that he's got a wallop and he might land a lucky one on Jim. And we'd hate to see the title leave the old U.S.A. Not so bad, was it?"

A few weeks later it was in the papers that Goulet and his manager, La Chance, was coming over. The picture people had made the Frenchman a sweet offer and they was no money to be picked up in France even for a champion.

"All I hope," said Moon, "is that he won't get seasick. Judging from his pictures, he ain't no side-show fat man at best and we don't want him to look no skinnier than usual or our match will be all wet."

Well, I don't know if he'd been seasick or not, but he certainly was a brittle-looking bird. The first time I seen him, up to one of the roof shows, I thought the guy that pointed him out must be mistaken. But it really was him—a pale, frail boy that if he'd went to college, the football coaches would of rushed him for cheer leader. As for him standing up in a box fight with the man that had sprinkled Big Wheeler all over Ohio, well, it was just a laugh.

"You may as well forget it," I said when I seen Moon. "Your show's a flop and you won't get no backer."

"Watch me," he says. "Give me time and a fair break in the luck!"

So one day he calls up the hotel where the Frenchman was staying and made a date with his manager, La Chance.

"Listen, Mr. La Chance," he said. "If you'll let me have a free hand, and you do what I say, I can make some real money for you and me both. Suppose I could get your man matched with

Dugan. How much would you want for your share?"

"I can't speak no English," said La Chance.

"How about two hundred thousand dollars?" said Moon.

This time he really couldn't speak no English. He'd swooned.

They called the house physician and brought him to and laid him on the bed.

"A heart attack!" says the Doc. "Don't let him get excited."

"All right," said Larry. "I guess I better go."

He started to follow the doctor out.

"Wait a minute!" says the sick man of Europe.

So Moon turned round and come back.

"My heart's all right now," said La Chance. "It was just the first shock.

"You made mention of a sum of money—two hundred thousand —was it francs?"

"I don't know nothing about francs," said Larry. "I asked you a plain question: Will your man fight my man for two hundred thousand dollars?"

"How much would our share be?" said La Chance.

"I'm talking about your share," says Larry. "Two hundred thousand for you, draw, lose, or get killed."

La Chance sprung at him with a kiss for both cheeks, but Larry ducked away.

"You've got to let me run this," he said. "You've got to put yourself in my hands and do everything I say."

"Absolutely!" says the Frenchman.

"All right," says Larry. "Now, in the first place, don't get the idear in your head that this is going to be a quick clean-up. It'll take time —maybe a year. What are you fellas going to do when you've finished your picture?"

"Well," said La Chance, "we thought maybe we'd stay over here and have a few fights."

"No!" says Larry. "You go right back home and don't fight nobody! You stay there till you hear from me. I think it'd be a good idear for you to have one bout in this country, to show that your man can knock somebody besides that English tumbler. But I'll pick out the man for you to fight and I'll let you know when I've got him. He'll be somebody that you can't help licking, not by no possible chance. You won't get much money for it, but it'll be advertising. Is that all right with you?"

"Oui, oui," says La Chance. "What else?"

"Nothing else," said Moon.

IV

Several months is supposed to elapse between these two acts. During this time Dugan has to eat, so he takes on a set-up out in Michigan and knocks him in three rounds, or two rounds longer than necessary. Also, they pick out a guy for Goulet to trim—old Tommy Fogel. This "fight" takes place over in Jersey and Tommy surprises them. He manages to stand up three rounds without his crutches. The Frenchman looks fast as a streak and everybody gets excited. People is saying to each other, "Even if he is a little light he may be just the kind of fighter that would give Dugan trouble. He's in there and out again like a flash and he's hard to hit. Jim ain't never faced a man like him. He's liable to run the big boy ragged."

A little w'ile after this great battle Jim and Larry get hungry again and they accept an offer of a hundred thousand to meet a big horse named Joe Barnes. Dugan has knocked him before and can do it again and they ain't much danger in taking him on, though some of the wise birds thinks different. They think Larry is risking the title because Barnes is a guy that fights five nights a week and he's always in shape and he's so tough that nobody ever did stop him except Jim himself. As a matter of fact, Larry ain't running no more risk than getting in a bath tub. Because w'ile all the wise guys know that Jim can punch, what they don't seem to realize is that he can take it.

Anyway, this bout with Barnes was in the Big Town and Jim trained for it on a ship and when he clumb in the ring he was still at sea. In the second round Barnes clipped him on the chin with all he had. And all he had wasn't half what he needed. After a w'ile Dugan got his land legs and begin to improve and he stopped Barnes in the twelfth with a funny-looking punch to the waistline. But they wasn't no time during the scrap when he looked like himself and I wouldn't be surprised if he was under wraps as well as in bad shape. However it happened, it made people think Jim wasn't the fighter his friends claimed; it made him look like he could be licked, and that was a boost for the Goulet match.

V

They's a big steamship man, Robert Crawley, that had a kind of a contract with La Chance and Goulet. The agreement was that if Goulet seen a chance for a big match Crawley was to be the backer. If he wanted to. If he didn't, he was to step out.

Well, Crawley's got a partner, Bill Guthrie, who Moon had met. So Moon phones them that he has been in communication with La Chance and La Chance says his man is ready to fight Dugan if a suitable purse is guaranteed.

"I thought maybe you'd like to talk it over," says Larry.

So Crawley and Guthrie said they would and Moon asks them to come up and see him in a couple of days.

"Now," said Larry to me, "I'm going way down town for lunch and you can come along if you want to. But if you don't like Spanish cooking you better stay home."

So I went with him to a joint off lower Broadway. They was a flock of Spanish dishes on the bill of fare, but what Moon ordered for him and I was plain ham and eggs.

W'ile the one waiter was out getting it, Moon left me and went over to the guy that had showed us to our table. They talked together for pretty near a half hour and I was through eating when Larry come back. He took a look at his food and passed it up.

"I've made a date with the head waiter for half past two," he says. "That's the soonest he can get off. If you haven't nothing to do you can go along with us."

"Where to?" I asked him.

"Shopping," he said.

"Well," I says, "I guess I better stick with you. When a man goes nuts he ought to have a friend along."

So the two of us walked down to the Battery and fooled round till it was time to keep the date. We dropped in at the restaurant again and come out with the head waiter and the greasy bird that had waited on us. We went over to Broadway and got a taxi. Moon give the driver his orders and we started uptown. We stopped at Livington's.

"Men's clothing," said Moon, and the man showed us where to go.

Well, to cut it short, we was in there an hour and when we come away our two waiter friends had bundles containing a complete new make-up—two silk hats, Prince Albert coats, gray pants, fancy shirts, ties that would knock you dead, and collars like Senator Smoot's.

"That's all to-day, boys," said Larry. "Here's twenty-five bucks apiece and you'll each get seventy-five more tomorrow. Don't forget nothing," he says to the head waiter, "and especially that envelope I give you."

So we left them with their packages.

I was amongst those present the next afternoon when Crawley and Guthrie showed up. Moon had sent Dugan away.

"Now," says Larry to our visitors, "we may as well get down to business. As I told you over the phone, I been corresponding with La Chance and he's willing to fight us if he can get his price. But he said I would have to let Mr. Crawley handle the promotion. So I said that suited me."

"It don't look like a match," said Crawley. "Goulet's a great boy, but look at the difference in size!"

Moon laughed.

"They's noweheres near as much difference as they was between Jim and Big Wheeler," he says. "And you know what Jim done to him!"

"That's all right," said Guthrie, "but your man weighs pretty near two hundred and when a man's that big he's big enough for anybody. But take a man that weighs two hundred and put him against a man that weighs round 165, and the difference counts. Look at Johnson and Ketchell!"

"Now listen," says Larry. "In the first place my man won't weigh 190 stripped; he may tip the beam at ten or twelve pounds more than that, but only in secret. In the second place, if the public demands the match, what do we care if the two men stacks up together like a pimple and a goiter?"

"That's true enough," says Crawley. "If the public does want the match."

"You know they want the match!" said Moon. "Or if you don't I do." And promoters wants it, too, from the number of offers I've had."

"Offers from who?" says Guthrie.

"I ain't at liberty to tell," says Larry. "But it don't make no difference anyway. You've got first crack at it on account of your contract. The question is, do you want it?"

"Yes, we want it," said Crawley. "That is, if we can get it at a reasonable figure."

"I'm listening," says Larry.

"Well, said Crawley," your man is champion and entitled to the biggest share. We'd guarantee you a hundred thousand and Goulet fifty."

"I see what you mean," says Larry. "You mean you don't want to handle it and you'll release Goulet."

"Where do you get that?" says Guthrie. "We don't mean no such a thing! We're making a legitimate offer and a good big one."

"You're kidding," says Larry. "I got a hundred thousand for the match with Barnes and that was just a workout. But forgetting me entirely what about Goulet? The least he'll take is two hundred thousand; and if you don't believe it, cable his manager."

Just then in come Larry's butler, or whatever he is.

"Two gentlemen to see you," he says.

"Who is it?" says Larry.

"Them two foreigners again," says the man.

"Oh, the two Cubans," said Larry. "Take them in the side room and tell them to wait. Now," he says, "where was we? Oh, yes, I was telling you what La Chance wants. If you don't care to take the trouble to cable, here's a letter from him."

And he give them a letter to read. When they'd read it he said: "You see what he says in there about you. He says Mr. Crawley has treated him O.K. and he wants him to have first refusal of this match. That's the only reason I've bothered you gentlemen. Confidentially, I didn't think you'd want to handle a thing as big as this. So just give us our release and they's nobody hurt."

"Who would you give it to?" says Guthrie.

"Well," says Moon, "I'm going to tell you men something, but I don't want it to go no further. They's two men in the next room that's been pestering me to death. I promised they'd have their final answer to-day, but I didn't expect them to get here till you fellas had left. When I got a release from you, I was going to phone Charley Riggs and tell him he could have the match at our figure, which is $500,000. That's the $200,000 Goulet demands, and $300,000 for me. I know he'll take it at that, but the only reason I'm going to offer it to him is to keep the match in this country. Because I've got a better offer from outside."

"Where at?" says Guthrie.

"Havana, Cuba," says Larry. "It's two bankers from there that's in the next room."

"I'd like to meet them," says Guthrie.

"I guess it'd be all right," says Larry, and he touched the button. "One of them can talk pretty fair English. He's the one I been dealing with. But the other one, I think, is the real money guy, though as far as understanding him is concerned, he might as well be a deaf mute. Show them two gentlemen in here," he says to the butler.

Well, they come in, dressed for a wedding.

"Hello there, gentlemen," says Larry, shaking hands with them. "I must apologize for keeping you waiting. I was busy with these two gentlemen here. Mr. Crawley and Mr. Guthrie, meet Senior Lopez and Senior Pancho, from Havana."

Senior Lopez pulled an envelope out of his pocket and waved it.

"I've had this tended to," he says, "and I guess you'll find it all right."

He handed the envelope to Moon and Moon opened it up. For all as I could see, it was a regular certified check.

"It looks all right," said Larry, and waved it towards Guthrie and Crawley. "Six hundred thousand fish," he says, "and I wished it was all mine. But I don't even know yet whether I'm going to let these gentlemen put it up or not. If the seniors will pardon me, I've got a little telephoning to do, and then you can have my answer, just as I promised. If I decide on Havana we'll take the check down town and leave it with one of the newspapers over night, and deposit it tomorrow."

"That satisfies us," says Senior Lopez, and Senior Pancho mumbled something that was probably Spanish for Swiss on rye.

"Now," says Larry to Crawley, "I know you and Mr. Guthrie will excuse me for hurrying you off. I wished we could of done business, but as long as we can't I've got to close with somebody else."

"Would you mind waiting a minute?" says Crawley. "Before you do anything, I'd like to have a word or two with Mr. Guthrie and talk to you a moment in private."

"Well," says Moon, "I've already kept the seniors waiting quite a w'ile."

"That's all right," says Lopez. "We don't mind a little wait as long as you ain't going to disappoint us."

"Then I'll take you in the other room," says Larry, and we left Crawley and Guthrie alone. In a few minutes they called Larry back.

"Now listen," said Guthrie: "You said something about cutting your price from $600,000 to $500,000 to keep the fight in America. You ain't doing that out of patriotism!"

"You bet I ain't!" says Moon. "If I do it, it'll be for two good reasons. One is that all I'll get anyway is my $300,000; the Cubans is so fair-minded that they want to see Goulet get just as much as me. The other reason is that Dugan's scared to death of fever and he thinks Cuba's full of it. He won't go there unless he has to."

"Listen," says Guthrie; "Mr. Crawley and I have decided to make you a flat offer of $500,000 for this match. If you and La Chance are satisfied with this we'll put up a forfeit of $100,000 to-morrow."

Moon waited a w'ile before he spoke.

"Would you guarantee to hold the match in America?" he says.

"Either here or in London," says Crawley.

"They's no fever in London?" says Moon.

"I should say not!" says Crawley.

"Well," says Moon, "if I can hold the Cubans off one more day I'll consider it. I could meet you to-morrow and you could deposit your check."

"That suits us," says Crawley, and they shook hands and left.

Larry joined us in the other room and ordered drinks all round.

"You boys done fine!" he says to the two seniors. "Here's the rest of your hundred apiece and I'm much obliged."

"Will we send you these clothes?" says Senior Lopez.

"No," says Larry. "You keep them for the next big fight."

"And how about your check?" says Lopez.

"Try and cash it!" says Larry.

"That's over," he says, when they'd went. "The next thing is to land Charley Riggs."

"What for?" says I.

"Why, to promote this match," said Larry. "He's the guy I've been after all the time, the only guy that's big enough to put it over. But I didn't dast go after him without something to show. When he sees that these birds is willing to put up half a million fish he'll know it's big enough for him."

"But how are you going to shake them out?" I asked.

"I don't care if they're shook out or not, as long as he's in," says Moon. "But you can bet they'll be glad enough to take him in as partner, and that's all I want. When I get him we're set!"

Well, as you know, he got him, and it wasn't no job to shake the other two out. When they talked five hundred thousand, they was over their heads. And when they begin thinking about expenses, and the conversation got up round a million, they was sunk.

VI

It was early spring when I run acrost Larry again.

"I been wanting to see you," he says. "What are you going to be doing in June?"

"I don't know," I said. "Just loafing, I guess."

"Well," he said, "would you mind doing your loafing at our camp?"

"What camp?" I asked him.

"Wherever we train," he says. "Somewheres near New York, I suppose."

"Where are you going to fight?" I asked.

"In Jersey," he says. "They's nowheres else we can. We got to be near the Big Town to get the money."

"How about all them offers?" I says.

"Oh, you mean the ones that's been in the papers?" said Moon. "Wasn't those a hit? A million dollars from Nugget, Nevada! Why, if a guy showed a nickel in that town, the whole twelve that lives there would blackjack him at once!"

"What do you want of me?" I said.

"Jim needs sparring partners," says Larry.

"I may look goofy to you," I said, "but I pass for all right round home."

"I was kidding," said Larry. "What Jim wants is somebody he can talk to and play rummy with. It's going to be a lonesome time for him and I don't know if he can stand it or not. But he likes you and having you there once in a w'ile would be a help."

"All right," I said. "I'll keep him company part of the time."

"You know," says Larry, "even the wise birds thinks this is easy money for Jim. But it's going to be about the toughest money anybody ever earned."

"What do you mean?" I says. "You don't think the Frenchman has a chance!"

"Don't be silly!" says Larry. "That's just the point. If it was like the Wheeler thing, where the guy was a big hulk that it might take some trouble to topple him over, why training for it wouldn't be such a grind. Jim would say to himself, 'Well, I guess I can lick him all right, but he's big and I better be in good shape. Because he might ————' You know how it was that time. But this is different. Here's a guy that may be the greatest man in the world for his size. But look at his size! And yet Jim's got to go ahead and work like he done for Wheeler. Even harder, because they's a lot more interest in this and people'll be watching us close. Jim could get ready in a week to knock this bird cold. But he's got to go through with five or six weeks of the toughest kind of work, which he knows ain't necessary. I've tried to convince him that they might be an upset. But he knows it's the bunk."

"Well," I said, "if I haven't nothing better to do I'll come round and try and keep him entertained. But personally, I don't know no work I wouldn't be glad to stick at for five weeks, not at them kind of wages."

VII

I landed in Jim's camp the second week in June. The day I got there he boxed with three of his partners. Two of them was big boys and he flattened them both.

We was all alone that evening and he opened up his heart.

"Goulet's got the right idear," he says: "Secret training. I wished we could pull that. My training would be such a secret that I wouldn't even find out about it myself. But Larry says no. I've got to show the boys I'm working so they won't think it's a farce. Like it wasn't a farce already! Anyway it is for me—punching the bag and shadow boxing and skipping the rope. You ain't got no idear how cute I feel skipping a rope! I suppose I ought to thank God they don't make me roll a hoop or dress dolls. But even skipping a rope ain't as bad as boxing with those heels! If I try not to hit them, the crowd thinks I ain't giving them a run for their money. And if I get my glove close enough to their beezer so they can smell it, over they go! Then the crowd thinks I'm too rough!"

"Well," I said, "they's only three more weeks of it. And think of the dough and the glory!"

"The dough part's all right," he says. "Whatever's left of it I can use. But glory! That's a laugh. You don't kid me with that line of talk. I've got the low-down on the whole works. Here I am, an American that's supposed to be fighting to keep the title in this country, and I doubt if they's a dozen Americans that ain't pulling for me to get knocked for a corpse. Sometimes I almost feel like I ought to let myself get licked. It would be doing everybody such a big favor and make them all happy. But how could I go about it? If the guy was big and had a real haymaker I could take one and flop. But I can't play dead from a kiss."

"You'll be surprised," I said, "if he nails you in the chin and drops you."

"Surprised ain't the word!" said Dugan. "I mean, if he drops me. I expect to get hit; on the chin too. Because I ain't no defensive fighter. I go in there to get my man and in order to get him I'm willing to take what he's got. And listen: I've been hit on the chin before, and not by children, neither. But I hardly ever lay down unless it's bedtime."

I asked him how long he expected the fight to go.

"Don't call it a fight," he says, "not when you and I are alone. Whatever it is will go a round or two rounds or three rounds, depending on how he behaves himself. If he wants to tear in and get it over quick, I'm willing. But no matter how long it goes—whether he lays himself wide open so as I can knock him in a round, or whether he keeps away for four or five—you can mark my words that they won't be no glory for me in winning. He's a great fighter now! A cave man! But after I've knocked him he'll be a bum. Because anybody I can lick can't be no good."

"You're brooding too much," I said.

"Let's play cards and forget it," he says. "Though it does me good to talk once in a w'ile. When I don't talk I worry."

"What about?" I asked him.

"Oh, the 'big fight,' " he says.

"But what's they about that to worry you?" I asked.

"Well, for one thing," he said, "I'm scared they won't put enough padding in the floor. I've read of cases where a guy got knocked and hit his bean on the floor and passed out entirely. And the guy that knocked him was held for murder. And another thing: I'm scared it may not come off after all. He may get sick."

"What would make him sick?" I says.

"Well," said Dugan, "he may read what the girl reporters has been writing about him."

VIII

You know what Barnum said. Well, he didn't go far enough. They like to be bunked, but what they like most of all is to bunk themselves.

Set round some night amongst the boys when they're easing their way through a bottle of near Johnny Walker at eighteen fish the copy. Pretty soon you'll hear this:

"Well, fellas, in another year we'll be leaning up against the old mahogany again, tipping over regular highballs or real beer."

And this:

"If they'd ever leave prohibition to a vote of the people! But they don't dast!"

Well, I was in New York for three days prior to the "big fight," and four or five days afterwards, and anybody that was there had to take a course in human nature. I didn't learn much that I hadn't suspected before, but whatever doubts I may of had was removed once and for all.

The plain facts was this: A good big man was going to fight a little man that nobody knew if he was good or not, and the good big man was bound to win and win easy unless he had a sunstroke.

But the little man was a war hero, which the big man certainly wasn't. And the little man was romantic, besides being one of the most likable guys you'd want to meet—even if he did have a Greek profile and long eyelashes.

So they was only one logical answer, namely that Goulet, the little man, would just about kill Dugan, the big man, maybe by a sudden display of superhuman stren'th which he had been holding back all his life for this one fight, but more likely by some mysterious trick which no other fighter had ever thought of before, because in order to think of it you had to have a French brain and long eyelashes. If Goulet wasn't going to win, what did him and his manager mean by smiling so much and looking so happy? Of course the two hundred thousand fish had nothing to do with it.

They's two reasons why I didn't talk back to them. One was that I haven't no breath to waste, and the other was that I don't like to make enemies, which you're bound to do that when you tell somebody something they don't want to believe. A lot of the fight reporters found this out. Contrary to the general belief, they's a good many American fight writers that knows more about fights and fighters than even Bernard Shaw. Pretty near all of them come right out in print and said Goulet didn't have a chance. In return for which they got a hat full of letters calling them every name that could get through the mails.

You seen the fight yourself. Personally, I haven't made up my mind whether Dugan done it as quick as he could, or whether he held back a w'ile to make it look like the guy was something more than a push-over. I ain't seen Jim to ask him. And I only seen Moon once, and then all he said was "Didn't I tell you!"

"Tell me what?" I said.

"That I was doing Charley Riggs a favor, coaxing him into this," says Larry.

Well, I guess he was. With all the trimming Charley took from one guy and another, he must of came out with a profit for himself and his backer of something like half a million. And not only that, but the way he handled it put him in a class by himself as a promoter. The big fights to come will be staged by Charley or they won't be big fights.

That's all, except a little incidence of a man that set beside me coming back in the tube.

"A great fight!" he says.

"Yes, it was," said I.

"The Frenchman showed up pretty good," he says, "though I had a kind of an idear that he'd win. I see now where I was foolish."

"How's that?" I asked him.

"Well," he said, "the way I've got it figured out, he wasn't big enough."

"By gosh!" I said. "I believe you've hit the nail right on the head!"

Mamma

(*Good Housekeeping*, June 1930)

The cross-town car came to a stop at the east end of Forty-second Street. One passenger stayed on, a woman of about thirty who had been riding, the conductor thought, from as far west as Broadway.

"We go back now, lady," he said.

She smiled at him, but made no reply.

"This is the end of the line," he said.

"Yes, I think so."

"Well, you must get off."

She smiled again, but was silent. The conductor went to the motorman.

"Should I put her off?"

"What is she, pickled?"

"I didn't smell no liquor."

"She must be crazy or a hophead. Or maybe she just enjoys the ride. You might ask her where she wants to go."

The conductor returned to the woman.

"Where do you want to go, lady?"

"Home," said the woman. "I must get home and bake a cake."

"Where is your home?" asked the conductor.

The woman just smiled vaguely.

"Do you live in New York?"

"I think so."

"Whereabouts in New York?"

She shook her head.

"In the city or in one of the suburbs?"

"I think so."

"Do you live over in Jersey?"

No answer.

"Out on Long Island?"

No answer.

"Up in Westchester somewheres?"

"Yes, I think so."

"Do you want to get off at Grand Central Station?" asked the conductor.

"Oh, yes!" She said it almost eagerly.

"Where is your purse?" asked the conductor.

"The woman took it, the woman that was standing next to me."

"Whereabouts?"

"In the store. She stood next to me in the store and took my purse."

"Haven't you any money or any ticket?"

"My husband will take care of me."

When the car, now well filled, stopped in front of the Grand Central Station, the conductor came to the woman and touched her on the arm.

"Here's where you get off," he said.

He escorted her to the platform and watched her alight and enter the station. He thought perhaps he ought to have put her in the care of a policeman. Still, if she did not "come out of it," some one in the station would notice her and take her in charge. There was no danger of her being robbed if she had nothing.

The woman, who would have been rather pretty if she had had more color and had not looked so tired, wandered uncertainly along the lane into the upper-level concourse. She acted like a sight-seer, walking around the concourse several times and stopping every little while to regard attentively some prosaic object such as a ticket window, a closed gate, the information booth. At length she went up the slope that led to the waiting room. She sat on a bench, sometimes observing the people near her, sometimes dozing, sometimes smiling to herself as if her thoughts were pleasant.

Late at night, when the waiting room was nearly empty, a policeman found her asleep and awakened her.

"It's time to go home," he said.

"I'm waiting for my husband," said the woman.

"Where is he?"

"At the office. He's going to stop for me and take me home."

"Where do you live?"

"My husband knows."

"Don't you know, yourself?"

"He'll take care of me."

"Do you live in the city?"

"I think so."

"What's your name?"

"My name? My name's Mamma."

"What's your last name?" asked the policeman.

"That's all—just Mamma."

"What's your husband's name?"

"Dad. He's at the office, but he'll stop for me; pretty soon, I hope. I must get home and bake a cake."

"I think you'd better come with me," said the policeman. "We'll try and find your husband."

The woman got up willingly enough, and the policeman took her outside and turned her over to a colleague.

"Steve, here's a lady named Mamma, and she's waiting for her husband, a fella named Dad. He was supposed to come for her when he got out of the office, but I figure he's been detained. You take her over to the Guest House, and if he comes here, I'll tell him where she is."

In the Travelers' Aid Guest House, the woman was given a bath, a nightgown, and a bed. But these comforts and a good breakfast failed to refresh her memory. At eleven o'clock next day she was still Mamma, waiting for Dad and eager to get home and bake a cake. And they took her to the city hospital's psychopathic ward.

"You must know where you live," said Miss Fraser.

"Yes," replied the woman.

"Well, tell me. We can't send you home till we know where it is."

"My husband knows where it is."

"Yes, but he isn't here."

"He'll be here this afternoon. He's coming for me, and he's coming early because it's my birthday. They're going to give me a surprise."

"Who are?"

"My husband and Brother and Betty."

"Who are Brother and Betty?"

"Why do you ask so many questions?"

"I'm interested in you," said Miss Fraser.

"Well, Brother is my little boy, and Betty is my little girl. They both had the flu. And Dad had it. And Doctor was frightened. He thought they were all going to die. But we fooled him. They all got well."

"What's the doctor's name?"

"My husband knows his name. My husband remembers everything."

"But we can't learn anything from him if you don't tell us where he lives."

"He lives at home, with me and Brother and Betty—at night, that is. In the daytime he's at his office."

"Where is his office?"

"He'll tell you that when he comes."

"But you see," explained Miss Fraser, "he isn't very likely to come because he doesn't know you're here. If you'll just tell me his name and how to reach him——"

"His name is Dad, and he's in his office because this is daytime."

"What does he do?"

"He'll tell you that, too. He remembers everything."

Miss Fraser gave way to Miss Parnell.

"I understand this is your birthday."

"Yes, and Brother said that he and Betty and Dad would surprise me with something if I would bake them a cake. I told them the surprise mustn't be very expensive, because we must save up to pay Doctor. Doctor will have a big bill, because he was there three and four times a day for nearly two weeks. But as long as everybody got well, what do we care how big his bill is? Are you a nurse?"

"Yes, I am."

"Well, I'm not a nurse. I mean I'm not a trained nurse, but Doctor said I should have been a trained nurse. He said I seemed to do the right thing by instinct. He said if it hadn't been for me, all three of them would have died—Brother and Dad and Betty. I didn't go to bed for a whole week. Sometimes I went to sleep standing up. Did you ever do that? It's a funny experience. But when it's all over, you don't mind what you went through, as long as everybody got well."

"Have you got any money? I mean, has your husband got any?"

"He makes a good salary, but we haven't saved. We have too much fun, I guess. The amount we spend for food, it's a disgrace for a family the size of ours. And Dad always wants me to look nice."

"Well, you need some new clothes and some new shoes and stockings."

"I guess you're right, but it's a queer thing, because I just bought what I'm wearing."

"How long ago?"

"Day before yesterday. And yesterday I was looking for some things for Betty when my purse was stolen."

"What store were you in?"

"I can't remember the name of the store—it's the same place I usually go. If I had my purse, I could tell you. But never mind; my husband will know. He keeps track."

The woman took a nap, and after it Miss Fraser renewed the siege.

"Can't you tell me now what your name is?"

"It's funny; everybody asks me that."

"But you don't tell anybody."

"Yes, I do. My name is Mamma. I told your sister."

"I have no sister," said Miss Fraser.

"She looked enough like you to be your sister, and she kept nagging the same as you do."

"Honestly I'm not nagging, but I do want to know your name and address so I can send you home. Brother and Betty are probably wondering what has become of you."

"No, they're not. They're at school."

"What school?"

"It's two blocks from where we live."

"What's the name of it?"

"Do you want to send your children there?"

"I have no children."

"Then why do you want to know the name of a school? You ask too many questions. When my husband comes, you can ask him anything you want to, but I'm tired of being nagged."

Dr. Phillips took a turn at "nagging." "Aren't you anxious to get home?"

"Yes, I am. I've got to bake a cake."

"Then why don't you try to remember your name and where you live?"

"Who are you?"

"I'm Dr. Phillips."

"Well, thank goodness we don't need a doctor. We did need one, but they all got well—Betty and Brother and Dad."

"Will you try to describe the house where you live?"

"House! We're not rich! We live in an apartment."

"Where is it?"

"That's all right. My husband will take me there. He's coming for me this afternoon."

"He can't very well do that, because it's evening now, and besides he doesn't know where you are."

"You're too fresh! We have our own doctor, and we're satisfied with him. If we want to make a change, my husband will send you word."

"Is your husband in business for himself, or does he work for somebody?"

"He's in an office. He has an office all to himself, and you can't get in to see him till the boy tells him who you are and what you want. And then he's liable to say he's out, if you're somebody he doesn't want to see. I don't imagine he'd want to see you; you ask too many questions. And those girls ask too many questions. It's people like you that make him so late. He has to stay at the office and answer questions, and it makes him late. He'd have been here long ago, if it wasn't for you. And I've got to get home and bake a cake."

That night Mamma boasted a little about her children and didn't seem to care whether any one was listening.

"Betty is smarter and gets along faster in school. She can skim through a lesson once and almost know it by heart. She finishes her home work in fifteen or twenty minutes and then helps Brother do his. Brother has brains enough, but he dreams a lot. He doesn't concentrate like Betty. He is more on the lines of a genius of some kind. Everybody says he'll be an artist or a poet or maybe a great actor. I don't believe he'd ever pass in school if the teachers weren't so crazy about him. That and the way Betty helps him with his home work. My husband says Betty will make a better businessman than Brother. I hope neither one of them will have to work as hard as my husband does. I suppose they will, though, if we don't turn over a new leaf and economize. We'll have to for a while, to pay what we owe Doctor. I don't imagine he'll charge us as much as he would if he wasn't so fond of the children. Betty's his favorite, and I think my husband likes Brother best. I don't know which I like best. They're both lovely!"

During her second day at the hospital, Mamma answered (if you could call it answering) most of the questions put to her, occasionally losing her temper and scolding her questioners for their inquisitiveness. For two weeks thereafter she would not open her mouth in the presence of a doctor, a nurse, or a volunteer social worker. She cried a little, smiled a great deal, and several times daily told other patients that her husband was coming for her "this afternoon."

In vain her picture was published in all the papers, along with the scant details of the case—the date she had been found, her approximate age, a description of her clothing. There were no inquiries for her at the police stations, the other hospitals, or the morgue, and policemen assigned to the task of discovering her alleged family reported failure. The psychopathic ward was beginning to regard her as part of its permanent equipment. And then—suddenly she recalled her other name.

"Carns," she said, and said it again, "Carns."

She said it loudly, and Miss Fraser heard.

"What is that you're saying? Is it your name?"

"Yes. That's it—Carns."

"What's the rest of it?"

"I don't know, but my husband will remember. He'll tell you when he comes for me this afternoon."

To Miss Fraser "Carns" sounded unreal, but in the telephone book she found five "Carnses." Four of them reported that all members of their families were present or accounted for. The telephone of the fifth was no longer in service.

Miss Fraser got off the West Side subway on upper Broadway and walked downhill to Riverside Drive. She stopped at an address listed in the telephone book, the address of the Carnses whose telephone had been disconnected.

It was an old apartment building, but the doorman was new.

"No, I never heard of nobody by that name," he said. "But you might maybe find out from the janitor. He's been here all his life."

The janitor was away—had gone up to the hardware store. Miss Fraser talked to his wife, who first wanted it understood that her husband was not a janitor, but a superintendent.

"The man at the door told me you had been here a long time," said Miss Fraser. "Did you know a family in the building named Carns?"

"Yes, and mighty fine people. A young man and his wife and two kiddies, a boy and a girl. The little girl was as smart as a whip, and the boy was so handsome that everybody turned around in the street to look at him. I never felt sorrier for nobody than poor Mrs. Carns. She was going to send me a postcard to tell me how she got along, but I guess it slipped her mind."

"Why were you sorry for her?"

"For losing her husband and two kids."

"Losing them?"

"They all three died of the flu two months ago."

Miss Fraser swallowed before she spoke again. "Where did Mrs. Carns say she was going?"

"No place specially. She was going to look for work, though I can't think of nothing she'd be fitted for. She couldn't be very choosey anyway, because I doubt if she had ten dollars when she left here, and she had to support herself besides satisfying all her creditors."

"Did she owe much?"

"She owed at least a month's rent, and she owed the doctor and the nurse."

"Oh, did she have a nurse?"

"The doctor told her she had to get one. She herself was the most useless, helpless woman you ever seen in a sick room."

Miss Fraser related her findings at the hospital.

"Well," said Dr. Phillips, "it's just a question of time till everything comes back to her. If she recalls her name, it won't be long till she remembers the whole business. And then she's liable to have something a lot worse than what she's got."

Mamma spotted Miss Fraser as she came into the ward, and called to her.

"Did you telephone my husband?"

"How could I?" said Miss Fraser. "I don't know his name."

"I told you his name. It's Carns."

"There's no such name," said Miss Fraser. "I looked in the book and couldn't find it."

"Maybe I've got it wrong," said Mamma. "Anyway he's coming for me this afternoon."

Cured!

(*The Red Book Magazine*, March 1931)

There was a fellow named Dick Streeter, and he had a nice wife, Mary Streeter. He also had a great job as a comic-strip artist for the Duane Syndicate, and a great thirst for all kinds of intoxicating beverages excepting light wines and beer. He was not the sort of fellow who could drink three cocktails before dinner and two high-balls during the evening, and then go to bed and sleep, and get up in the morning with a normal appetite for breakfast and live through the day, until cocktail time, without giving alcohol a thought. He was a fellow in whom one cocktail or highball created a demand for a hundred or a thousand more, and during the days or weeks when he was consuming them, the very idea of breakfast or any other meal was disgusting.

Dick and Mary were frequently invited to dinner parties at the homes of various friends. At first Dick drank all that was offered him at these parties, and sometimes went so far as to take a few drinks without being asked. Along about eleven o'clock in the evening he would become quite tiresome, and then it would get to be one or two o'clock, and everyone, including the host and hostess, would want the party to break up; but Dick would insist on staying on and on until he was fairly pushed out the door. It didn't take him long to realize that he was an unwelcome guest in the best homes when he was drinking, and it didn't take him much longer to realize that he would rather stay home when he wasn't.

Undoubtedly the host and hostess and the other guests found him pretty tedious when he had had a few too many. Just as undoubtedly it was no great fun for him to sit around, cold sober, from half-past seven to midnight, and listen to anecdotes, jokes and stories which he had heard a score of times before, and watch the normal husbands and wives toy with one highball for an hour, enough time for him to have got rid of nearly a dozen.

Gradually he became party-shy, and when an invitation came,

Mary replied that she was sorry, but on the date designated, Dick would be in Lancaster on business, Lancaster being a place where Dick never had any business and probably never would have. As a rule the hostess said, well, wouldn't Mary come without Dick, and they would get an extra man. When Dick persuaded Mary to agree to such an arrangement, he felt pretty good. He wanted Mary to have fun, but he knew he just didn't fit in, any way you looked at it. On such occasions Dick would usually go to bed early with a book. Sometimes he would even work a little, though it was unnecessary for him ever to touch pencil or pen to paper, for he had an understudy named Sammy Burns who, for a paltry two hundred dollars a week, could and did draw his cartoons for him so efficiently that no one except brother cartoonists could tell the difference, and they weren't likely to squeal.

Now, when a person is a cartoonist, he gets to know people whom his wife never meets, or if she does meet them, she doesn't like them. Dick had a number of pals who, queerly enough, found him bright and amusing when he was drinking, and a bore when he wasn't. It was natural that he should seek out these pals when he started on a bender. They sang with him; they laughed at what he said; and they saw nothing odd about a person's ordering another highball all around while the glasses were still half full of the last one. Moreover, very few of them ever spoke of food or seemed in a hurry to get home.

This gang of good fellows usually hung out at Clayton's, which had a bar and tables and pretty good stuff—that is, you could take two drinks of it without bursting into tears. Mike Clayton claimed he got it off a boat. Some of the customers suspected that the boat was a tanker, but what was the difference, so long as the effect was not fatal? To Dick it didn't taste any worse than what he had been wont to consume at private houses, and the advantages of Clayton's over these were several: you didn't have to be polite to anybody; you could stop or interrupt an anecdote or story any time you felt like it, without causing resentment; you could order all the refreshments you wanted and no one would suggest by word or look that you were taking too many; you could play bridge (though you seldom cared to), and the penalty for a revoke was general laughter instead of points against you above the line, a fishy look from your partner and uncouth expressions of triumph from your opponents; you could sing with singers who didn't think bass was the melody pitched an octave below, or that tenor was alto.

None of Dick's cronies at Clayton's was woman-crazy. They all had a deep affection for their wives and if they didn't get home for a day or two, it was merely because the trip was too much of an effort. Dick, for example, lived up in Westchester County, nearly thirty miles from town. It was a tedious and expensive ride in a taxi, and the trains always left just ten minutes before you could catch them; the trains, moreover, always carried two or three acquaintances who wanted to talk, and with whom you didn't want to talk at that particular time.

Well, on an occasion when Dick had been on the wagon for over two months and had golfed himself into a state of almost uncomfortable healthiness, Mrs. Colton, who was Mary's best friend, called up and said she was going to have just eight people (including herself and Mr. Colton) for dinner the following evening, and she hoped Dick and Mary would come. Mary gave her the customary answer—that she would love to come, but she would have to ask Dick, who wasn't in (he was, too), because he might have to work on his Sunday page or something. Could she call back later on? Yes, she could.

Mary asked Dick; and he, well aware that Mary was fond of the Coltons, said sure, tell her we'll come.

"But you know, dear," said Mary, "that you have to go to town tomorrow morning."

"What's that got to do with it? The contract is made out. All I'll have to do is sign it, and maybe talk a little, and I can catch the two forty-five back."

"Are you sure you'll be all right?"

"Of course I will! What do you mean?"

"Oh, just that sometimes you run into some of your friends, and you don't catch trains that you intend to catch."

"I'll catch that one, all right. Don't worry," said Dick.

So Mary telephoned Mrs. Colton and told her she and Dick would be tickled to death to come; and the next morning Dick went to town to sign his new contract with the Duane Syndicate.

"You certainly look fine!" remarked Mr. Watson, who owned the syndicate. "How long do you expect to keep it up?"

"I don't believe I'll ever take another drink," said Dick.

"I hope you don't. If you were a fella like me, who could take it or leave it alone—"

Dick stopped in at a barber shop in a midtown hotel, and had a haircut, a shave and a shine. Then he started walking along toward the Grand Central Station. It was too bad he hadn't chosen another street, because the street he did choose was the one on which Clayton's was located, and just as he was about to pass the place with a keen sense of righteousness, a mounted policeman's horse mistook itself for a pedestrian, stepped up on the walk and planted a hoof right on Dick's new shine.

"You so-and-so!" said Dick to the jockey.

"Why don't you watch where you're going?" retorted the jockey.

"Why don't you tell your horse it isn't walking a beat?"

The policeman made no reply to this, but rode off. Dick looked at his ruined shoe and limped upstairs to Clayton's.

Mike welcomed him cordially. So did three of his best pals—Joe Gale, Rudy Miller and Paul Stroud. He showed them his shoe, and they sympathized with him briefly, cursing policemen in general. They made jocose remarks about his coat of tan and his long stretch of good behavior. And they asked him to have a drink.

"I can only have one," said Dick. "I promised my wife I'd catch the two forty-five."

"What's she giving, a tea?" said Rudy.

"Anyway, it's only two o'clock now, and if you can't take more than one drink and still catch the two forty-five, it's time you were applying for a pension," said Paul.

"It isn't that," said Dick. "But if I take more than one, I'll want a dozen, and I've got to get home cold sober, because I'm going to a party tonight."

"Did you have any lunch?" asked Joe.

"No, I didn't," denied Dick.

"Boys," said Joe, "he's lying to us. He looks like a man who'd had lunch, and I bet he had breakfast too."

"I did have breakfast," admitted Dick.

"All right," said Joe, "you had breakfast. Now, I want to leave it to these boys. Boys, what do you say about a man who confesses he's had breakfast?"

"There's nothing much you can say about him, except he's a man that's not to be trusted."

"Did you enjoy your breakfast?" demanded Paul.

"I didn't mind it," said Dick. "I'm getting used to it."

"But listen," said Joe; "if you ever have any children, how are you going to explain to them that there was a time when you enjoyed your breakfast?"

At half-past two, Dick had had four drinks and said he would have to rush to catch the train.

"You can't go home with that shoe," objected Paul.

"No, and you can't go home without it," said Rudy.

"Why," suggested Joe, "can't you have a couple more light ones and then get a new shine over at the station and take the three thirty? What's the matter with the three thirty, anyway? Do you hate the conductor or something? Or have you got a case on the two forty-five?"

"I told Mary I'd make it."

"You don't want to stagger Mary by making a train you said you'd make."

"I'm in pretty good now, and I want to stay that way."

"Anyhow, you can't get the two forty-five," said Mike, "—not unless Lindbergh's waiting for you downstairs."

"I'm afraid I have missed it," said Dick, "but you can bet I'll get the next one."

"You mean the next drink," said Rudy. "What's the trouble, Mike? The service here is terrible!"

"I'll have to call up Mary and tell her the lawyers were late or something."

"Let me call her up," suggested Joe.

"Yes, that's a sweet idea!" said Dick.

He had brought Joe out to the house one day a long while ago, and the hostess had not urged Joe to repeat his visit.

"I wouldn't care much," said Dick, "if the party were anywhere else but at the Coltons'. Mary likes them, and they like her. They even like *me,* when I'm not drinking."

"You're not drinking now," protested Rudy. "You've only had four, and two more won't hurt you. You can just take it easy and catch the three thirty, and by the time you get home, nobody'll know you've slipped."

At twenty minutes of five, Dick said he wanted to telephone and went into the booth. He didn't want to telephone, but it was necessary. He sat and stared at the instrument awhile, and did a little quiet thinking. He could catch the five ten or even the five forty and be home in time to dress for the Coltons' party. But he knew that his wife and everyone at the Coltons' would know he had fallen from grace and would be mad at him. He also knew that he could not sit through the party without a drink, and he had sworn never to imbibe again in the presence of any of Mary's friends.

Desperately he took off the receiver, called his number, dropped in the required number of coins, and waited.

"Hello," said Mary.

"I thought I'd call up—"

"I'm surprised you even did that," said Mary.

"The lawyers were late, and there were a couple of mistakes in the contract, and we've been getting them straightened out."

"Yes. You sound like it. What day do you think you'll be home?"

"I'll be home tonight if you don't scold me. But I do wish you'd get me out of going to the Coltons'."

"Don't worry about that! I'll get us both out."

"But I want you to go. They can easily get somebody to fill in. And you'll have a good time."

"You just leave everything to me," said Mary, and hung up.

Dick returned to the table, where two fresh highballs were waiting for him.

"Well," said Joe, "how did you come out? Did you square it?"

"Sure. Everything's fine. But we'd better have another drink."

"You'd better wait till you catch up with yourself."

"All right," said Dick, gulping down one of the highballs. "And how about a little harmony?"

Rudy started it:

When you wore a tulip, a big yellow tulip———

Three hours later, Joe remarked: "You ought to send a card of thanks to that mounted horse policeman."

" 'Mounted horse policeman,' is good," said Paul.

"You know what I mean," said Joe. "I mean that policeman that stepped on Dick's horse."

"That's even better," said Paul.

"I'd break his jaw if I had him here," said Dick.

"Who? The horse?"

"Anybody."

"I'm telling you that you owe him a vote of thanks," said Joe. "If it wasn't for him stepping on your horse, you'd be eating dinner. You couldn't help yourself."

"I don't want any dinner," said Dick.

"You bet you don't! Not now! You're human now. But if it hadn't been for that policeman, you'd be fighting a squab."

"Don't mention the word!" said Paul with a shudder. . . .

Dick reached home at eleven o'clock the next night. He had a pint on each hip for use in an emergency—Mary had been known to lock up the supply and hide the key. This time, however, she had left the cabinet open and had gone to bed and to sleep, which was a disappointment to Dick, who still wanted to talk, though he had been up nearly forty hours. There was nothing for him to do but take a couple more shots and go to bed and talk to himself.

Mary did her talking when Dick woke up the following afternoon.

"I've done something that I know you won't approve of, but I can't help that. Experience tells me that you're started on another long spree, as you call it, and you'll keep going till you're sick if we don't try something radical. I was with Myrna Evick yesterday, and I didn't mention you at all, but she just said casually that she had a brother who used to drink for weeks at a time, and common doctors didn't do him any good, and finally her father heard of a Dr. Wendell, a kind of psychologist and psychiatrist, who specialized in that kind of thing. And they called him in, and her brother was just as much of a skeptic as you are, but in two weeks Dr. Wendell had him won over so that he wouldn't even look at a drink; he hasn't taken one since, and that was five years ago. I called Dr. Wendell up this morning, and he's coming to see you this afternoon, and I hope you'll at least be polite to him."

"I wish I had a shave," said Dick.

"I imagine," said Mary, "that he's accustomed to seeing men without shaves."

Dr. Wendell, a large, foreign-looking gentleman with a walrus mustache, drove up to the Streeters' house in an expensive car, greeted Dick and Mary in a gruff voice and invited Mary to remain in the room during the interview. He asked Dick a hundred questions about his parents and the rest of his family, who all, it happened, had been and were as nearly perfect as people get.

"Why is it you drink?" inquired the Doctor.

"Because I like to, and because it gives me a kind of mental release."

"A release from what? Are you depressed about something?"

"No sir."

"You're a cartoonist, aren't you?"

"Yes sir. But I'm not depressed about my cartoons. I hardly ever look at them."

"Now, when you start to drink, do you make up your mind in advance that you're going to, or does it come on you suddenly?"

"It comes on me suddenly. Something happens that drives me to it."

"What happened this time?"

"I'd just had my shoes shined, and a mounted policeman's horse stepped on one of them."

"That's sufficient cause," said Dr. Wendell. "You must be careful to keep away from mounted policemen. Or else you mustn't get your shoes shined."

There were more questions and answers, and then Mary put in a word.

"Doctor," she said, "my husband claims that this isn't just a bad habit. He claims it's a disease."

"He's perfectly right, madam," said Dr. Wendell, and Mary wished she hadn't spoken.

Well, it was finally agreed that Dick should take a room in a hotel in town, where the Doctor could visit him daily and see that he kept straight. And that Mary should go to her aunt's in Maine and stay there until Dick, thoroughly cured, summoned her home.

For more than two weeks Dr. Wendell called on Dick every afternoon about four o'clock and found him thin but sober. The reason he was thin was that he hadn't eaten anything. The reason he was sober was that he had been out of bed only long enough to have a bath and a barber. At five o'clock, after the Doctor had gone, you could find him at Clayton's with Joe and Rudy and Paul, singing, *"I want a girl just like the girl that married dear old Dad,"* or one of its contemporaries. At four o'clock every morning he disgusted his pals by leaving them and going back to his hotel to sleep.

When the third week began, he realized suddenly that Mary's absence was harder to bear than being stepped on by a mounted policeman's horse.

He said to Dr. Wendell:

"I'm all right again now, and I want to send for my wife. I want her to get here the day after tomorrow. If you'll give me something that will insure me a good, long nap we'll call it a cure and the credit belongs to you."

Then he sent Mary a telegram and received a day letter in reply:

ARRIVE ON THURSDAY MORNING NINE
O'CLOCK PLEASE CALL UP OLGA TELL
HER TO HAVE HOUSE READY LOVE.

Dick stayed away from Clayton's on Tuesday night. In fact, he stayed in bed from Tuesday night until Thursday morning. He got up at half-past seven Thursday morning and had a bromide and a cup of clam broth and a haircut and shave, but no shine.

The people waiting for incoming trains at Grand Central smiled a little wistfully at the warmth of the greeting between Mary and Dick.

"You look grand!" said Mary.

"Not half as grand as you do," said Dick. "Have you had breakfast?"

"No."

"Neither have I. And I'm hungry," said Dick. "We'll have time to get something and still catch the nine fifty-eight."

"Dr. Wendell's a great fella!" said Dick, as he choked down some wheatcakes.

"You'll have to admit I had the right hunch," said Mary.

Going out on the suburban train, Dick said:

"Would you like to have the Coltons over tonight, for dinner and maybe play some bridge?"

"Oh, no, dear. Let's just stay home together, alone."

Dr. Wendell was released and paid off a month ago, and Dick hasn't been to town since. So the cure is beginning to look permanent.

Bob's Birthday

(*The Red Book Magazine,* November 1933)

This is my first attempt at writing a story, and I would not have courage to make the attempt only for a friend of Bob's who is editor of a magazine named Mr. Bishop encouraging me to make the attempt, and also because there is nothing I would stoop so low as to make money in order to relieve some of the burden from Bob's shoulders as he seems to be carrying everybody in the world's burden on his shoulders. At first I thought I would try and write a detective story about a mystery, but he said to write about a subject I am more conversant, I mean Mr. Bishop, and he suggested a story about some incident in my home life. So he being the editor, I am taking his advice and writing a story about an incident in my home life, and I only wish it could be more exciting, but all I can do is hope that we will soon have a murder in the family or somebody will die so that when I write my next (?) story it will be really exciting with a murder or at least an inquest in the plot.

Our name is Tyler and my brother Bob is 17 years of age and a born musician and plays the saxophone and clarinet in Belden's Orchestra and makes arrangements for the orchestra of new pieces and Mr. Belden pays him a salary of $150.00 per week. How is that for only 17 years of age? But it is just awful the way he has to work and has been supporting the family for two years, ever since my father lost his position with Kemp and Warren. During the daytime Bob is either making records or writing arrangements or attending rehearsals, and from dinner time on they play engagements at some restaurant till 3 or 4 o'clock in the morning, and they broadcast every Wednesday night and several weeks every year they play engagements at some theater like the Paramount or Capitol or Palace.

It is funny sometimes how different a person's plans turn out than the way they planned them. Two years ago Bob was a junior in high school and desperately in love with Kathleen Dennis, whose father is president of Dennis & Co. and has a chair in the Stock Exchange

Market. No girl could help loving Bob, and Kathleen loved him and they were engaged, but her father did not like him just being a musician though even at that time Bob had offers from Mr. Belden and other good orchestras to join their orchestras. But in order to please Mr. Dennis, Bob said he would graduate from high school and then work his way through Yale or some big university by forming an orchestra like Rudy Vallée and would learn some profession like medicine or a lawyer, and Mr. Dennis liked this idea because he said it showed that Bob had the right stuff in him, and he said that it would take 8 or 9 years for Bob to carry out this idea and by that time I guess he thought Bob and Kathleen would be tired of each other, though I am 14 years of age myself and have lived with Bob all that time and never got tired of him. But Kathleen said that was different because a sister might get so she could not bear the sight of her brother and what could she do about it, but if it was her husband she could get rid of him.

Anyways my father lost his position and Bob not only had to give up his plans for college, but also quit high school and go with Belden's Orchestra, and he has been supporting my mother and father and myself ever since because my father does not seem able to secure another position and Bob says positions are very hard to secure these days especially when a person tries to secure them by playing contract every afternoon and spending all their evenings at the club like my mother and father and my Aunt Lucille and Uncle George. They say they go there to forget and pretend things are like they used to be, and I would say there is very little difference at that, judging from the noise when they come home.

I forgot to tell you about my uncle and aunt. Their name is Marshall and Uncle George is my mother's brother. He lost his position about the same time my father did his, and every time they cannot think of anything else to quarrel over, they quarrel over who lost his position first. My father claims he did and Uncle George claims he did and you would think that Congress was going to award the Legend of Honor to whomever could prove they had been out of work the longest time.

Anyways it was 3 or 4 months ago when my mother told Bob she had good news for him, that Uncle George and Aunt Lucille had decided to come and live with us and they would pay $25.00 per week, and though it meant that Bob would have to sleep on the divan in the living-room, he did not mind that as he never has time to sleep more than 2 or 3 hours and he is so dog tired that he says he could sleep on an arpeggio. He knew Uncle George's habits and rightly figured that he would not add much to our grocery bill because when he was out of a job he would only eat a light breakfast at home around noontime and go to the club for dinner and take Aunt Lucille with him the same as my father and mother or anyone else when they are drinking. But what Bob did not know was that Uncle George came to live with us because the people where he rented his apartment put him out for not paying his rent and he had no more money than my father himself and like my father, he picked up the habit of borrowing gin money and taxi money from Bob, so that at the end of 3 months he had actually borrowed more than he owed us for board and lodging.

During the week before last, Belden's Orchestra had their first vacation in over a year and a half, due to them ending an engagement at the Crawford, and Mr. Belden arranged for them to take a week off before they begun their new engagement at the Maples. It was not really a vacation for Bob because he had to make arrangements for 5 new numbers and rehearse, and they did their regular broadcast on Wednesday night, but at least he was able to be home almost every other evening except Wednesday, and Mother promised that she and Dad would stay home for dinner 5 evenings that week just so we could get acquainted again. I can remember when they used to stay home 2 or 3 evenings a week and play backgammon or even read, and it was fun having them because they acted as if they liked us and enjoyed our company even though we were only their children. But that was a long time ago.

Secretly I hoped to myself that Aunt Lucille and Uncle George would keep on going out as usual. It only takes 1 drink now to make Uncle George as bad as he was the night before, and his conversation is always on 1 of 3 subjects, none of which are likely to add to the gayety of the occasion. Either he is asking Bob for $10.00 more or he is bragging about how long since he lost his job or he is quoting some violinist friend of his who says that real musicians look down on people who play the saxophone or clarinet. Bob is one of the best-natured persons in the world, but it is awfully hard for him to just laugh and take that last crack without replying when there so many things he could say, especially to Uncle George. He admits that a saxophone is a kind of a mongrel instrument as he calls it, but nobody can play a clarinet as Bob plays it by just greasing their hair like Rudy Vallée. Besides, where would Uncle George and Dad get their gin if Bob had decided to spend these years in Europe learning to be a second Kreisler?

Well, my mother begged off for Monday evening, saying that she and my father and the Marshalls had been invited to the club by Mr. Gaines and they could not afford to refuse because there was a chance that Mr. Gaines might offer Dad a position. I did not see how he could very well do this as Mr. Gaines has no position himself, but there is no use arguing with Mother. They gave the same excuse for Tuesday night, only this time Mr. Sterrett was host and it was Uncle George who might get the job. No alibi was necessary for Wednesday, when Bob had his broadcast date, and on Thursday, Mother just said I would have to forgive her again, she had forgotten Bob and me and made an engagement at the club with the Lavelles. But I insisted on no excuses for Friday because it was Bob's birthday, and I also made her give me her word that she and Dad would buy him some kind of a present, even if it only cost them a dime of all the money he had loaned them in the past 2 years.

Personally I took some money of my own which I had saved up towards some clothes that I would simply have to have if Kathleen Dennis invited me for a week-end at Southampton as she promised, and I bought Bob a copy of the Life of Richard Wagner, a great German composer, and got Olga to make him a birthday cake.

There is two items that I have forgotten to mention, which shows how unexperienced I am as an authoress, and one of them is that Kathleen and Bob were still in love with each other all this time, but Mr. Dennis would not permit Kathleen to call it an engagement on account of the uncertainty of Bob's plans and you can hardly blame him as it looked like Bob would hardly be able to support a wife for some time to come in addition to Mother and Dad and myself and Uncle George and Aunt Lucille. The other item is my grandfather, who had a position as book-keeper with Silvers & Co. which paid him enough to pay for his room and board at Mrs. Hackley's, and he was still able to put a little in the savings bank every week so he would have enough to keep him when he was no longer able to work. That is, we thought he was one person whom we would not have to worry about, but it turned out different.

Well, the rest of my story is kind of embarrassing for me to put down in black and white. My father and mother and the Marshalls did not get home from their Thursday night party till 8 o'clock Friday morning. Mother and Aunt Lucille spent Friday in bed and came to Bob's birthday dinner in their kimona. Dad and Uncle George got up late in the afternoon and went out somewhere, Dad first borrowing $10.00 from Bob. I did not expect either of them to come home, but they did, at 8 o'clock, when the dinner was completely spoiled, and they brought Bob two presents, a bottle of gin and Grandfather.

Well, if there was ever a "happy birthday," Bob's was it. There was Aunt Lucille in her kimona and Uncle George with two days growth of beard neither of which were expected or wanted. There was Mother and Dad, who were welcome heaven knows, but not the way they felt or looked. There was Grandfather, who must have been rooming a couple of nights in a coal chute and celebrating some occasion of his own, because all he could do was take a drink of gin whenever they passed him Bob's "present," and no matter what you said to him, his answer was "Hotcha!"

If anybody had been hungry there would not have been nearly enough to go around, but even before the meal started, Bob and I were the only ones who could look at food without getting sick, and it was not long before our appetites were gone too. When Olga brought in the birthday cake, everyone suddenly remembered that it was Bob's birthday and congratulated him, that is if you could call Grandfather's "Hotcha!" a congratulation, and Dad got up and made a speech which was news to us and not good news either. He told us that Grandfather had joined the ranks of the unemployed three months ago, of which he and Uncle George were charter members, and that all of his savings had been spent paying for his room and board while he had sought in vain for a new position, that his landlady would give him no more credit and finally, to make a long story short, he (Dad) was giving him (Grandfather) to Bob for a birthday present. He added that it would only be for a little while as Grandfather is now 62 years of age and very few of the Tylers live much beyond eighty.

Almost before my father had finished speaking the doorbell rang. Well, it was Mr. Dennis and Kathleen.

They had come, so Mr. Dennis said, to wish Bob a happy birthday, and Kathleen had brought him a box of fudge which she had made herself. I knew that they had really come to spy on us, I mean Mr. Dennis, not Kathleen. To spy on us and to let Kathleen see what a mess she would be getting into if she ever married Bob.

She saw and she heard, and it did not take more than a minute. Mother and Aunt Lucille, sitting there in dirty kimonas, looking as if they had forgotten to brush their hair or even wash their hands. Dad and Uncle George and Grandfather, all of them dirty and unshaven and much the worse for gin. Bob standing up, trying and failing not to look ashamed.

"You are lucky to catch us all home at once," said my father. "It would not happen only for it being Bob's birthday."

"Bob is a fine young man," said Mr. Dennis. "You are fortunate in having such a good son."

"And you will be fortunate in getting such a good son-in-law," said my father.

"I hardly think it will come to that," said Mr. Dennis. "I would not ask Bob to assume any more financial responsibilities than he has already."

"If you were half a man," said my father, "you would relieve him of those responsibilities. Here is my brother-in-law, George Marshall, and myself and my father, all out of jobs through no fault of our own and all capable of filling any position that may be vacant in your office or any position you might create for us. It is men like you who are to blame for present conditions in this country. And now you come around here and hint that you are not going to allow your daughter to marry my son. Well, listen, Mr. Dennis, I will beat you to it. I would not allow my son to marry your daughter, not if she was the last girl in the world."

"That's talking!" said Uncle George.

"Hotcha!" said Grandfather.

"Come on, Kathie," said Mr. Dennis. "I think we have stayed at least long enough."

They went without saying good-night to anyone, not even Bob. Dad seemed to think he had done something wonderful and both

Uncle George and Grandfather were praising him for what they called "speaking up."

When I could not stand it any longer, I ran into the living-room and threw myself on the divan. Bob followed me and patted me on the shoulder and told me not to worry.

"Worry!" I said. "But with Grandfather here, where will you sleep?"

"Well," he said, "it will hardly matter tonight because I do not expect to feel like sleeping. And thanks to you I have got Old Man Wagner, so I would rather read than sleep."

That is the story of Bob's birthday and I could go on and tell you what we did about the sleeping arrangements with my grandfather added to the family, but I am afraid the story is already like what Mr. Dennis said about his stay at our house, it is "at least long enough."

Poodle

(*Delineator*, January 1934)

Now, I won't tell you who I am, but if you want to ferret it out for yourself, call up Information and inquire for a fella that's married to a woman named Mary who says that when her husband's drinking he talks a great deal too much. When he ain't drinking, he won't talk at all. Mary always gets mad at him when he's drinking, so she must figure that if he talks at all, it's too much. Like a Vice-President or something. I don't mean to imply that Vice-Presidents drink; in fact, I understand that their parents have warned the saloons not to sell it to them because statistics show that we're losing thousands of shade trees every year on account of kids, coming home from late parties, driving into big maples and elms to save their brake bands.

Where were we? Oh, yes. I was going to say that Mary's got all the best of it in our team. I have no objection to her drinking. I'm in favor of it, up to a certain point. If she stops before she comes to this point, why it don't do any good. But if she keeps on till she gets there, she falls asleep and quits talking.

Outside of me, the great sorrow in Mary's life is not having insomnia. It just about kills her to think that there's seven or eight hours out of the twenty-four when she ain't talking. I've tried to tell her she talks in her sleep. She won't believe it because she always wakes up depressed.

I'm certainly out of talking practise; I keep wandering off the subject, if I was ever on it. Well, let's begin all over. I meant to say that every Christmas up to last Christmas, Waldron's always gave their employees a bonus of ten percent, and believe it or not, that meant six hundred dollars to the fella that's promised to rock you to sleep. As a matter of fact, it didn't really mean a dime; I just kept the check till I got home, and then I endorsed it and turned it over to Mary and she went ahead and spent it whatever way she wanted to, which was to help pay for a new car because the one she bought last year had cigaret ashes on the running board.

174

But when we girls and boys opened our envelops on the twenty-fourth of December this last ult., we got a big surprise. It seems the old man had received a mash note from the Secretary of the Treasury and he'd read between the lines and found out that there was a temporary slump in business, and the only way to offset it was to turn over our bonus checks to some deserving charity on Wall Street. He enclosed a substitute for same in the form of an order on a couple of haberdashers, one for women and one for men, calling for fifty dollars' worth of pearl-handled suspenders for the high-salaried guys like myself and scaling all the way down to five-dollar certificates for the office boys and the little blond kid who had been playing guessing games with the telephone switchboard for three weeks.

Well, during the first week of my married life I'd passed a resolution to never tell Mary any bad news, and the result was that I'd practically become a mute except when I made a few local stops on the way home from the office. But this time there was no way of concealing the facts or even stalling long enough to not spoil the spirit of the occasion. Mary never made much of just an ordinary homecoming. Other days of the year, she generally managed to suppress a wife's natural urge to rush to the door when she heard her handsome husband's hoof-beats crunching up the gravel walk. On Christmas Eve, however, she always risked the danger of taking cold by waiting for me on the front steps.

Maybe it would have been better this time to telephone before I left town and give her a hint of what had happened. I know that nothing could have been worse than the way it was. I handed her the envelop without a word of warning and when she'd read the contents often enough to realize that it wasn't a joke, she let out a yell that would have waked up a porter and looked so much like she was going to faint that I went in the kitchen and told the girl to let the cold water run.

I won't attempt to remember all the bright ideas she had when the first shock was over. One was to hire a lawyer and sue Mr. Waldron for the six hundred on the grounds that he had given it to me so many Christmases that it was really a part of my salary. Another one was to threaten him that if he didn't come across, I would spread a report that we were saving money by buying an inferior grade of raw materials. Still another one was to appoint myself head man among the employees and organize a strike, which we wouldn't have to go through with, of course, because it's pretty near impossible these days to fill vacancies in a high-class establishment like Waldron's.

When you've been Mary's husband eight years, you know that the only way to win an argument, or stop one, is to agree with everything she says. After you've yes-ed her a couple of times, she'll change sides. Then you change with her. If she jumps back, you jump, too, and if she goes neutral, you do the same. She finally gets disgusted and picks out another subject, but whatever subject she switches to, it's bound to be better than the one she was on.

She gave up plotting how to fleece Mr. Waldron after I'd cheered every suggestion she could think of, and the next problem was what to do with my fifty-dollar order on Norton's Store for Men; that is, what to do besides what the old man intended for me to do.

It was a long while before Mary convinced herself that the certificate wouldn't do her any good. It said right on it that you couldn't turn it in for cash, and Norton's is one place a woman might as well stay out of unless she's got a boy friend. She had already bought me a carton of her kind of cigarets and she was giving a record of "Tea for Two" to Jack Ingram. It's her favorite piece and the Ingrams have got a phonograph and we're over there three or four nights a week. Anyway, she finally decided to give me my certificate, and if I only had a new suit of clothes to go with this shirt and tie, I'd be a pretty good-looking fella.

The Ingrams were the first people we met when we came to New York. As far as I know, they're the only people Mary ever met outside of the man that's got the Bayside agency for Parker automobiles. We were going to rent an apartment in town till we could afford a little home in some suburb, and the idea was to stay at a hotel while Mary looked the place over. We happened to pick the Hotel Lindsay, and that's where the Ingrams were living, waiting for their house to be finished out in Bayside.

Well, it only took Mary and Edith Ingram twenty minutes to cement a beautiful friendship and I'd have had to like Jack even if he was a Collector of Internal Revenue. Instead of that he's a harmless kind of a fella and a good talker if you're interested in blooded cattle. He never owned any and it looks now like he never would, but he subscribed to a couple of magazines that tell you how to bring up an ox and you can get along with him if you say "Wonderful!" in the right spot and don't keep dozing off the way you've been doing.

Jack had a good job with the Boland Drug Company, which paid him for knowing something about chemistry, not cows. He was getting seven thousand when we met him and they boosted him to seventy-five hundred before the crash. Edith had some money of her own and when their house was ready, they owned it clear.

Of course, Mary went along two or three times to help Edith superintend the finishing touches and we spent the first week-end with them after they moved in. Right then and there Mary lost all interest in New York apartments. It was Bayside or bust, and maybe both. She knew we couldn't buy or build, but she found a place for rent and we've been there ever since. Evenings when we didn't go to the Ingrams' house, they'd come to ours. Sundays in the winter time, they just meant six or seven hours' extra gayety, and in the summer, a drive in the latest model Parker sedan, with me and Jack in the back seat and Mary at the wheel, on whatever road she thought we'd find the worst jam; me jealous of Edith for being able to sleep; Jack always wishing we'd get stalled in front of a stock farm, and never getting his wish, and everybody but Mary hoping there'd be a cloudburst next Sunday at a quarter to two.

When the Ingrams built their house, they didn't build a garage. They decided to wait till they could buy a car. Mary decided to buy a car because the place we rented had a garage and the rent would have been lower if it hadn't had one, so if we didn't use it we were cheating ourselves. This saved the Ingrams a lot of trouble and expense. I had to get to New York earlier than Jack and my train left Bayside a half hour ahead of his. But after Mary had driven me to the station, she'd go and get him. Then, during the rest of the day, she'd taxi Edith around the village or wherever else she had errands to do. For all that, I'll bet there was many a time when Jack and Edith wished they had their own car so they could stay home Sundays.

Christmas Eve, it was the Ingrams' turn to come and see us. Mary said I mustn't tell them about our little surprise; they liked us so much that they'd feel pretty near as bad as we did, especially Edith, who could be so sympathetic sometimes that it was almost impossible not to get up and sock her in the jaw. You see, the difference between my regular salary and Jack's was fifteen hundred dollars, but his firm had never even given him a pocket comb for Christmas, let alone a check, so if Edith didn't know our secret, Mary could still take advantage of her only annual chance to gloat, and I will state in behalf of my Mary that she can outgloat any two women I ever met, and doesn't need to speak a word. Twice during the evening Edith brought up the subject herself. She asked me how it felt to be a millionaire. I said I wished I knew, but Mary flashed a smile that would have fooled a whole lot less dumber dame than Edie. Mr. Waldron had raised the bonus instead of repealing it—that's what you'd have thought, seeing Mary smile. She acted like a child with a new flask, except every so often some speech of Edith's would remind her that the Boland Drug people didn't believe in Santa Claus; then she'd sober up for a minute and look ashamed, as if she'd laughed out loud at a disarmament conference.

Well, Jack's concern remembered him the last day of the year. They gave him his freedom and a nice note telling him how sorry they were to lose his services; they knew he wouldn't have any trouble finding another job and not to hesitate to call on them if his future employers wanted a recommendation. Jack realized that there wasn't a chance of him landing anything in his line at even half what the Boland people had paid him, so he and Edith moved out to Chicago where his brother owns a couple of hotels and he's going to run one of them, or maybe it's the elevator. They left their house with a real estate man, and he's supposed to hold onto it till he can get what it cost them; in other words, he's supposed to hold onto it.

Mary felt terrible losing Edith, but she did have the satisfaction of one final gloat the night before they went away. That happened to be the seventh of January and the seventh of January happened to be my birthday. And without knowing anything about it being my birthday, Mr. Waldron called me in his office that afternoon and made a speech which I'm still wondering why he made it. He said he understood what a blow the bonus thing must have been to the employees; it had probably spoiled their Christmas; it had spoiled his Christmas worrying about it; he hated not showing his appreciation of our loyalty in the usual way, but business conditions didn't warrant his keeping everybody on the payroll, let alone giving us a bonus of ten percent. However, I was the most valuable man in his employ and it wasn't fair for me to be treated like the riffraff and he intended to more than make up to me for the six hundred dollars I hadn't got; it wouldn't be in the form of a bonus, but my salary check would be different from now on; and finally I must treat this as strictly confidential.

Well, I gulped and thanked him and went back to my desk, where I spent the rest of the afternoon trying to guess what for and how much. I was so baffled that when it came time to quit, I happened to go to a saloon instead of the station, and I caught the six-fifteen instead of the five-twelve.

As I told you before, and maybe you believe me by now: when I drink, I talk too much. And when I drink, Mary gets mad. On this particular evening, she wasn't any too good-natured to start with; she doesn't like for me to come home one train late, to say nothing of two, and Edith always felt so sorry for her when I'd had a couple of drinks that it looked like the gals' last evening together would find the sympathy all on the wrong side. But the reception I got broke down my morale and I took three drinks before dinner in place of the two I intended to take, and that extra drink was what made me tell Mary everything Waldron had said and put her in a position to send her best friend away thoroughly whipped.

The old man hadn't stated how much my raise was to be; just that it would more than equal six hundred dollars. Mary insisted on me guessing and I guessed seven hundred. That didn't satisfy her at all, so I made it eight hundred and fifty. But she's the kind that you give her an inch and she'll take the Lincoln Highway, and by the time the Ingrams showed up, she had me getting eight thousand a year, five hundred more than Bolands were paying Jack before they fired him. Not only that, but she appointed me general manager and if the Ingrams had stayed an hour longer, she probably would have made me Waldron's partner. Edith was the silentest I ever saw her. If she'd opened her mouth she'd have screamed.

You've been drowsing and not listening, but I'm going to tell you the rest of it just the same. My pay checks for the last three weeks in January were no different from what they had been before the old man spoke his piece. Mary had told the Ingrams that the new scale was to become effective on the fourteenth. When it didn't, and when the twenty-first and the twenty-eighth went by and still no signs of action, she said the old boy must have forgot all about it and I ought to remind him. I convinced her that this wasn't the year when the best people considered it stylish to insist on raises in salary; the thing for me to do was keep my mouth shut and indulge in silent prayer.

That brings us to the comedy relief, or the love interest, or something. Waldron left for Florida Monday night, the thirtieth of January. He didn't call me in to bid him goodbye, but when I got to the office Tuesday morning, there was a mash note from him saying he regretted that a sudden change in plans had prevented him seeing me in person, and a sudden change in the business outlook had rendered it necessary to reduce expenses fifty per cent; I was the highest salaried man in his employ and it was simply impossible to pay me what I'd been getting; on the other hand, or maybe the same one, he wouldn't insult such a valuable and important employee by asking me to take a cut, so this was a notice that he would have to worry along without my services after February the fourth, and he hoped I'd understand that he, and not I, was the one who would really suffer.

You must bear in mind that I hadn't squawked about the Christmas surprise and I hadn't asked for a raise or ever hinted that I thought I was worth more than he was paying me. He had made his speech and his promise without any threat or suggestion from me. That's why the entire proceedings are a jigsaw puzzle with all the pieces missing; that's why I haven't averaged two hours' sleep per night from the last day of January till now, and I envy you every cat-nap you've enjoyed since I began this monolog.

Now I may as well admit that I was afraid to break the news to Mary. She was already in convulsions over the salary proposition. To report that my future earnings would be nothing per annum instead of seven thousand, or eight, or ten—well, you don't go up to a ravenous wolf and tell him they took the diner off at Jackson.

I was in a tough spot and it was necessary to practise deception, which is as foreign to my nature as rolling on a duck's back. The system in our family has always been for me to give Mary my check and for her to give me ten dollars a week for subway fare and lunch and side trips to the old Spanish missions. At the end of the month, she makes out a check for the next month's railroad ticket, but she makes it out to the Long Island Railroad Company. That didn't matter anyway, because if my secret was to be a secret, I had to go to town and come home on my regular train, job or no job; besides, I could think of many a more economical way of spending the winter than to hang around the house all day long and wait for Mary to run out of hallelujahs.

If I hadn't been scared of rousing suspicion, I'd have done at least one thing different: I'd have changed morning trains. The train I always take is like most trains—it carries more than one passenger —and there's a fella that's been getting on with me at Bayside every morning since the Boer War, who I never knew his name and don't know it yet and don't want to know it, but he got the idea somewhere that he and I were old schoolmates and he must sit by me or behind me or in front of me, or stand in the aisle alongside of my seat, and keep up a conversation every minute of the trip or I would feel neglected and lonesome. Years ago I gave up trying to shake him off: silence and cold stares and insults, they just seemed to draw us closer together.

I've got nothing against the fella except that I do like to read the papers in the morning, even when there's no news. With him always asking questions and expecting answers, I didn't find out till a couple of weeks ago that Byrd was back home or Mussolini had swum the Channel.

Another risk I couldn't afford to take was in regards to being called up at the office; I mean, after February fourth. Mary hardly ever phoned, but she might. I had to fix it with the switchboard gal to say I was out or in conference and couldn't be disturbed, and was there any message? The gal was as dumb as they come, but she would lie for me because I never squawked when she made a mistake, which was every day from eight-thirty to five, with a half hour off for lunch, where she probably got somebody else's order.

When Mary gave me my allowance the morning of the sixth, I realized I'd better go light on lunch myself; it don't take more than two or three hours to answer all the help-wanted ads, and in the middle of winter, with the kind of weather we've had, you get bored waiting for time to go home. You ain't in any frame of mind to read, except the ads, so the Public Library is no good. The waiting room in the Long Island station, or any other station, or the lobby of a hotel—any place that's indoors and free—they all lose their kick after a few days. Twice I spent a nickel riding to the end of the subway and back; it gave me a headache and it wasn't much fun and it didn't take long enough. It came down to a choice between the talkies and the speakies, though there wasn't really a choice. Ten dollars don't last forever in a place like this, and in my case, the explanation when I got home would have lasted the rest of my life. Well, I've seen every cheap talkie in town and most of them twice in one day.

When I got home at the end of the first week of "vacation" I didn't have to excuse myself for the check not being bigger than usual, but I had to explain why there was no check at all. As I've already said, I'm not an expert at deception; just the same, Mary believed my story and liked it better than anything I'd told her since the night I broke the news of the phantom raise.

It appears that Mr. Waldron had decided to pay me my new salary monthly instead of weekly. I would receive my next check the first of March and another the first of April, and so on. This was the orders he'd left with the cashier, but the cashier hadn't stated how much the monthly check would be and I hadn't had the nerve to ask. He probably took it for granted I knew and I would feel silly admitting that I didn't.

I was afraid Mary would be sore about this. She was just the opposite. I never saw her enjoy herself as much as she did that night, dividing different amounts by twelve and then multiplying to see if they came out the same way. Of course it couldn't be as little as five hundred a month because that would only mean the six thousand I'd been getting without the ten percent bonus and he'd promised me more than six thousand plus the ten percent. The lowest it could possibly be was six hundred a month or seventy-two hundred a year. If it was any figure between sixty-six hundred and seventy-two hundred, what was the sense in paying me by the month instead of by the week? But even seventy-two hundred wasn't much more than sixty-six, and the chances were that it would be seven hundred a month, which made eighty-four hundred a year, or nine hundred more than Jack Ingram got before he got fired.

She had money in the bank and she didn't mind advancing me ten dollars every Monday morning till the new deal went into effect.

Maybe I ought to have felt mean, filling her full of hopes that were headed for a nose dive. But it was fun for her while it lasted, and temporary peace for me. Maybe I *did* feel mean, but if you knew Mary—anyway, I don't feel mean now.

I wish I'd kept a list of the jobs I tried to get and didn't get and couldn't have held onto them if I'd got them. "General sales manager, protected territory, photographic equipment—probable earnings twenty thousand for the right man"; "Tall American headwaiter, maintenance and a hundred a month, must speak German"; "Silk examiner and analyst, thoroughly experienced, thirty dollars a week"; "Manager for a New York City credit clothing store, large city experience essential"; "Photo retoucher," and I hardly ever touch a photo, let alone doing it twice; "Young man for exterminating, must live in Westchester and own an auto"; "Superintendent-gardener for 75-acre Nassau County estate"; "Experienced travel-bureau manager with following"; "Mechanic, typewriters, all-around man, inside or outside, thirty-five dollars per week." I'm pretty sure I'd rather be outside a typewriter than in one, but they didn't give me a chance to choose; they hired the second all-around man that was after the place, and I was about Number 27 in a line of forty.

I applied for positions that I don't even know what the words mean: "Galalith" for instance, if that's how you pronounce it; and "Furniture tracer, to locate furniture skips"; and "Fanfold biller," "Silk disponent," and "Beveler." I even went to an address in Twenty-first Street where they wanted a man to cut boudoir dolls; if they'd engaged me, I wouldn't have known whether to use a razor or an ax. But I needn't have worried; at least twenty guys were waiting when I got there and they took one of the first four or five.

Now try and stay awake long enough to listen to what happened today. I came in town as usual, with my boy friend sitting in the seat in front of me, but with his neck twisted around so he could face me while he asked what I thought of free wheeling and relativity and a half dozen other subjects that a year-old child could tell you all about. The papers only had three new want ads I could answer in person and I wasn't qualified for any of the jobs they offered even if they gave me a trial. Just the same I answered them so as not to spoil my record. The first place I went was on West Thirty-fourth Street, where a watch company wanted a collector. They had him before I arrived on the scene, but I wouldn't have stood a chance anyway; I'd have to admit that I'm thirty-four years old and haven't collected a watch since I graduated from high school. I was also too late at the next stop, on Third Avenue, 'way uptown, where a German had advertised for a private tutor to learn him to speak English. The fella he had engaged was talking to him in German and they were getting along so well that they'll probably wind up by not fooling with English at all.

Finally I lost out with a concern that was looking for an intelligent young man to operate addressograph and graphotype machines, laundry experience preferred. The position was no longer open—they never are. Outside of that, and not being young or intelligent, or having any idea which machine was which, the job was right up my street. I've had plenty of experience with laundries.

This part of the performance was finished at ten and I spent the next two hours writing to people who wanted their ads answered by mail. That's really the best way to go job-hunting. You don't have to listen to thirty or forty hard-luck stories from bozos that are as bad off as you are, or pretend you're pulling for them to land the same job that you hope to land for yourself. You don't have to act indifferent or force a smile when the master of ceremonies announces that "there's no need detaining you gentlemen; the vacancy has been filled." And when you've written your letter and dropped it in the box, the suspense is over. You know you'll never hear from it again and some lucky fifteen-dollar-a-week secretary will soon be tossing it in the waste-basket.

It was a little past noon, hardly twelve hours ago, I got through with my day's "work" and nothing to do till train time, and I was headed for Felton's Restaurant where the Fifty-Cent Blue Plate Lunch is just as bad as other places, but it takes them a lot longer to serve it, and crossing Forty-second Street I heard a couple of women say, "Oh, let's go to the Paramount! Paul Whiteman's there this week," only I guess they didn't both say it, but one was enough —I'm a sucker for Whiteman's music—and the other woman said, "If we go now, we can hear him twice"; I certainly had no right to overlook a bargain, and it was a safe bet that no matter how long you hung around Felton's, they wouldn't serve you two blue plate lunches for one fifty cents. Next thing you know I was settling myself in a seat that alone was bigger than the theaters I've been haunting, and though I didn't get to hear Whiteman twice or even pay proper attention to him the first time, I can't complain of my bargain, and I only wish some of my brother unemployed, who I've chummed with mornings for pretty near a month—I only wish they could get the same kind of a break.

A newsreel was showing a bunch of Greeks, all twins, fishing for sponges at Tarpon Springs, Florida, when the guy next to me nudged me in the elbow and said, "Well, Poodle, how do you like the big town?"

I gave him a dirty look, never having seen him before in my life, but he just smiled and came at me again.

He said, "Are you too proud to talk to the home folks?" he said. "Or don't you like being called your old nickname?"

So I said, "Listen, Cuckoo," I said, "you've got me mixed up with some other dog. You and I are strangers," I said, "and it suits me fine to continue the relationship."

So he said, "Your parents would hate to see the change in you," he said. "They came of a good family, but they weren't too good for other people," he said. "They never would have got the swell head just because they live in New York."

This didn't go so good with me; I just had to set him right on my opinion in regards to the metropolis. I said, "People don't get the swell-head on account of living in New York. They get embarrassed, unless they're crazy, like you."

So he said, "I'm not crazy, Poodle," he said, "but I *am* under observation."

"Why not?" I said. "You're talking as loud as a Congressman, and even sillier."

So he said, "I mean I'm under observation at Graves' Hospital, on Fifty-seventh," he said. "I don't want you to mention that when you write home."

"I'm not liable to," I said. "I don't write home because there's nobody left to write to, and if I did, I couldn't mention you because I don't know your name."

He dropped his voice to a shout.

"I'll tell you my name," he said, "though you know it as well as I do. I'm Phil Hughes. There!" he said. "How does that strike you?"

"It's prettier than Poodle," I said, "but it's the first time I ever heard it."

So he said, "I haven't any idea why you want to keep up this sham. Your mother's son couldn't be very bad, but if you're mixed up in a shady business of any kind, I won't squeal on you," he said. "I won't even say I saw you if I ever go back to Oconomowoc."

I asked him if that was where we came from and he said, "Just as if you didn't know!" So I asked him what was my name and he said, "Ben Collins, the same as your dad's, but everybody called you Poodle because you looked like a poodle and still do." I thanked him and then I said, "Now listen once more: my real name is none of your business. But it ain't Ben Collins and nobody but you calls me Poodle or ever called me Poodle much as I may look like one, and besides that, the only Oconomowoc I ever heard of is in Wisconsin—there couldn't be two of them—and I was never west of Parkesburg, Pennsylvania, in all my life."

So he said, "You better not talk so loud, Poodle, or they'll put you out," he said. "You've got some reason for changing your identity. I don't like to pry into your affairs, though I'd like to know what you're doing and I hope it's honest for your mother's sake."

So I said, "I'll tell you. I'm making an honest effort to hear Whiteman's band, but the competition has got me licked." So he said, "I'd like to know what you're doing for a living," and I said, "I'll tell you another piece of truth: I was making an honest living, but I ain't making any living at all right now because I lost my job." So he said, "If that's true and you can prove it's true, I'll give you a job, but we'll have to leave here and go somewhere else to discuss it." And as the ushers reached the same decision at the same time, my pal, Phil Hughes, and his pal, Poodle, marched out of the theater to the strains of "Rhapsody in Blue."

If the fella wasn't old, close to sixty; if I wasn't convinced that he really thought he knew me, or if he'd talked like a bum or dressed like one, I'd have shaken him off when he first started talking, and I'd have alibi-ed myself to the ushers and stayed in and seen the show. But he wasn't trying to put anything over and he had me pegged for somebody who he was acquainted with, just like the fella that shadows me mornings on the train; only this new fella is crazy enough to be interesting, and not a pest that drives you crazy yourself with childish questions and remarks.

I'll be through in a few minutes; I want to get some sleep, too. I thought that when he saw me in broad daylight, he might realize his mistake and admit it. But no; I was still Poodle on Seventh Avenue and still Poodle when we got out of the taxi at Graves' Hospital on Fifty-seventh Street. He took me up to the seventh floor and introduced me to a nurse as Mr. Collins, a young man he used to know in Oconomowoc. He asked the nurse to send for Dr. Gregory. The nurse said that the doctor was somewhere in the hospital, and he said to send him to his room. The room is a nice, big room and full of books about travel in this country and Europe.

While he waited, Mr. Hughes said that he was allowed to go out alone after nine in the morning provided he reported at the hospital for lunch and was in for good by five in the afternoon. The doctor had been after him to employ a companion to go around with him daytimes, not because there was danger of him doing anything rash, but to keep him from spending too much money. If I wanted the job, I could have it because it would make him feel good to think he was helping my mother's son. I told him again that he had never seen my mother, that my name wasn't Ben Collins or Poodle Collins and didn't even begin with a C, and that Pennsylvania was the closest I'd ever been to Oconomowoc. He said, "Some day you'll trust me with your secret, but you can't fool me and we'll just let it go at that." I told him what I had been getting at Waldron's and he said he would pay me seventy-two hundred dollars a year, and the first month in advance. In my pocket right now I've got his check for five hundred, and the money I've been spending tonight is part of a hundred-dollar bill he gave me in case I needed cash, as I certainly did. It wasn't the doctor's business how much he paid me, but he wanted the doctor's approval of me as a man.

Finally the doctor showed up and Mr. Hughes introduced me to him: "Dr. Gregory, this is a boy from my home town. We used to call him Poodle Collins and now he resents the nickname and denies the rest of it. But if he meets with your approval, I'll take him as a companion, and we've already agreed on terms."

The doctor said he would like to talk to me alone, and we went out to some visitors' room or something and I thought that as soon as I told him the truth, Poodle would die the death of a dog and I'd be as far out of a job as I was this morning. But get this: the doctor said his own name was Tyson, not Gregory, only Mr. Hughes insisted that he was Dr. Gregory and that he'd known him in Cleveland, where Dr. Tyson has never been. Mr. Hughes makes Dr. Tyson's checks to cash because Dr. Tyson doesn't like to endorse them with the name Gregory. This check I've got is made out to cash because I'd have trouble establishing myself as Ben Collins or Poodle and Mr. Hughes won't believe my name is anything else. Dr. Tyson said that if I was on the level it didn't make any difference what my name was or where I came from; he wanted Mr. Hughes to have somebody with him when he's wandering around, to prevent him buying the corner of Forty-Second and Fifth Avenue and starting a rival Radio City. He gets a big monthly check from a trust fund and he tries to get rid of it as fast as he can. My six hundred a month may save him six times that amount and spare Dr. Tyson a lot of worry.

The fella is harmless and no bad habits. He likes to go to matinees and picture shows and baseball in the summer. Won't that be tough, if Poodle can hold his job! And Dr. Tyson thinks I can if I pretend I came from Oconomowoc and know everybody I'm supposed to know, though the doctor says their records show that Mr. Hughes didn't live in Oconomowoc and only spent a couple of summers there.

The doctor naturally wanted references and the only one I could give him was Waldron's, with the old man still in Palm Beach. But he telephoned to the treasurer and the vice-president, and what they said must have satisfied him. If it hadn't, I'd have gone down there and shot up the joint. I was the best man they had; so Mr. Waldron told me himself—three weeks before he canned me.

So that's about all. I'm a seventy-two-hundred-dollar day nurse named Poodle. I spend eight hours a day with a crazy person that pays me and the rest of the time with one that doesn't. Only she ain't around just now, and maybe she won't be for quite a while. Because it seems that she called up Waldron's a half hour before my regular lunch hour today and Waldron's had a new switchboard gal, which I don't blame them for, but the gal they fired had forgotten to leave instructions with the new one protecting me, and the new one had never heard my name, but said to wait and she would make inquiries. Evidently she told Mary the truth, which was that I hadn't been connected with the place since February fourth. So when I got to

Bayside this evening, there was no Parker sedan to meet me at the station and for the first time in months I had to use my key to open the Love Nest door. On the table in the hall there was twenty dollars and a note. It's short and I'll read it to you:

"I am going home to my mother and I wish I had never left her and never had met a man like you. I did not know there was such people in the world, people who can deliberately lie and lie to the person they have promised to love and cherish and who have made as many sacrifices for you as I. I do not know and certainly don't wish to know the name of the woman with whom you have been associating all the weeks when you pretended you were still at work. When you have given her up and when you have secured a position and can support a true and loyal wife as she should be supported and when you have convinced me that you are through once and for all with the lies and deceptions and frauds and infidelity which you have been practising and laughing in your sleeve at the loving wife who has sacrificed her whole life to make you happy, perhaps then and only then I may perhaps come back and resume my own humiliating position as your slave whom you have treated worse than the harems of Italy and Europe. Until that time I ask for you to not communicate with me in any way, shape or manner as you will receive no reply. Kindly be careful not to throw ashes and lighted cigarets on the floor and I imagine that when this money which I am giving you runs out your huzzy will gladly supply you with ample to supply your needs extravagant as they may be and as I know they are. Please do not insult me further by bringing that woman into this house."

Well, I guess Mary deserves a vacation and I'm going to let her have one at least as long as the one I've enjoyed; maybe a couple of months longer.

I've told you that when I drink, I talk too much. And it works the other way, too. When I talk too much, I drink. So let's not quit just yet. Get rid of those four in front of you and take a fresh one on old Poodle. Every dog must have his night.

Widow

(*The Red Book Magazine*, October 1935)

John Winslow was sick for only two days before he died. That is, he was sick in bed for only two days. His heart had been bothering him for a long while, racing at an alarming speed if he drank too much coffee, or smoked too many cigarettes, or went upstairs in a hurry. He had spoken of it to his doctor, to his brother and to his wife. But he had always told everyone else he felt fine—being rather reticent, for one thing, and for another, knowing that the inquirers into the state of his health would not be listening to his reply.

He took to his bed early on a Sunday evening, feeling anything but fine. He died Tuesday night. Mrs. Winslow telephoned to his brother Ed; and Ed and Mrs. Ed came over and stayed in the house with her. Mrs. Ed kept saying: "Keep hold of yourself, Margaret." She said it so many times that Mrs. Winslow was at last unable to keep hold of herself any longer, and cried on Mrs. Ed's shoulder for several hours. Mrs. Ed (Alice) told her husband that it was a good thing Margaret had "cried it out"—crying was so much better than suppressing your grief. Ed wondered why, if that were true, Alice had said, "Keep hold of yourself, Margaret," so often; but Ed had the Winslow reticence and wondered in silence.

Ed called up his office Wednesday morning and announced he would be unable to come to work the rest of the week. He assumed the management of the funeral and notified the papers. Margaret and Alice received many sympathetic visitors Wednesday afternoon and Thursday. Most of the visitors told Alice, as they were leaving, that Margaret was one of the bravest women they had ever seen, and was bearing up beautifully. Alice explained that Margaret had cried it out on her shoulder for several hours and had got it over with, which was much better than trying to hold yourself in.

"She may break down at the cemetery," said Alice, "but I don't believe she will even then, because she has already cried it out on my shoulder."

There were a few men among the visitors. They awkwardly expressed their sympathy to Margaret, shook her hand and they went into another room to talk to Ed, with whom they felt more at home. The women were sorry Alice was there. They felt they would have had a much better chance of making Margaret cry if they had caught her alone.

"You're perfectly wonderful to be up and seeing people," said Mrs. Hastings to Margaret. "If anything happened to Frank—I mean if he was taken away from me—well, I'd want to die too, or disappear and never see anybody again."

"I should think," said Mrs. Somers, "you ought to be in bed resting; you'll need all your strength for Friday. I know that if anything happened to Paul, I'd refuse myself to everybody and just hide. But I suppose things affect different people in different ways."

"I'm only going to stay a minute," said Mrs. Gordon. "I just wanted to tell you that you have all of my and Joe's sympathy, and we only wish there was something we could do. But there isn't anything, is there, dear?"

"No, thank you," said Margaret, "Ed and Alice are attending to everything. They're wonderful. But it's nice of you to offer just the same."

"You're lucky to have Alice and Ed," said Mrs. Gordon. "My sister Julia was all alone when her husband died, and she lived up in Minneapolis, so it was two days before I could get there. You never met Julia, I guess. You were away when she visited me. She had friends, of course; but friends aren't like your own family. Bert —that was Julia's husband—he was a wealthy man, had a half-interest in a big garage, and he left Julia comfortably off. But a person doesn't think of money at a time like this."

And when Mrs. Gordon was leaving, half an hour later, she said: "If there *is* anything I can do, or Joe either, don't hesitate to let me know."

Mrs. Bishop, failing to make Margaret break down, did it herself, and had to be consoled out of the house by Alice.

Mrs. Milburn had buried one husband and spoke with more authority than the rest.

"You will find that time is a great healer. When Archie died, I felt like life just couldn't go on for me. If it hadn't been for my religion,

I believe I would have made away with myself. I honestly mean it. I would have. For weeks and weeks, when people talked to me, I simply didn't hear what they said. I was in another world. I couldn't think of anything but Archie, and how much his passing meant to me. I couldn't reconcile myself to living without him. My friends did everything they could to keep my mind off; they were afraid I would go crazy or have a breakdown. Finally I did get really sick and had to have a doctor. It was Dr. Sampson, in Louisville so of course you don't know him. He was perfectly wonderful to me; he seemed to understand things, and he gave me perfectly wonderful advice. He told me my illness was partly physical, because I wasn't eating or sleeping, but it was mostly mental, and he recommended me to travel and get away from home. He said a change of scene would be my salvation—that, and getting away from things that were constantly reminding me of Archie.

"Fortunately, I had money enough to do what he said, and I went to Miami, and that was where I met Fred. I really went there on account of the climate more than anything else—I hate cold weather; and I had no intention of seeing people or going out, though it was nearly five months after I had buried Archie; but there was a married couple stopping in the same hotel where I was stopping—I mean some people I knew, the Beldens, from Frankfort, Kentucky, and they simply insisted on me going to a party at the Casino. They had a terrible time coaxing me into it; I made every possible excuse; for one thing, I'd only brought two evening gowns. But they insisted and insisted till—well, Flora Belden acted like she was going to be mad at me if I didn't say yes. So I went with them and met Fred—it was the beginning of a new life. Archie still has his place in my memory and in my heart, but there is room for Fred too. So you mustn't give up, Margaret. Time will do wonders for you, and a year from now this may all seem like a bad dream that never really happened."

Several ladies besides Mrs. Gordon and Mrs. Milburn mentioned money in the course of their condolences, and an outsider might have thought there was some curiosity regarding how much John Winslow had left. Margaret knew, but did not tell. There was eleven hundred dollars in a checking-account, eight hundred in a savings-bank, and twenty-five thousand dollars' life insurance. He had also carried an accident policy for fifteen thousand dollars which was now, of course, worthless.

Mr. and Mrs. Fleming called together. Mrs. Fleming said the news had shocked her, that she had no idea there'd been anything the matter with Mr. Winslow—he had always looked so well.

"I had no idea myself," said Margaret. "He never told me anything. I guess the suddenness of it was what makes it so hard."

"Just what did the doctor say it was?"

"Heart trouble was all he called it. And it was a surprise to him too. John had seen him about other things, things like sinus and head colds, but had never mentioned his heart, though Dr. Hyland says he must have known about it for years."

Mr. Fleming sneaked, as soon as he could, into the room where Ed was handling the male contingent. He got there in time to hear Ed replying to a query by Mr. Somers:

"Oh, yes. Jack knew his heart was wrong. He often spoke of it to Margaret and me. And he consulted Doc Hyland. Doc told him to cut down on smoking and coffee and lay off whisky entirely. And rest all he could. Well, Jack did quit drinking; he never drank much, anyway. But he wasn't the kind of a fella that would rest or take any care of himself. He couldn't even walk slow, no matter if there was no hurry about him getting places. He was like a three-year-old colt, nervous and high-strung."

The mention of a three-year-old colt reminded Frank Hastings of the pathetic story of his visit to Saratoga the summer before. A drunken man had given him a tip on Jim Dandy in the race that was supposed to be a duel between Gallant Fox and Whichone. Frank, it seemed, had been inclined to bet on Jim Dandy because of the odds, but the drunk was such a pest that he had changed his mind.

The other men in the room had heard the story many times and had laughed at Frank's serio-comic way of telling it. They laughed at it now; in fact, they were putting on a show of light-heartedness that was in decided contrast to the scene in Margaret's stronghold. The men did a lot of laughing, and seldom mentioned John Winslow's death. There was no concerted or individual attempt to make his brother cry. . . .

Funeral services were held in the house on Friday. Alice protested at first, saying it was bad luck for anyone to go away on Friday, but Margaret pointed out that John had really gone away on Tuesday night.

The casket was much too small to hold all the floral tributes. Alice told Ed that the one which probably cost most was what she called a "Gates Ajar," sent by the Fred Milburns, though a spray of roses embellished with ferns must have set the Gordons back twenty dollars. There were other rose sprays, of course, and a plethora of lilies and carnations.

A mixed quartet from the Winslows' church sang two hymns; rather, they sang "Just As I Am" as well as a mixed quartet can sing anything when there is no piano or organ to accompany them and they fought a losing battle with "In the Hour of Trial," owing to the fact that Miss Wells, the soprano, pitched it three tones too high for her own good or that of Mr. Standing, the tenor. It was abruptly decided by a vote of four to nothing to put the Amen after the second verse.

The Rev. Miles Langdon read the service and toasted the deceased in a twenty-five-minute talk. One of his paragraphs was to the effect that nobody ought to feel sorry for John, who had gone to his reward and finally attained happiness, a statement that may have been true but was not very complimentary to Margaret. Mr. Gordon and Mr. Hastings, two of the bearers, were dying for a smoke, and heartily wished the Rev. Langdon could be muzzled.

Margaret knew that tears were expected of her, and two or three times she was close to them; she and John had lived together for six years; she would miss him. But she managed to keep hold of herself by thinking of other things—how had the local florists managed to corner the world's carnations in so short a time? Was Mrs. Hastings crying because it was John's funeral and not Frank's? And why hadn't Dick Randall called or written or telephoned? Perhaps he had telephoned and Alice had just not told her. Did Alice suspect something? She couldn't *know* anything, because there wasn't anything to know. At least, not much.

Twelve cars were in the procession that went to the cemetery. Margaret had a hard time there, because Ed cried, and so did two of John's men friends. John must have been nice if men liked him that well. She felt sorrier for them than for herself. And she had always hated to see men cry. . . .

She was home at last, and Alice and Ed were still with her. She had hoped they would go to their own house and leave her alone, but it was useless to suggest this to Alice. The latter was one of a large majority of human beings who believed that when you have lost one near to you, you must not be allowed to seclude yourself for at least a week.

On Saturday, Margaret inquired whether it was necessary to reply to the letters and telegrams of condolence she had received.

"Yes," said Alice, "but not for another day or two. Wait till you feel more like it. They are all there together in the top drawer. I wish I could answer them for you, but that wouldn't do."

In the end, they were all there together in the waste-basket, and Margaret had not answered any of them.

On Sunday, Alice persuaded Ed that it was time to talk to his sister-in-law about her future.

"Your rent," said Ed, "is paid up till the first of next month, and there won't be any trouble getting you out of your lease after that. Of course you don't want to stay on here; you can't afford to, anyway."

"No."

"You'll have to rent a room at Miss Brent's or Mrs. Logan's or some other place where they're reasonable."

"Yes."

"John didn't leave hardly any debts. When you've paid off the few he did leave, you'll have somewhere around twenty-six thousand dollars. What you've got to do is invest it in high-grade bonds or maybe first mortgages. You can get six per cent and be perfectly safe. Let's see: Six per cent on twenty-six thousand is—six times six is thirty-six, and six times two is twelve, and three to carry makes fifteen. That gives you an income of fifteen hundred and sixty dollars a year, or twelve into fifteen is—let's see—one hundred and thirty. You'll have a hundred and thirty dollars a month, and that's enough to live on and save a little besides if you're careful."

"It's just as well you haven't any children," said Alice, who had remarked two days previously that it was too bad Margaret had no children, because they would have been such a comfort and given her something to live for.

"I forgot about the State tax," said Ed. "The State will take a small percentage of your inheritance, but not enough to make any difference. If the amount was a hundred thousand or more, the Federal Government would cut in."

"Well, then," thought Margaret, "I ought to get consolation out of the amount not being four times as much as it is, but it seems odd the State should punish me because John had heart trouble."

"If you want me to," said Ed, "I'll look up possible investments and attend to all that part of it for you."

"I wish you would," said Margaret. "I'm helpless when it comes to business."

"And I," said Alice, "will see Miss Brent and Mrs. Logan and try to get you a decent room at a decent price."

"You're awfully good to me, but please don't make anything too definite. I may want to go away for a while."

"Where would you go?"

"I have no idea. I just think maybe a change of scene will help me. Don't worry. I'm not planning an expensive trip."

"Well, I hope not," said Alice. "You must remember that every cent counts from now on."

Ed went back to work Monday, and he and Alice returned to their own home Wednesday evening, having decided that Margaret could be safely left alone. Margaret, lying awake after they had gone, did a lot of thinking. She thought a little about John, and how nice he must have been to win those men's love and respect. She recalled his having often spoken of his heart, and she wondered vaguely why she had paid so little attention, or been unable to believe he was not feeling all right.

She thought regretfully of next Saturday night's costume party at the Hamlins', a party which was an annual affair, but to which she and John had never been invited till this year. She thought of the Elizabethan costume she had rented, and how pretty she looked in it and how pretty Dick Randall would have told her she looked in it. If John could have postponed his death for two weeks!

And she thought if it were ordained that John was to die, he might just as well have died by accident. That would have meant fifteen thousand dollars more in insurance, or about forty thousand dollars altogether. Six times four is twenty-four—twenty-four hundred dollars a year instead of fifteen hundred and sixty, or two hundred dollars a month instead of a hundred and thirty. . . .

But she thought most of Dick Randall: of the first time they had danced together, and he had said things that made her warm inside;

of the first time he had kissed her, and she had pretended to be shocked but was thrilled; of the other times he had kissed her as she had not been kissed for years and years; of how he had said over and over again: "If you were only free!"

Well, she was free now, and had been free a week, and she had not seen him or heard from him, though she knew he was in town. Perhaps it was delicacy of feeling that was holding him back. Perhaps it was fear of Alice and Ed. Or fear of what people would say.

He would know tomorrow that she was alone, and he would telephone, or come to her, or something. There was nothing for her to do but wait.

She waited a day, a long day, and then called him.

"Dick, what's been the matter?"

"What do you mean?"

"I thought I would see you or hear from you at least."

"Listen, Margaret: I hate funerals, and I figured you would have enough people bothering you without me. I did send flowers."

"Yes. They were lovely."

"I just don't know what to say in a case like this. There's nothing I *can* say. If there was anything I could do for you, I'd do it."

"You might come and see me. I'm all alone."

"Well, I'll try to, sometime."

"I don't mean 'sometime.' I mean now."

"I've got a lodge meeting tonight."

"All right, if your lodge is more important than I am."

"Of course it isn't. But I've got to be there. It's an installation."

"You could come here for a few minutes first."

"Well, if you want me to. But it can only be for a few minutes."

"All right."

"Are you sure you're alone?"

"Very sure."

Dick waited till it was quite dark before he rang the Winslow bell. Margaret opened the door, and he came in and shook hands. They sat down in the livingroom.

"As I told you, I never know what to say in a case like this. About all there is to say is that I'm sorry, Margaret—terribly sorry," said Dick.

Margaret made no reply, and there was an awkward silence.

"I've only got a minute to stay," said Dick.

"Before you go," said Margaret, "I wish you'd tell me why you're acting so funny."

"What do you mean, funny?"

"Well, Dick, two weeks ago, at the Flemings', we were on different terms than we seem to be on now."

"I don't think so."

"You know so. And I just want to know why."

There was another silence. Then Dick looked at his watch and then he said:

"I guess you must have got me wrong, Margaret. You and I had some pretty good times; we flirted a little, and we both enjoyed it; I did, anyway. But it's all different now. I should think you'd understand that."

"I'm trying to, but I can't."

"I may as well make myself clear, then: John and I were in the Rotary together, and I got to know him pretty well. I got to like him pretty well, too. There's no man in this town I like better than I liked John. He was twice the man that I am. It broke me all up when I heard he was dead. I cried for the first time in twenty years. And as for you and me, why, now that he's gone, of course there can't be anything between us like there was before. I'd always be thinking of him, and—"

"You'll be late for your lodge, Dick."

Margaret, alone again, did some more thinking. The insurance money would be paid to her, not to Ed. She could give Ed as much or as little of it as she liked. She could keep what she wanted for a trip. She thought that Mrs. Milburn's doctor's advice about a change of scene was very sensible. But she certainly did not want to discover another Fred Milburn, and she would steer as far away from Miami as possible. She wondered how much it would cost to go to Los Angeles.

Second-Act Curtain

(*Collier's,* 19 April 1930)

They were trying out a play in Newark. The play was to open in New York the following week. Washington had liked it pretty well and business had been picking up in the big New Jersey metropolis until a full house at a rainy Wednesday matinée had just about convinced the authors and the manager that they had something.

The three were standing in the lobby before the evening performance.

"We'd be all set," said Mr. Rose, the manager, "if we just had a curtain for the second act."

The authors, Mr. Chambers and Mr. Booth, walked away from him as fast as they could go. Neither of them wanted the blood, even of a manager, on his hands; and they had been told so often—by the manager, the company manager, various house managers, the entire office staff, every member of the cast and the citizens of New Jersey and the District of Columbia—that they lacked a second-act curtain (just as if it were news to them), that both had spent most of their prospective profits on scimitars, stiletti, grenades and sawed-off shotguns, and it was only a question of time before some of these trinkets would be brought into play.

After a while the good folks from the Oranges and Montclair began looming up in such numbers that Chambers and Booth thought Mr. Rose's mind might be on some other subject and they ventured back into the lobby.

"Boys," said Mr. Rose, "we've got a hit. If we only—"

Chambers grabbed Booth by the arm.

"Come here a minute," he commanded, and Booth obeyed.

"Now, listen," said Chambers, "we're not going to find a second-act curtain by watching another performance of this clambake. Let's leave it flat for tonight and go to our respective homes and do a little real thinking."

Chambers' respective home was a mansion in the lower sixties.

Booth's was a hotel room in which he had spent nearly all of the summer working, because he found it impossible to work out on Long Island where everybody else was having a good time. The collaborators parted at the Thirty-third Street terminal of the Hudson Tube and Booth went first to a speakeasy to buy himself some thinking powders and then to his room—the number doesn't make any difference because each is equipped with radio, and all you have to do to avoid it is not open the drawer of the table by the bed.

Booth's room was not an expensive room. It was a $4.00 room and opened on a court, and the people in the other rooms opening on the court were nice and friendly and hardly ever pulled down their window shades, no matter what they were doing. For three days the room right across the court from Booth's had been occupied by a comely and frank lady of about twenty-six, so Booth took a powder before settling down to real thinking. The room across the court was dark. Booth got into his thinking costume, consisting of pajamas, slippers and bathrobe, had another powder and decided he had better eat something.

While waiting for the food, he began a letter to somebody at Syracuse University who didn't know him and wanted him to make a speech. He discovered that the *I* key on the typewriter had gone blooey from overwork, rendering him mute. The food came and he sat on the bed to eat it. There was a knock at the door and in scampered a chambermaid not a day over fifty.

"Are you sick?" she said.

"No," said Booth. "Why?"

"Well," said the chambermaid, "there was a woman sick in this room a couple of weeks ago and I thought maybe she was still here."

"You're the only woman in this room," said Booth, "and I hope you're not too sick to leave."

"It's a funny thing," said the chambermaid, "but I came in a room along this hall one time, it must have been last spring, and there was a man and a woman both in there, both sick. And they knew me because I worked in a hospital once and they were both there, too."

"Marriage might regain something of its former sanctity," observed Booth, "if husbands and wives were always both sick together."

"I'll just turn down your bed."

"No. Let it alone. I'll fix it when I get ready."

"Well, I wouldn't sit around like that or you'll catch cold."

"Good night."

Booth finished eating and looked around the room for reading matter.

There were three books—Heart Throbs, a collection, by Joe Mitchell Chapple of Boston, of favorite bits of verse or prose of well-known Americans; Holy Bible, anonymous, but a palpable steal of Gideon's novel of the same name, and the Insidious Dr. Fu Manchu, by Sax Rohmer. Booth had seen them on the desk all summer, but had been too busy to read when the *I* key was working.

He took another powder and started in on the insidious Chink, but the author's quaint method of handling direct discourse ("Too small by inches!" he jerked; "The pigtail again!" rapped Weymouth; "Is 'Parson Dan'?" rapped Smith; "But," rapped Smith; "Got any theory?" he jerked) was a little too much for frayed nerves. "It is all right," he rapped to himself, "for a guest to bring a book like this with him, but there certainly ought to be a penalty for leaving it in the room."

Holy Bible began too slow and after another powder Booth dived into Heart Throbs, only to be confronted by the complete text of Home, Sweet Home. Now out in the town where Booth's family was spending the summer the natives had pointed with pride to the house where Mr. Payne, who wrote this famous lyric, used to live. If the natives had ever read the whole thing, they probably would have burned the house instead of pointing to it.

Turning over a few pages, however, Booth came across a poem that soon had him fighting to keep back the tears. It told about a mother who often cried at the memory of the good times she used to have, before she was married and gave birth to a little one, but who felt all right again when the little one reminded her of her present blessings by climbing on her knee—

> *And she says and twists a curl:*
> *"I am Mamma's baby dirl!"*
> *And the while I bless my lot*
> *Whispers: "Mamma had fordot!"*

And another whose first stanza ran:

> *When you see a man in woe,*
> *Walk right up and say, "Hello!"*
> *Say, "Hello!" and "How d'ye do?*
> *How's the world been using you?"*
> *Slap the fellow on his back,*
> *Bring your hand down with a whack;*
> *Waltz straight up and don't go slow,*
> *Shake his hand and say, "Hullo!"*

For a brief moment Booth considered dressing again, engaging a taxi, driving to Chambers' house, waltzing straight up to Chambers' room, bringing his hand down with a whack on Chambers' shoulder and saying, "Hullo, and how d'ye do, and how's your second-act curtain?" But he hadn't had enough powders.

While the waiter was removing the tray, he took another one and looked across at the opposite room. Strangely, the shade was down.

Booth lay on his bed, with glass and bottle beside him, for half an hour. Inspiration came to him. The second act should end with a song. But he'd better call up Chambers and get his approval.

"Why, sure," said Chambers. "Only it's got to be damn' funny."

"Have you had any ideas yourself?"

"Not yet. I've been reading. You realize, of course, that a line or a piece of business would be better than a song unless the song's damn' funny."

"But I can't think of a line or a piece of business."

"Then go ahead with your song, and be sure it's damn' funny."

Booth hung up and took a drink. In a room devoid of musical instruments he had to compose a song that would be a curtain, would make an audience laugh, would be damn' funny.

He looked across the court and saw the light in the girl's room flash on and then off.

He pictured her as a buyer from St. Louis or Cincinnati. She worked hard all day while he attended rehearsals, or while he sat there in his own room and attempted to think up lines dumb audiences would laugh at, as substitutes for lines that they wouldn't. He wondered whether she was dumb.

In the evening she came back to her $4.00 cell, and perhaps

changed her clothes and went to a picture, or sat in the grill or on the roof and dined alone and wished there were someone for her to dance with when the orchestra played Here Am I.

After her solitary dinner or the pictures, she probably went to bed and read the confessions of John Gilbert and Rudy Vallée until she fell asleep.

It was a shame, thought Booth, that the conventions and his arduous work kept him from calling her up and perhaps taking her to dinner or a show, or merely carrying on friendly conversations with her so she would not be quite so homesick.

He fell asleep and was awakened by the telephone at half past two.

"Listen," said the voice of Mr. Rose, "we've got a show if we find a curtain for that second act. They liked everything but that tonight. You fellas have got to dig up a curtain by tomorrow."

"I think I've got an idea."

"Well, I hope it's good."

Booth began to hum different people's tunes to himself. Tunes lots of times suggest words; it's customary and much more satisfactory to get the tune first—

He looked across the court once more. The lights were on, only the thin shade was down, and he could see a man in shirt sleeves standing in the middle of the room.

"Well," thought Booth, "she's married and I've been wasting all my sympathy. A girl that's married may not be having a good time, but at least she isn't alone."

For some reason, however, he felt resentful and the drink he took was three times as big as its predecessors. So, she was married—

Suddenly there flashed into his head one of the prettiest tunes he had ever heard. He grabbed a piece of music manuscript paper and wrote a lead sheet of half the refrain.

"It will be all the better," he thought, "if I can get some silly, incongruous words to such a pretty melody as this."

He set down what he considered an amusing line and was at work on a second when the telephone rang again.

"This is Rose. I was thinking maybe you'd better tell me something about your idea for a curtain."

"It's a song. I've got it half done."

"You might just as well quit working on it. We can't drop on a song. It's got to be a gag."

"But suppose the song is a gag—"

"No, I tell you we can't ring down on a song. We've got too many of them. This is no musical. Just forget that idea and work on another."

Booth tried to answer, but Mr. Rose had hung up.

"Whether we ring down on it or not," Booth said to the bottle, "we can use it somewhere."

But in the middle of the third line of the lyric a terrible hunch came to him. He had heard the tune before. Where? Why, back at home in the Episcopal church choir. Only there it had been in nine-eight or something, and now it was four-four. "The strife is o'er, the battle done."

"I won't give up till I'm sure," he said to himself.

There was one composer in town who, chances were, would be up at this time of night, five or ten minutes past three. It was quite a job to grab hold of the telephone, but Booth finally managed it.

"Well, whistle it or hum it, but do it quick because I'm working," said Mr. Youmans.

Booth whistled the refrain, though whistling was difficult.

"I like it very much," said Mr. Youmans.

"But isn't it a hymn? I seem to have heard it in church."

"It's a hymn all right," said Mr. Youmans, "but I don't think you heard it in church. I'm sure I never did."

"No. I can imagine that."

"But I can tell you where you did hear it."

"Where?"

"Do you remember the morning you came to my Great Day rehearsal? That's where you heard it. It's the Negroes' hymn that opens the second act."

Booth tore up his sheet of music paper and looked across the court. Clearly visible was the silhouette of the gentleman putting on his coat and hat.

Booth lunged for the telephone again.

"I'll call her up," he thought. "I'll tell her I'm sorry her husband has to go to work so early."

The operator answered in a voice as thick and sleepy as his own.

"Listen," he said, "what's the number of the room right across the court from me?"

"I don't know, and if I did I wouldn't tell you."

"But I've got something important to say."

"You sound like it. Anyway, you tell it to me and I'll deliver the message."

"All right," said Booth. "You tell her I've been in my room alone all evening, trying to think up a second-act curtain. And I can't think of one."

At seven in the morning he was aroused by strange noises that issued forth from the telephone receiver, which was off the hook, and the cord of which was looped around his neck.

"Will you please hang up your receiver?" said the operator.

"I will if you'll send me the house detective."

"All right."

A house detective appeared before Booth had a chance to get back to sleep.

"Officer," said the latter, "there was somebody in this room last night."

"It looks it."

"When I came in, I brought a full bottle of pretty good stuff. I had my dinner, I worked a little and read a little, and then I went to sleep. Ten minutes ago I woke up to find the bottle empty and the telephone cord twisted around my neck as if someone had tried to strangle me."

"Go back to sleep," said the detective, "and give me time to run down clues. I think we will find that both crimes—the emptying of the bottle and the displacement of the telephone receiver—were the work of one man."